INFERNO

TALES OF HELL AND HORROR

Design by Deborah Golota.
Cover by Zagladko Sergei Petrovich.
Edited by Charles P. Zaglanis.

FIRST EDITION
10 9 8 7 6 5 4 3 2 1
Published in October 2017
ISBN: 9781934501818
Printed in the U.S.A.
Published by Elder Signs Press
P.O. Box 389
Lake Orion, MI 48361-0389
www.eldersignspress.com

INFERNO

TALES OF HELL AND HORROR

BY ANGELINE HAWKES

ELDER SIGNS PRESS
2017

For C.H.F.—All of my love forever and always because you saved me from life's inferno.

CONTENTS

The walls of the city of Dis, encompassed by the River Styx, surround the lower parts of Hell. These circles are guarded by Demons.

The Seventh Circle is guarded by the Minotaur and is divided into three rings
The Eighth Circle of Hell is located within a circle named Malebolge, which translates as "Evil Pockets". The sinners here are guilty of deliberate evils. This circle is divided into ten ditches reached by bridges that cross over each ditch.

DITCH 1: SEDUCERS
THE INJUN MEDICINE OF CUT NOSE

DITCH 2: FLATTERERS
CEAD MILE FAILTE(100,000 WELCOMES)

DITCH 3: PAYING FOR HOLY OFFICE
BEC DE CORBIN (CROW'S BEAK)

DITCH 4: SORCERERS
IT ALL COMES UNDONE

DITCH 5: CORRUPT POLITICIANS
JUDAS RENEWED

DITCH 6: HYPOCRITES
BETWIXT THE HILLS A SONG COMES CALLIN'

DITCH 7: THIEVES
ASHES TO ASHES, DUST TO DUST

DITCH 8: FRAUDULENT ADVISORS
A PLACE TO REMEMBER

DITCH 9: SOWERS OF DISCORD
GATE OF THE GODS

DITCH 10: LIARS
MADAME ZENIA'S HOUSE OF SPIRITS: CASH ONLY

The Ninth Circle of Hell is a lake of ice Dante names "Cocytus". Each sinner is encased in depths of ice ranging from waist high to complete immersion. This circle is divided into zones.

ZONE 1: TRAITORS TO THEIR KIN
BROTHER'S KEEPER

ZONE 2: TRAITORS TO THEIR COUNTRY
HE REVEALS DEEP AND HIDDEN THINGS, HE KNOWS WHAT LIES IN THE DARKNESS

ZONE 3: TRAITORS TO GUESTS
SCOURGE OF THE FOREST

ZONE 4: TRAITORS TO LORDS & BENEFACTORS
ACELDAMA: FIELD OF BLOOD

AN IMPORTANT MESSAGE TO THE READERS

WELCOME SINNERS!
Not true? You're sin free? Honest and pure, wholesome and nice to everyone, friends to all and enemy of none? Sure you are. And I'm Mickey Mouse.

Let's be perfectly truthful for a change. Pure and wholesome don't read books like this, with titles like *INFERNO: Tales of Hell and Horror*. If they read anything at all it's their family BIBLE. Or the latest newsletter from the 700 CLUB. Think about it for a second. Do you really want to be considered a non-sinner? They're the dull ones, the people who go to sleep at nine o'clock at night—because they want to! Remember that old saying you first heard in high school (or grade school if you lived in a big, big city), that "all the interesting people end up in hell."

It's true. Don't believe me? Then read this book. Angeline Hawkes might not have an inside line to heaven and hell. But she might. We'll discuss that exact point somewhat later in this short but insightful introduction. Ok, maybe just comparatively short and insightful by a non-famous but incredibly honest author. What sort of free advice do you expect in a book priced so reasonable? The Ten Commandments explained in depth by Dean Koontz? Or perhaps you were looking for Stephen King on the true meaning of good and evil? For the price, consider Bob Weinberg a bargain. At least that's what I've been telling my wife for the past thirty something years.

The best thing about this book is that it gives you a nice variety of sins to read about. There are big sins, huge sins, moderate sins, and even a bunch of small sins. There's no story of someone cheating on their taxes but I'm positive that Angeline is merely saving that for her sequel to this book, the cleverly titled INFERNO 2, starring Bruce Willis. Not to mention another humorous but insightful introduction titled "Another Word to the Wise Who Ignored the Message in the First Book." Which, by all such measures, probably includes everyone who is reading this exercise instead of rushing onward to read the good stuff. In any case, keep reading because I have some secrets that are going to surprise you. Not to mention surprising Angeline, her husband, her family, and her publisher. Who's bad? I'm baaaaaaad. (Short Michael Jackson tribute, since he died the past weekend. Imagine having to write a story about which circle of hell he's going to end up in? Is there a specific spot for abusers of plastic surgery? Or for fathers who name their children, Prince, Paris, and Blanket?)

Returning to your regularly scheduled introduction, let's at least mention some of the excellent stories in this book. Or, in simple terms, the reason you've bought this collection.

There's some wonderful tales of destruction. First and foremost among them are two different but equally fascinating descriptions of the fall of the Temple of Babel in ancient Babylon. Did you know that there were aliens from another dimension involved in that disaster? Neither did I, but Angeline paints a convincing alternative picture of what happened thousands of years ago. And gives a much more believable explanation of what happened to Shadrach, Meshach, and Abednego. The other story, for the sinners among us not into science fiction, has plenty of sex.

Another tale of destruction is titled "Judas Renewed" and it's the most modern story in the book. In fact, it could be taking place a few years in the future. Or it might have already taken place on an alternative Earth, assuming that there's an alternative hell for politicians there. Which, going by the nature of politicians, seems to be a pretty logical and believable premise. Read this one and shiver.

Want to read about monsters? After all, this is a book filled with horrors and hell is filled with creatures of the night and worse. There's a noble vampire in these pages, and a man accused of being a werewolf. There's a number of horrifying babies that should never have been born. Still, they're not the worst of the worst.

The true monsters in this volume are the human ones. Take, for example, the phony fortune teller who squeezes the last pennies from those poor women looking for hope where no hope exists. She deserves her fate and more. Then, there's Bobbie Sue, who defines sloth and suffers a bad case of heartburn because of it. Teoticua is a man obsessed with blood and he gets more than a fill of it. Plus, there's a Viking chief who makes Grendel look like a pipsqueak. I suspect that none of these sinners paid their taxes either. That's perhaps the only thing they have in common. This is not a bunch of people you want living on your block and not mowing their lawn.

This book being concerned with hell and the circles within it, there's sins for every taste. Looking for deception? Meet Charlie. How about lust? Talk to Fujiwara. Want to meet a greedy, lustful, heartless villain? There's Count Lorza Graf, a man who surely belongs in the pits. As does the killer named Otto Goethe, and the priest name Father Conn. A word to the wise—don't get too fond of any of the characters in this story collection. They're all here for a reason, and good deeds aren't high on the list. Though some of the most fascinating and horrifying tales are those of good people doing what they think are good deeds, only to have them turn out terribly wrong.

Actually, one of the most fascinating and appealing aspects of such a story collection is rearranging the contents of the book in a way that makes sense to you. In other words, deciding what sins deserve what punishments and where the sinners should be located. Does the nasty young Charlie deserve to be in the first circle of Hell, and does the noble but misguided Lucifer, star of the morning, deserve to be in the ninth circle? Is the devil really that much worse than the priest who bribes his way to become cardinal? It's a question we don't normally ask ourselves, but this book raises the point and does so very effectively. Does the King of Babylon who sacrifices numerous people from his kingdom to save the world from demons deserve our praise or our scorn? There's no problem despising Fujiwara, Lord Nathaniel, or Count Graf, but are weak-willed individuals, merely looking for happiness and being bent to evil like Simon, or Julian Deveraux so deserving our contempt? Are they really much different than people we read about every day in the newspaper? The world is filled with sinners. Hell is crowded with them. Let's face it. In the grand scheme of things, heaven is relatively empty. And it doesn't have movie theaters or television or radio stations. Or so I've been told by pretty good sources. After all, we know everyone in the entertainment industry is in hell. $10 a movie ticket? They deserve to suffer.

Now that I've given away the names of all the evil characters in the book, it's time for me to reveal the final truth. Oh, and don't worry about the names stuff. All of the characters in this book except for an angel or two is evil, so I really didn't give away anything important. I mean, what did you expect in a book named INFERNO? Sweetness and light? Nobody ranks very high on the sweetness table in this volume.

Enough mindless chatter. Now for the promised secret. If you've been following the career of the author of this book, a certain Angeline Hawkes, you might have noticed that she has a particular fondness for stories dealing with heaven and hell. That she writes about sinners with conviction and a certain honesty that rings amazingly true. If you're someone like me, paranoid and suspicious of everyone wholesome and pure, then you can't help but wonder? Then you look at her most recent author photograph and think she sure doesn't appear to be as old as she claims. Plus, I've heard her husband tells people she's his angel in disguise. And reading her blog, along with writing massive amounts of intelligent, entertaining fiction, she sews, bakes cookies and drives her kids to school every day without complaining. That's saintly behavior even for a parent. Still not seeing where I'm going with this? Then take a look at her first name. Duh. Angeline. Or, more to the point, Angel-in-e. E? Obviously it's an abbreviation, most likely for "exile." Angeline is really *Angel in Exile*. I dare not speculate on exile for what? I'll leave that to the movies. But when you read this book, learn from it. There's going to be a test and it's one you don't want to fail.

Studying hard:

Robert Weinberg
June 30, 2009

INTRODUCTION

T*HE DIVINE COMEDY*, WRITTEN by Dante Alighieri between 1308 and 1321, is considered the central epic poem of Italian literature, and is one of the greatest works of world literature. Written in the first person, the poem tells of Dante's journey through the three realms of the dead: *Inferno*, *Purgatorio*, and *Paradiso*. The Roman poet Virgil serves as Dante's guide through Hell and Purgatory. Beatrice, the focus for Dante's affections since childhood, guides him through Heaven.

Dante's *Inferno* presents a unique view of Hell. In the *Holy Bible* and in the *Holy Koran*, Hell is captured in terms of torment and unimaginable torture. We know that Hell has many circles, or levels, as described in 2 *Peter* 2:4: *For God did not spare angels when they sinned, but threw them into the lowest hell and imprisoned them in chains of deepest darkness, holding them for judgment.* Dante uses poetic license by labeling and assigning sinners to each circle.

The *Holy Bible* gives many descriptions of Hell: lake of fire (*Revelation* 20:14); worms that eat the body never die, and the fire is never put out (*Mark* 9:48); Upon the wicked he shall rain snares, fire and brimstone (*Psalm* 11:6); outer darkness: there shall be weeping and gnashing of teeth (*Matthew* 25:30); And he opened the bottomless pit; and there arose a smoke out of the pit, as the smoke of a great furnace; and the sun and the air were darkened by reason of the smoke of the pit (*Revelation* 9:2).

The *Holy Koran*'s descriptions of Hell run parallel to the biblical version: Garments of fire have been prepared for the unbelievers. Scalding water shall be poured upon their heads, melting their skins and that which is in their bellies. They shall be lashed with rods of iron. (*Koran*

22:19-22:23), For the wrongdoers we have prepared a fire, which will encompass them like the walls of a pavilion. When they cry out for help they shall be showered with water as hot as molten brass, which will scald their faces. (Koran 18:28-29); Begone to the Hell which you deny! Depart into the shadow that will rise high in three columns, giving neither shade nor shelter from the flames, and throwing up sparks as huge as towers, as bright as yellow camels (*Koran* 77:20-77:50).

Near the end of Dante's *Inferno*, he passes through the last gate of hell, which bears the famous inscription: *Lasciate ogne speranza, voi ch'intrate*; or *Abandon all hope, ye who enter here*. No matter what your religion, Hell is a place of eternal lament and suffering, a place reserved for those who do wrong in the eyes of God.

THE ASSIGNMENT: OBADIAH GETS A PROMOTION

OBADIAH SAT ON THE hard, marble bench, listening to the echoes of the cavernous building that housed the Agency of the Celestial Order of Angels. The foyer, though pleasantly decorated, was cold. He'd been waiting for a ridiculously long time and he began to wonder if he'd noted the wrong appointment time. Bored, he stared at the gold-lettered, black granite sign hanging above the office door: Hell Census Task Force. Until today, he wasn't aware that Heaven even *had* a Hell Census Task Force. If he had his wish, he'd still be ignorant of its existence. His mind continued to return to the image of his desk with the unfinished reports stacked in neat piles. He should've brought something to work on, but Suriel might interpret that as rude. Seeing how Suriel was the Angel of Death, he wasn't exactly a Seraph anyone wanted to offend. *Not that Suriel can kill me or anything*, Obadiah thought with a chuckle.

Angels filed in and out of the door with purpose. Reluctantly, Obadiah shuffled into the office again and toward the receptionist. She spotted him before he made it half way to the desk.

"Suriel isn't ready to see you yet," she said, clicking the top of her pen in a frantic, and very annoying manner.

"Do you have *any* idea *when* he *will* be ready to see me?"

She rolled her eyes and was about to speak, when the door to Suriel's private office opened unexpectedly. Suriel's presence made the room immensely brighter. He didn't address the receptionist, but instead pointed at Obadiah. "Are you the angel Obadiah?"

"Yes." Obadiah said, eyeing the brilliant red robe Suriel wore. All of the Seraphim wore red robes. It was their uniform of sorts. Not that they needed a red robe to distinguish themselves from other orders of angels. Their four heads and six wings did a fine job of announcing their elevated status. The Seraph was calm, but a harried expression crossed the face that spoke to Obadiah.

"Come inside. I have an assignment for you."

Obadiah followed the Seraph into his office. The angel's four faces were busy reading something atop the desk, but Suriel pointed to a chair. Obadiah sat. All six of Suriel's wings folded backward as he sat behind his own desk and then focused a pair of eyes upon Obadiah.

"Congratulations, you've been promoted to the Hell Census Task Force."

"Thank you, I think. To be honest, until a little while ago, I didn't know Heaven had a task force dedicated to a census for Hell."

"Not a widely known fact as the task force is only needed every few thousand years. Mostly we process complaints from Hell and Purgatory." Suriel tapped on his desk impatiently. "I'm very busy today, as you've probably surmised by the constant stream of comings and goings in this office; so, let me cut right to the heart of the matter and give you your assignment."

Obadiah laughed. "Wow. Fast work. I don't even have a desk yet."

Suriel smiled politely. "We have one for you, don't worry." He pushed a large book across the desk in Obadiah's direction. "Your job will be to record a random sampling of sinners, one from each division of Hell. The census of Hell has been woefully neglected. The last time the agency oversaw the census it was someone's less than stellar idea to allow a human to perform the task. Hmm–" Suriel shuffled through a stack of papers. "Ah, yes, the human was named Dante. His escort was Virgil."

"I've read that report. Wasn't it leaked to a human publisher? It's considered one of the greatest works of fiction of all time."

Suriel looked annoyed. "Fiction, huh? Well, I don't keep up with these things, too much to do. My census takers have already combed through the legions in Hell recording the data required: number of souls per circle, number of females, males, ages, races, all of those details. You will provide the 'fleshing out' details. We need to have documented case files to produce should Yahweh have questions."

"What sort of questions?" Obadiah asked.

"He's a curious Father. When you tell him we have X amount of souls in circle X, he'll most likely ask about the average crime, offense, or what have you. Though it would take an eternity to record every condemned soul's offenses, we can take a random sampling and produce that sample for the Father to review."

"I see. A few years back I helped process a similar project for promotions into Heaven from Purgatory. There were several random case files that I assisted in verifying."

"Excellent. Then you have a good idea of what's necessary. You're being assigned a demon to serve as your guide through Hell. He'll be given the proper documents, and whatever else is required, of course. I'll need your findings filed in triplicate on my desk in three days." Suriel began shuffling papers again.

"Three *days*?" Obadiah's tone was incredulous.

Suriel stopped shuffling, and turned all four faces to Obadiah. The faces glowered, eyebrows knit. "In *three days*, our Lord was *crucified* and *resurrected*. Surely, *you* can do something as *simple* as walk through Hell and record one story from one miserable lost soul in each of Hell's divisions? I'm not even sending you in alone. No numbers to crunch. All you have to do is pick someone and write down their woeful tale."

Obadiah sighed. *I'm not the son of God*, he thought, but didn't say it aloud. "You're right, of course. I was out of line. Who will be my escort?"

"His name's Azubah. Very helpful demon, I'm told."

An elevator to the right of Suriel's desk made a whirling noise and a green light suddenly illuminated. *Bing Bing.* The double doors slid open.

"Ah, there's your elevator now. Here's the book in which you will record the information gathered. Here's a pen." Suriel handed the necessary items to Obadiah. "I'll recall you to Heaven upon completion of your task or within three days, whichever comes first. Do try to complete your assignment on time."

Obadiah stood. He hadn't been expecting a promotion or transfer to a task force he didn't even know existed. And then once informed of this decision, he wasn't expecting to be sent into the field so suddenly, but clearly this wasn't up for discussion. With no other options, Obadiah put on his bravest face, and advanced toward the elevator to Hell. "What if I need anything while I'm down there?"

"You'll be fine. Don't worry so much. The proper channels have been notified. You shouldn't have any problems. I'll see you in three days." Suriel waved and smiled. His other three faces were immediately occupied with other matters contained within the documents atop the desk.

Obadiah stepped into the elevator, turned and watched the doors shut smoothly before his face.

FIRST CIRCLE:
LACK OF FAITH

OBADIAH STARED GRIMLY AT his escort, the demon Azubah. The guide wore a look that clearly said he'd much rather be doing other things than leading this angel through the circles of Hell.

"I'm really sorry for this inconvenience, Azubah, but Suriel is demanding this census. You know how the Celestial Order is: cross your t's and dot your i's."

Azubah trudged on with no response, the *thud thud* of his walking stick beating the packed earth of the path.

Obadiah frowned, not enjoying his assignment, or the blatant cold shoulder he was receiving from the demon. "At any rate, I've got a deadline of three days, so I won't be taking too much of your time."

"Hmph. Three days?"

The demon's guttural voice startled Obadiah from his random thoughts. He hadn't expected a reply. "I protested, of course, but Suriel reminded me that in three days, Christ was crucified, died and resurrected. He said surely I could record one meager sampling from each level of Hell in that time if our Lord could do so much more." Obadiah sighed.

"I understand your frustration. We hear the three days example a lot down here too."

Obadiah nodded, knowingly.

"We're almost there. Pick your specimen, ask only what you need, and then we'll depart. Lucifer wants you in and out with as little interruption as possible."

Obadiah entered the first circle. A field stretched as far as he could see, and in the distance cattle of bizarre origin loomed. A long line of souls drifted toward a castle. Sitting on a rock, watching the procession, a young boy, not more than eight years old, stared with hollow eyes, a smug expression on his face. Obadiah was surprised to behold a child in Hell. "That one," he said, pointing to the boy.

The demon's shrunken, black wings twitched on his back as he went to the boy. The child followed Azubah to the angel holding a book and quill.

"Who are you, child?" Obadiah asked.

"Charlie."

"Charlie what?"

"Don't know that I 'ave another name."

Obadiah looked him over from head to toe and sighed. "And for what offense are you here in Hell, so far from our maker?" Obadiah scratched at the blank page with his pen.

"I'm told, I 'ave no faith," the boy said. He sounded doubtful of his charge. "I don't believe a god can exist that allows a child to be abused as much as I was in life, short as it was."

"How old at the time of mortal death?"

"Six. Give or take a year. Don't remember ever 'earing my exact age." The boy sounded old, as only death could age him.

"Cause of death?"

"Lungs filled with coal dust. Slow and painful."

"Punishment?"

"You're looking at it, mate, though I do steal out from time to time to deliver a few souls to death when I get a chance. Women are the easiest. They always want to mother me, save me from my misery."

Obadiah stopped writing and looked at the boy. "I might have to put an end to *that*. Would you tell me your story?"

The boy yawned, stretched himself out against a rock, and shook his head in the negative. He stared out at the wandering line of souls with the obvious intent of not fulfilling the angel's request.

Azubah boxed his ear. "Willful child! His lack of faith chains him here, *and* to his place of death. He has many tales to tell, but I'll give you one."

FROM THE LIPS OF A CHILD

Clara wrung her hands, twisting the handkerchief into a wet knot. The child sitting before her was delicate, with tiny, bird-like bones, fragile like an expensive china doll in a shoppe window—yet, he was filthy and rugged from life. Smudged black from head to foot, the only patches of white flesh were those rubbed clean by his soot-smeared hand. For an English child, he seemed a bit unfamiliar with the bathing process.

He was old beyond his years, eyes sunk deep in the hollows of his face: a little coal-smudged skull dressed in a blackened suit of skin.

"And then what happened, Charlie?" Clara asked, as the little boy, not more than seven, suddenly grew silent.

Charlie looked at the little cottage, and back at Clara as if suddenly confused. "Where'd that 'ouse come from then?" He pointed to the rose-covered cottage with a skeletal-thin finger.

"Why, it's always been there. That was my Grand-mum's cottage up until the time of the Great War." Clara smiled, fondly remembering tea in cracked teacups painted with tiny blue flowers.

Charlie paced, a scowl cast over his little features. His babyness faded into the stern countenance of an old man, stooped and worried by the burdens of time. "There's nothing supposed to be there but a path leading toward town."

Clara grew puzzled by the boy's strange behavior. "Charlie, where's your mum?"

The boy sighed, and sat on the tree stump once more, a look of resigned determination set on his features. "Me mum died when I was little. I don't remember 'er face. Sometimes I 'ear 'er singing in me 'ead." Charlie smiled. "She used to kiss me on me 'ead and call me Charlie-boy."

"What a sad thing. What of your father? Where's he?"

Charlie shrugged. "Don't think I 'ave one."

Clara pressed no further. What was she to do with this poor child?

"Don't make me go to the work'ouse, Miss Clara! James told me what they do to boys there!"

"Workhouse? What are you talking about, child?"

"James told me the sweeps'll come get me there."

"Sweeps?" Clara shook her head. Most of the homes around here bricked their fireplaces and converted to heaters of various sorts a long time ago.

"James once told me of a boy who got stuck in a chimney and died.

'is body stank so bad they looped a rope around 'is dead ankles and pulled 'im out in pieces!"

"Charlie!" Clara gasped.

"I'd rather be the trapper I am for the rest of me life than be caught by the sweeps!"

Trapper? "Charlie, do you mean to tell me you work in a mine?"

"Course I do. 'ow else you think I got so black?" He brushed a liberal amount of coal dust from his body.

"But, the mines have been closed for more than half a century. Tapped out."

Charlie laughed, a babyish giggle that immediately made Clara want to hold him to her bosom in a motherly embrace. And, yet this child seemed so—old. *Poor motherless babe!*

A glint flashed in the man-child's eye, as if he was remembering a very clever thing. He smiled a thin-lipped grin, soot cracking in the lines of mirth. Charlie stretched. "You don't realize 'ow bright the sun is until you're 'ere a bit." His voice trailed away.

"Charlie, would you like to come home with me for tea?" Clara asked, then turning to look at the cottage, "Or we could have a picnic here, if you'd like. I often come here when I want to be alone."

The boy studied her face. "Naw, you'll just try to clean me up and take me to church where some fat man will tell me all about 'ow god loves the little children. 'e don't love nobody. Especially not me. I'm bad, I am. I cuss as much as the rest of the men down there in the 'ole, and I pinch food every chance I get."

Clara's mouth was agape, shock permeating her being. This mere child sounded like a world-hardened man of sixty. "Jesus *does* love all the little children! And our Father loves us all as well! And besides, I hardly think pinching something to eat when you're hungry is going to make God not love you. You're just a little boy."

"Naw. 'e jest loves rich folks. James told me 'ow it all works."

Clara frowned. "Just *who* is this James? He knows *quite* a bit about things."

"James and me, we work the trap in the mine. We talk, whisper really, not allowed to talk, but it's really dark and I get scart."

"Charlie, I can help you."

"Won't 'elp none. James says it's either the trap or the work'ouse for orphans like us."

Clara reached for his little hand, but he jerked away before she could make contact. "I once had a little boy, but he grew up into a fine man and was killed in the war last year. Seems every generation a new war catches us. First the Great War, and now this one–"

"What war you talking about?"

Clara shook her head. "*What* war? Charlie, only the worst thing that ever happened to the world. Didn't you hear the planes? *The bombs?*"

"See, I told you god don't love no one."

"No, you're wrong. God had a greater plan for my son. He's walking in a beautiful garden in heaven right now."

Charlie bent over, laughing. "You believe that rot?" He leapt from the stump, came closer, and poked the air with a skinny finger. A sinister look crept over his visage and he spit as he snarled his words: "There's *no* god, lady."

Clara was horrified. *Who was this little monster?*

"If there was a god, me mum would be alive. I'd 'ave a father. Mr. Weatherby wouldn't bugger me arse before he give me my bread at night, and I wouldn't be damned to 'ell."

Clara's hand flew to her mouth. "Charlie!"

"It's true. Mr. Weatherby 'e says to me every night: *Charlie, me boy, every man gots to pay the piper. Nothing in this world comes free. You want this 'ere bread and my pecker gots an itch that needs to be scratched. Now bend over and drop them britches and spread yer rosy little bum wide.* 'e says that most every night. Sometimes I mouth the words as 'e says them. Just like clockwork that old bastard."

"My goodness, you poor boy!"

"Naw. Me arse has gotten used to it now. Besides, when yer 'ungry, you don't much think about anything else but puttin' food in yer belly."

Clara felt tears roll over her cheek. She dug around in her pocket for her handkerchief. "I'll go to the authorities over this, mark my words! Those are horrendous crimes, Charlie!" she whispered, voice raspy and choking from her sobs.

Charlie laughed. "What? You gonna tell the coppers? They won't bother with the likes of me. Throw me in the work'ouse is what they'll do. If they don't bugger me too. You see, that's how I know there's no god. There's nobody out there that 'elps a dirty, poor boy like me. You been 'anging around those rich folks that tell fairytales. That's all this god is: a fairytale."

"Charlie, you're so wrong. Come home with me. Let me show you that there's a god and that there are people who can love you and protect you."

"You jest want to give me a bath!" Charlie turned and ran toward a thicket of trees. "Gotta catch me first!"

She watched him go, then picked up her purse and ran after him. "Charlie!" She saw him head toward a deep pit, wood barriers fallen away with age and neglect. "Charlie!" Now she screamed, urgently concerned for the child's safety.

Charlie mockingly laughed and stepped over the pit. She lunged—losing her footing on the loose soil. The little boy disappeared in mid-air. Too late for Clara: she plunged, screaming, into the black maw of the earth, knowing she'd soon see her son—a *good* boy.

SECOND CIRCLE: LUST

D ISMALLY, OBADIAH FOLLOWED AZUBAH through the field and to a barren land. A great wind blew from every direction. He wrapped his wings around him protectively, clutching the book to his chest. "What is this place?"

Azubah held onto his walking stick as a gale force wind knocked him sideways, nearly colliding with the record keeper. "Second Circle. Those punished for the sins of Lust. Pick your subject quickly. I don't like the winds here."

Obadiah's brows rose at the demon's confession. The wretched souls around him were blown like autumn leaves on the wind. It was hard to see who was who in the whirlwind of dust and debris. A disturbed man in a silken robe blew before him like a fleshy tumbleweed, colorful silk flapping in tatters. "Him!"

Azubah opened his massive arms, catching the man in an embrace, holding him with all his strength lest the winds snatch him away. "Be quick! I don't know how long I can hold him!"

Obadiah rattled off his reasons and questions and held firm to his pen as the man unfurled his story.

FLESH OF MY FLESH

Pink blossoms flew like a rain of petals, stirred by a gentle breeze from the trees, dotting the old path. Fujiwara Kazuma had wandered to this grove alone to think on his brother's death, only to discover the path leading to a beautiful garden surrounding a stately *shinden-zukuri*. Sitting among the shedding cherry trees, was a young woman strumming a biwa of inlaid wood and mother of pearl. She sang in a voice strong and clear, moving Fujiwara to tears with its beauty.

Fujiwara ducked behind a flowering bush and peered between the branches, watching the woman sing. She was exquisite. Perfect. Her kimono was arranged neatly around her, not a hair out of place, her beautifully painted lips mouthing the words of a sorrowful song. He listened for a while, wiping his eyes at the song's sad story. The more he stared at her, the more he burned with desire for her. He focused on the well of her throat, so delicate, so pure. To touch that flesh—his own flesh rose to the occasion and he parted his *shitagi* and grasped his swollen manhood. Careful not to shake the bush that hid him, he imagined her naked body, supple and inviting beneath him. She stood, gathering her biwa, right as he reached his solo climax. He gasped.

The woman, startled, looked from her biwa to see Fujiwara hiding in the bush, awkwardly fumbling with his *shitagi*, listening. Her eyes betrayed her fear.

"Don't be afraid. Play. Sing! Your voice is beautiful and your playing divine." Fujiwara sat on a bench, pulling his *shitagi* into place.

She lowered her eyes demurely, sat again, and politely resumed her song. Fujiwara's heart pounded against his ribs. His palms broke into a sweat. He felt light-headed. All of these things were due to his uncontrollable want for this woman. She was perfect in every way. He slipped to his knees and crept closer to her. She watched him, but continued singing. Just as Fujiwara thought he was close enough to embrace her, she leapt from her repose, clutching her instrument, and ran into the house. Fujiwara felt foolish, but his lust was insatiable and he burned with desire for the nameless woman.

The next day, and the next, he returned to listen to her singing. Sometimes he hid in the bushes and pleasured himself. Others he greeted her, and asked to sit on the bench in the yard and listen. In the process he learned her name was Marisaki Katsyori—and that she was unmarried. Immediately, he envisioned himself as her husband, watching himself caress her unblemished flesh.

As time passed, Marisaki let him kiss her, and Fujiwara's wooing continued until it grew cold outside in the garden, and the flowers were long gone. "My family has gone to visit friends; you could come inside so we could be warm," Marisaki said, sliding the door open to admit Fujiwara. The poor girl was impeccably groomed and to leave her guest, cold, outside was almost as bad as inviting him inside without a chaperone. As Fujiwara didn't offer to leave, he left Marisaki with little choice but to admit him and close the door against the bitter winds.

She disappeared into the house and returned with a bamboo tray and a green porcelain tea set. Hand shaking, she set two teacups onto the low table between them, and poured the golden tea. She smiled shyly and made small talk. This was the first time they had been alone within the confines of a private building. Only the garden had seen their company previously. Marisaki looked nervously about her as if hoping her family would come through the door. Her wrist shook so violently she could barely get the cup to her lips.

"I make you nervous, being alone?" Fujiwara asked.

"Yes. It's inappropriate for us to drink tea without my mother or sister here with us."

"Why did you let me in then?" He seemed aggravated at her behavior.

"How could I allow you to remain in the cold outside? You didn't offer to leave my garden. What sort of daughter would I be to my father if he knew I had turned away a guest with such rudeness?"

Fujiwara laughed and set his cup on the table. He slipped his hand around her wrist. "You are not so young."

Marisaki recoiled at his touch. "Please!"

"I've kissed you once."

"I should not have let you do that. I'm a weak woman and in my weakness, I allowed you liberties you should not have had." She lowered her eyes, looking away.

Fujiwara put a finger beneath her chin, turning her face to him. "You are so beautiful. A face like porcelain painted by a master."

"Please, Fujiwara, we must not–" She attempted to wriggle her wrist from his grasp and jerked her head away from his hand. Fujiwara grabbed her delicate jawline with his hand. His face twisted into an angry expression, which evoked immediate fear from Marisaki's eyes.

"Must not—what?" Fujiwara prompted her to finish her statement.

"You must let me go."

"Must I?" he said. He used his other hand to jerk her kimono open, revealing the shift beneath. Marisaki fought his affront, pushing at his hands, and struggling to fix her clothes.

"Stop it!" She shouted now and tried to stand, but Fujiwara jerked her by the arm, pulling her back to her seated position. She threw herself onto the bamboo matting beneath them, and covered her face. Black smudges dribbled over her cheeks, smearing the white paint as she cried tears of shame.

He seized the silk of her kimono and ripped at her obi, loosening the long belt. Laughing, he unfurled the length of fabric and tossed it aside. Marisaki ran from the room, kimono billowing loose, with Fujiwara on her heels. She ran through the hall, opening and closing sliding panels, until there was nowhere else for her to go. Backing against the wall, she clung to her silk robes, and shouted at him to leave. Her black hair tumbled around her shoulders in disarray, but to Fujiwara she never looked more beautiful.

With a hard rip, her kimono was gone. He pounced upon her, shredding her simple shift with the strength of a warrior. The fabric was nothing more than a rag when he finished. Marisaki covered her most private parts with her hands, shrieking, crying.

Fujiwara pinned her to the ground and forced open her quaking thighs, and then stole her maidenhead, all the while professing his desire to make her his wife.

When he released his desire, and collapsed panting atop her, Marisaki lost her fight and lay silently beneath him. He got up.

Slowly, she gathered her kimono around her, her eyes dry of bitter tears, and she flashed eyes of hate in his direction.

"Now, we should wed." Now she was his. Her father had no choice but to relinquish her to him in marriage or she would live with her shame forever.

Because his actions were dishonorable, Marisaki begged him to never speak of her to anyone. "If you speak of me to *anyone*, I'll be taken from you—*forever.*"

"I'll speak to your father about our marriage," he said.

Marisaki looked horrified. "You must not! His wrath is legendary and he'd refuse you for he has told me since I was a little girl, that he'd kill me before he allowed me to be wife to any man. That's why I stay here, hidden away in our *shinden-zukuri* surrounded by the garden."

Fujiwara didn't know what to do. He knew that loving her body in secret the way he did was cowardly, but what choice did he have? His every thought was of her beautiful face with the cherry red lips, her almond eyes, and delicate hands—the vision of her burned his loins and he lived for the moment he could be beside her.

Time passed and another spring arrived. She had kept their secret, not telling anyone of her rape and shame. Fujiwara continued to force himself upon her whenever the opportunity arose, but something was different about the union. Gone was the thrill of the conquest. Gone was the perfection of slipping within her silken folds. Marisaki laid beneath him with a face like stone, motionless, until he climbed off.

Still he persisted in his desire to wed her. "Please, Marisaki, let me speak with your father! I cannot live without you. Our love isn't a shameful thing to hide. I want to shout of our passion from the mountains, but you bid me keep our secret."

"You call this love? How can you speak of love when you force your way into my temple and take what was never yours?" she said, a sneer twisting her red lips.

Back at his own home, Fujiwara's father began discussing marriage plans for him. A friend of long-standing had a suitable daughter and Fujiwara's father insisted upon a match.

Marisaki! he thought, devastated. That night he stole away and found her strolling through the garden as if it were daylight.

She recognized him in the shadows and stopped walking. "Why do you come here?"

"I cannot be away from you."

"Your sin and my shame will be discovered. I'm pregnant. Our son will be born a bastard. I am nothing but a whore to you and to the world."

He was surprised at her confession. "I'll speak with your father. Surely he'll discover this and cast you out! This secrecy is madness! We can be wed and no one will have to know that I got this child upon you in shame."

Marisaki laughed a musical, lilting laugh. "My father and mother have gone on to our ancestors. It's just me here tending their shrines now. There's no more fear from my father."

Scowling, Fujiwara was bewildered. "What happened? What about their funerals–"

"Ssh, no more questions. If you want me, you must come live here with me out of the shadow of the world. I care not for prying eyes."

"But, I need to tell my family. We need to have a ceremony–" but then Fujiwara remembered his father's wishes and that another bride was being arranged.

"No! You must not speak of me to anyone! If you do, I'll commit *Jigai*! If you speak of me outside this property, I'll leave you forever!"

Fujiwara would do anything for her, to love her, to touch her, to have her; so he said nothing. Even when his friends began asking where he was all of the time, he said nothing. His father reprimanded him for forgetting his duties, but all he could think about was Marisaki, his beautiful blossom. For want of her he would neglect all.

Her ebony tresses, silken robes. Her slender legs, and naked flesh. Pert nipples the color of cherries, and lips softer than any rose. He was consumed with desire for her and did whatever she asked just to lie with her. Except live alone with her in her house in the garden. Every time he saw her, she said the same things. Why should he have to live in her home, in secret? Why should he have to do these things? He took her when he wanted and she no longer resisted. She was full of his son in her belly. She was his. Why should he have to bow to her wishes? Didn't she realize there were ways things must be done? Surely there was an honorable way to settle all, to convince his father of his need for Marisaki and to persuade her of his need to act honorably where his family was concerned.

His father pressed him on the matter of the arranged marriage.

"Later. There's plenty of time. I'm still young. Let the girl stay with her mother a while longer," Fujiwara said.

His father wasn't amused. "You behave like a boy! It's time to have sons. Your sisters are all married and they're younger than you. Your brother is dead and will issue no seed! The Kazuma family needs heirs!"

Fujiwara didn't know what to do. In order to make his father happy, he had to defy Marisaki's wishes; and in order to make Marisaki happy, he had to avoid his father and defy his wishes.

• • •

Marisaki gave birth to a healthy boy. While she was sleeping, Fujiwara gathered the boy in a blanket and slipped from the house. Surely, his father would understand that he must wed Marisaki and put aside this other arrangement now that he had a son. Surely, Marisaki would understand the need for marriage and honor now that she was a mother.

His father stood before his house talking with Fujiwara's friends, Naiki and Mitsuse. They grew silent when Fujiwara approached with a bundle in his arms.

"Father, I must show you why I can't marry the bride of your choosing. This is my son!" He pulled back the blankets to show his father the infant.

Inside the blanket was nothing but a pile of brittle bones.

Naiki and Misuse laughed, thinking it a joke. Fujiwara frantically searched the folds of the blanket, tiny bones falling to the ground. His father jerked the cloth from his hands.

"What's this? You bring this rag to me full of bones? Your son? What sort of trick is this?"

Fujiwara dropped to the dirt, his knees in horse dung; he picked up the tiny bones, clutching them to his chest, sobbing. "My child; my son!"

The other men grew quiet, staring at the weeping spectacle Fujiwara made in the dirt as he ran his hands through his disheveled hair, and clawed at the ground to retrieve each bone. Babbling like a madman, rotting rag of bones in his hands, he led them to the garden.

"Marisaki!" he shouted between gasping sobs. To his father, he said, "She's inside, sleeping."

Naiki seized Fujiwara by the shoulders. "What are you talking about? Sleeping where? Are you mad?"

Fujiwara turned to go inside the house and saw that the grand *shinden-zukuri* was nothing more than ancient ruins overgrown by an untended garden. He dropped the bits of skeleton and yanked the hair at his temples in bereavement. Running around the garden, and through the remains of the house, he returned to his father and friends, falling on the ground, shrieking for his loss. "Marisaki! Marisaki!"

Mitsuse wandered behind a cherry tree. "Here! Over here. Here's your Marisaki!"

Fujiwara's face lit up and he ran to Mitsuse, only to find a crypt with a golden biwa hanging over it and the name *Marisaki Katsyori* written below. "How can this be?" He fell to his knees, tracing her name with his fingers.

"This woman's been dead for two hundred years, Fujiwara," his father said, a look of confusion on his wrinkled face.

Fujiwara ripped open his *shitagi* and pulled out his *tanto*, plunging it into his abdomen before anyone knew what he intended. He drew the dagger across, his face unmoving save for the tears that coursed over his cheeks. Naiki slid his sword from his scabbard with a hiss and sliced the head from his friend's shoulders, not wanting to let him commit *seppuku* unassisted.

The sound of blood gushing from Fujiwara's body filled the otherwise peaceful garden. Pink blossoms flew like a rain of petals, stirred by a gentle breeze that carried a tinkling sound of laughter—eerie and far away—a lilting, musical laughter that whirled around the three men as they stood there, watching the ghastly scene—Fujiwara's blood-smeared hand touching the name of his ghostly lover.

THIRD CIRCLE: GLUTTONY

OBADIAH FOLLOWED AZUBAH DOWN the treacherous mountain pass. Azubah carried a single torch that cast eerie shadows on the cold stone around them. The sounds of rain and hail mingled with the low moans of lost souls reached their ears. Three howls ripped the rhythmic chorus of the falling hail. Obadiah froze in his tracks. Azubah, sensing that the angel was not immediately behind him, turned around. "What is it?"

Obadiah rubbed his arm to erase the shivers. "What's that howling?"

Azubah laughed. "That's Cerebus. He guards the third circle. You should turn back now if a little howling frightens you."

"I'll be fine."

"Things will get a lot worse, fair one," Azubah said, his tone mocking. He reached into the leather bag at his side and pulled out a map. Handing the torch off to the angel, Azubah squatted on the ground, holding the map flat with one hoof and a hand. On the map, he pointed to the path they were on. "See, here's where we are. Here's where we've been." He tapped the map. "The closer we get to here–" The demon jabbed the core of Hell with a black talon. "–the worse things are going to get. Things as in punishments, conditions, the type of souls condemned for all eternity to suffer great miseries and horrific infliction." Azubah looked up at Obadiah, who clutched the torch tightly. "Now, we're going to hear howling, and screaming, and shouting and all manner of atrocious sounds. Not to mention insidious weather, less than savory characters both guarding the souls and the souls themselves. If you don't think you're up to snuff, you might consider turning back now and have Suriel send someone else. This isn't going to be pleasant by any means."

Azubah stood and rolled the map, returning it to his pouch.

Obadiah's face revealed deep frown lines. He sighed as he handed the torch back to the demon. "I'll be fine—go on, I'm coming." Obadiah squared his shoulders and pressed onward, thinking: *If God be for thee, who can be against thee.*

As they neared the gate, Obadiah saw the three-headed dog, Cerebus, pacing on the path. The sounds of hail were much louder now.

"Who's this?" the dog said, growling between clenched teeth, gums bared, saliva pooling beneath its heads.

"Suriel sent him. Name's Obadiah. He's recording samples of offenses and stories from random souls in each circle. Part of the larger census," Azubah said, shrugging.

"Make haste here, angel. I don't like disruptions on my level." Cerebus continued to growl, but moved aside so Obadiah and the demon could pass. "You might need this–" The dog reared back one of its heads. Something large, round, and shiny flung through the air from the mouth.

Obadiah tried to catch it, but the circular object came too quickly, knocking him backward into a craggy ravine. He clutched the item, a bronze shield that had seen better days, and climbed from the ditch to the path. He eyed the massive dog with a frown. "What's this for?"

Cerebus kicked open the gate onto the scene of a harrowing hailstorm. Lying in the mud were the souls punished for the sins of gluttony. Hailstones pounded the sinners mercilessly, yet they didn't bleed, nor could they die. The pain must be intolerable. Obadiah at once realized the need for the heavy shield. "I believe *thank you* is in order, then," he said, teeth clacking with the cold.

Azubah led the way, his tough leathery hide no worse for wear as hailstones pummeled him. He shrugged them away as one would a fly.

Obadiah held the shield over his head, the barrage of ice clanging, constantly reverberating above. "I'll be quick," he said to the demon, who seemed more bothered with the mud splashing over his goat legs than with the blasts of hail.

The angel stood, holding the shield overhead, shivering, as the demon fished around in the mud near a puddle of bubbles. Azubah pulled up a man by a dripping feather cape once a brilliant hue of yellow.

The man wore jade earplugs, and scowled at his visitors. "What do you want?" Mud dribbled from his mouth as he spoke. Above him, words unfurled on a hazy scroll: the man's name. Obadiah wondered if this trick would happen with all of his interview subjects. He read the man's name and continued.

"I'm Obadiah, sent by the Celestial Order of Angels. I'm a part of the Hell Census Task Force. I've been sent to collect random stories from each circle of Hell. You are Teoticua, Moche warrior-priest, are you not?"

"I am," the man answered in a haughty tone.

"Tell me your story, please."

"Why should I? What do I receive in return?"

Azubah pounced on the hail-scarred man. His razor sharp talons ripped the bronze flesh, but no blood issued forth. Teoticua put a finger in the gashes and withdrew it, looking puzzled.

"You will talk, sinner, or I'll be forced to do something severe," Azubah hissed, spittle coating the side of the man's face.

Teoticua eyed the demon with a superior expression, but turned to the angel with a more cooperative attitude. "I'll tell you my story as long as you keep your *beast* away from me."

Azubah snarled at the cocky man. Obadiah sighed and waved the demon back. Teoticua made a pathetic attempt to straighten his sopping feather cape, and then, head held high, readied himself to speak. Obadiah propped his shield over a crevice in the mountain, shielding his book and his body from the freezing hail, and prepared to write.

DRINK OF MY BLOOD

Teoticua licked his slender fingers; sticky crimson blood ran over his arms in thick rivulets, coursing over jade rings and silver bracelets. Stomach gorged to full capacity, he reclined on a stone couch, woven pillows cushioning his respite. The body of a muscular man, clad only in a beaded belt and tattoos worn since his coming of age, was sprawled belly up on an altar. Two priests in yellow macaw feathered robes caught blood delivered into golden goblets from the multitude of obsidian blades plunged into the enemy warrior. The man was unconscious now, breathing his last.

"Bring me the heart," Teoticua commanded, a glint in his eye. "Bring me his heart and his strength will be my strength."

The priests sunk the stone blades into the blood-drained man; one rattle of breath gasped from him and he was dead. His heart was torn out, twitching, and offered, on a platter, to the warrior-priest. Teoticua seized the pulsing organ and sunk his teeth into it. Blood spurted from the wet muscle, painting the warrior-priest and prince's face in blood. Sated for the time being, he sank into the cushions and fell asleep.

Huactictic walked through the much-decorated corridor toward the sleeping prince. More warrior-priest than ruler, Teoticua assumed minor responsibilities under his brother, the Lord ruler. Until now, his brother tolerated Teoticua's immense appetites for women, feasting, and dance, but his constant blood gorging was getting out of hand. Two hundred enemy warriors ago, Teoticua promised to make those prizes last; but his uncontrollable appetite for blood and power drained the hundreds in a matter of months. Now, the Lord ruler had sent Huactictic to deliver a tablet with restrictions for Teoticua's enemy body count.

Upon waking the prince and delivering this missive, Huactictic could see that Teoticua wasn't pleased.

"He says what?"

Huactictic bowed low, near groveling on the polished stone floor in front of Teoticua. "The Lord ruler demands that you fast for ten days from all blood products. If it bleeds you are not to eat it, nor consume it in any way."

Teoticua was outraged. "Does he know the power that surges through me because of the blood and hearts of these beasts he calls men?"

Huactictic began to reply.

"Silence! Tell the Lord ruler his requests cannot be complied with. He must not know the rewards of such feasting."

"It's the *amount* of feasting the Lord ruler is angered with," the emissary said.

Teoticua clasped a dripping heart above his open mouth, wringing from it the last drops of blood. His hands were covered with coagulating blood. His skin smeared with brown dried streaks. "Go now," he ordered the emissary of his brother. "Tell the Lord ruler that I'll find my own sources from now on."

Huactictic scowled, but backed away from the chamber. The Lord ruler would not be pleased.

• • •

Teoticua stretched languidly after his nap, and recoiled, startled, at the sight of the beautiful woman sleeping beside him. Rubbing his eyes, jade earplugs bobbing, he assured himself that, yes, she was indeed real.

"Woman?" he said, in a tone that demanded she awake.

The woman shifted legs of bronze and opened eyelids painted heavily in red. She smiled a sultry smile and then rolled on top of him. "Are you *hungry*, Teoticua?" She straddled his naked body.

"Who are you? You're not one of my women. How did you get in here?"

The smile again. She tilted her head one way and back the other in an avian fashion. "I go where I please."

Anger flashed in the warrior-priest's eyes.

Then she laughed. "Do you not know who I am?"

Teoticua lay back as she guided him into her, rising with each of his thrusts. Her long talon-like nails scratched across his chest leaving scarlet ribbons in their wake. Her hips plunged expertly down, her breasts swaying with the rhythm of her movements until at last she arched her back, writhing in rapture. Teoticua found his pleasure, and the woman rolled from him and stood. He crossed the chamber and sat on his engraved jade throne watching her suspiciously. "Who sent you and for what purpose?"

"I told you, I go where I please." She picked up a gold goblet from a low table and neared him. "I've come to offer you blood sweeter than any you've yet known."

At the mention of blood, Teoticua forgot his suspicions and leaned an interested ear to her. "First, tell me your name."

The woman smiled, teeth inlaid with dots of jade. "Tilco Quetza."

The name wasn't familiar to him. He knew of no one with such a name. "From where do you come?" *A nearby village, perhaps?*

"From the skies, from the sun," she whispered, circling his throne. She ran talons over his arm and placed the goblet beneath. Blood poured into the cup. Teoticua started to protest, but Tilco Quetza placed a finger on his lips and filled the cup. "Drink." She pressed the gold between his lips and he drank.

Wiping his mouth on the back of his hand, he smacked his lips. The blood was sweet.

"It's the blood of a thousand warriors," she said, and a pair of magnificent yellow wings unfurled behind her.

At the sudden spectacle, Teoticua leaned as far back on his throne as he could. Fear filled his eyes. She laughed, and while doing so, her feet transformed into the crooked feet of a bird, giving her an unsteady gait as she neared him again—and slit his other bicep, filling the cup once more.

"Drink, prince!"

Teoticua gulped the blood, his blood, from the cup. "More!"

"More you shall have, for yours is an appetite never quenched by the common blood of your enemy."

A sliver of flesh from his thigh, a piercing of his side, a slash of his calf, everywhere and all over she drew her razor-sharp talons and filled his golden cup. And he drank. "More," he demanded, head swimming with the pureness of the blood.

Tilco Quetza flapped her brilliant wings and filled his cup again, and again. Sparkles like a storm of stars danced against an ebony sky. Teoticua's heart slowed but his hand stretched forth. "More please, it's so sweet." His voice a whisper, "I'm so tired."

She laughed; flitted and fluttered around him. His flesh carved like a bird at a feast. He cared not that his skin was a tapestry of cuts and slivers. He only craved the blood that was so sweet. The last plunge of the talon pierced his slowly beating heart, and she wretched it from his blood-sodden breast, holding it dripping before her. With jade-laden fangs she ripped the muscle in two and slurped the crimson nectar. "No more, my prince," she whispered, and flew from the stone temple.

FOURTH CIRCLE: GREED

U P A JAGGED MOUNTAIN and to a lofty precipice, Obadiah and Azubah trudged. At the top of the mount, the sounds of grunting and over-exertion filled the air in a constant chorus of labor. Condemned souls of every nation and time clustered together in what seemed like teams, shoving great boulders up the mountain and into the huge stones being pushed by an opposing team of souls. Once the huge weights rammed into each other, the boulders crashed down the mountain and the shoving, pushing sort of tug of war began anew.

The souls forced to participate in this torturous sport were weary and ragged. Clothes hung in tattered shreds, draped and tied in knots, fabric beyond repair. More than one soul slipped and fell beneath the monstrous boulders, flailing and shouting in agony as the jagged rock beat them into the ground. After a few minutes the crushed sinner would dig out of the mud and resume his or her place shoving the assigned boulder.

Obadiah watched, fascinated, by the agonizing repetition. Impatient, Azubah singled out one striking figure that paused alone beside a stone. "You!" the demon quaked, black leathery wings twitching from red flesh that smoldered with heat.

The soul pointed to his chest, and walked toward the mismatched pair. The man was very tall, broad-shouldered and wore a hardened expression that revealed a life of authority and war. His clothing was indiscernible beneath the layers of mud and caked on, dried vegetation. The man's beard was matted from centuries of dirt. His shoulders slumped as he exhaled, weary from his perpetual, meaningless task of shoving his assigned boulder. His eyes met Obadiah's without flinching, and his eyes silently sized up the demon and angel before him. Everything about him bespoke a man used to getting what he wanted reduçed to a man who was no longer in any position to ask for anything.

Azubah was anxious to move on, and so, without ceremony, announced: "This angel has been taxed with the burden of assisting in a census of Hell. Tell him your tale so that he might satisfy the order of Suriel, the Angel of Death."

The aristocrat cleared his throat and in a thick, German accent said, "Very well, but it isn't a pleasant one."

"I'd be very surprised if it were," Obadiah said opening his book.

GROSSE MESSER
[BIG KNIFE]

The lands of Count Lorca Graf extended in every direction as far as the eye could see. Rolling hills of forested acres lined the sides of a winding road ending at a castle drawbridge. Count Graf was an iron-fisted ruler who demanded high taxes and the bulk of all crops. Even if he had more food than his household could devour, he still mandated the same allotment choosing to let the grains rot in his storerooms than ease the burden on his subjects.

Treasures of unexplainable beauty found their way to his coffers and the fairest women of the land fell victim to the Count's lascivious nature—never to be seen again. He took what he wanted and destroyed any who stood in his path.

On the borders of his lands lived a widow, a Countess in her own right, who had a beautiful daughter. Count Graf sent a messenger to negotiate a marriage with the fair maid, but the Countess refused to entertain such a notion. Count Lorca Graf's reputation of greed and debauchery preceded the messenger.

"Tell the Count that my daughter isn't interested in marriage at this time, but we're honored by his desire to negotiate," the Countess, wanting to be perceived as gracious and not repulsed by his character, instructed the messenger. "We wish him good will."

The messenger returned to the Count with the message. Lorca Graf wasn't happy. Not being a man to take no for an answer, Lorca tried a different tactic: sending a fine carriage full of gifts—sumptuous gowns and fabulous jewels—all for the maiden, if she'd only agree to be his wife.

Again the widow refused to negotiate, returning his gifts untouched, and this time without a message. The Count flew into a rage, insulted by the Countess's blatant cold shoulder. He wasn't accustomed to being denied. He took what he wanted, and what he wanted was the girl. Damn her virtuous manners and damn her hag of a mother. Graf sent for his favored knight, a massive figure of a man, a warrior, scarred and weathered.

"I want the Countess of Auerbach's daughter. Seize her and bring her to me."

The knight shook his head. "The Countess of Auerbach is a witch. To take her daughter will bring naught but trouble."

"Who says she's a witch? By what proof do you say this?" Lorca thought perhaps he could have the old shrew accused of witchcraft and confiscate her lands, castle, and child.

"By her own hand. Do you not notice that the flowers stay in bloom year round on her lands? And, though she's over sixty, she looks as young as her child?"

Lorca laughed. Countess Auerbach didn't look sixty, but she was nowhere near as youthful as her daughter. He waved his hand, dismissing the notion of witchcraft. "Peasant superstitions. Bring the girl to me."

The knight stood his ground not wanting to tamper with a known consort of the Devil. He'd rather deal with the wrath of the Count then doom his immortal soul with a witch. "No, I cannot. If you want the maid, you'll have to take her yourself." The knight left, despite the Count's lack of dismissal. Lorca cursed until the knight's bulky outline was no longer visible in the dark corridor.

Lorca fumed for days until he devised a scheme. Anxious to carry out his plans, he called for his finest carriage and a team of black stallions. He had himself driven to Countess Auerbach's castle.

The maid, the fair Lizelle, was sitting on a blanket, braiding a wreath of flowers, when the black carriage came to a halt not far from her. With a smile and a trusting nature, the young woman walked to the carriage.

She stood before the door. "Good day! May I help you? Have you lost your way?"

The carriage door burst open, and Lizelle recoiled instinctively from the sudden motion. Count Graf leapt from the carriage and onto the girl, tearing her clothing, and savagely used her in the dirt like a tavern whore. When he was finished brutalizing the woman, he threw a sealed letter atop her bloody, naked flesh. "Give that to your mother. It's our marriage agreement. Now that I've taken you, your honor demands you wed me."

Lizelle wiped her tears and with dirty hands, gathered the tatters of her dress, and the letter, and sobbing, ran inside the castle.

Count Graf shouted at the driver. "Home!" and the carriage and horses rumbled off in a choking cloud of dust.

• • •

Days passed into months, but the Countess of Auerbach didn't return his proposal. Having exercised the limits of his patience, Graf made plans to return to her castle in the morning, and retired for the evening.

Deep in the night, a servant knocked upon his door. "Count? Count?"

"What is it?" he called from his bed.

'There's a knight at your door, a crusader, he seeks shelter."

"Let the man in. Wait in the hall. I'll be down momentarily." Count Graf dressed hurriedly and met the crusader in the great hall, ordering a lavish meal prepared and set before him no matter the hour. "Tell me traveler, to where do you go?"

The knight drank deeply from his goblet and then, walking to the fireplace, warmed his hands before the fire. "I'm bound for home in southern France. I've been gone too many years in the Holy Land."

"What bids you return?" Graf asked, genuinely curious.

"At long last, I acquired a jewel of such value that, once sold, I will restore my family's fortunes and live the remainder of my life as a king."

Graf looked the traveler from head to foot, wondering where this valuable gem was. "What is it? Did you find this gem in the Holy Land?"

"A ruby. A ruby of grand proportions. Never have I seen such a jewel!"

Graf wanted to see the stone, but his guest hadn't offered to show it. "It's a very long journey from Jerusalem to France, where do you hide such a valuable gem that the highwaymen fail to find it?"

The knight only laughed.

The Count could think of nothing but laying his eyes upon this marvelous ruby. "Where does it rest now, as we speak?"

"I carry it in a beautiful wooden coffer, but Count, I'm sorely tired and wish to rest my weary head. Do you not have a chamber where I can sleep for the night? I'll be gone in the morning and won't trouble you any further."

Count Graf smiled. "You're no trouble. A crusader in my castle!

You're an honor to welcome." He stood, gesturing toward the stone steps. "Come, I'll show you to a bed chamber."

The knight followed behind his host, and reaching the room, thanked him, and closed the door. Lorca immediately began to plot and scheme, thinking of ways to steal the jewel from the traveler. Such a man couldn't be very smart traveling so far, unprotected, with no one or thing save a single sword at his hip to guard the gemstone. After a few hours, Lorca crept through the corridor and to his guest's bedchamber.

Listening at the door, he heard the telltale sounds of snores from a man heavy in sleep. He pushed the door open softly, and in his hose, tiptoed into the chamber. There on the table sat an exquisite coffer of olive wood and brass. Quietly and steadily, Lorca lifted the lid of the chest: it was *empty*.

"Are you looking for something?" a voice in the darkness asked, gruff and low.

The Count jumped, surprised by the crusader's sudden alertness. "I—I—no. I was making sure you were sleeping comfortably."

"What does my slumber have to do with my coffer that now rests in your hands?"

Count Graf sat the chest on the table. He backed away. "I only wanted to see it."

"*Steal* it, you mean?"

"What?"

"My ruby. You wished to steal it just as you took the Countess Auerbach's maiden daughter?"

"I—What? How do you know this?"

The crusader emerged from the shadows. "I will show you my ruby."

Lorca forgot about the maiden of Auerbach and the unyielding Countess and happily smiled. "Oh yes! Show it to me!"

The crusader sprang upon the Count, a huge knife grasped in one hand, and with the force of ten men rent the robe from the count's body, plunging the knife into his chest. Before the shocked Count could perish, the crusader's manly form shrank and assumed its rightful shape as the Countess of Auerbach.

"W—w—witch," Graf murmured with his dying breath.

The witch shoved her hand into Count Graf's chest and yanked out his pumping heart. With a cackle of approval, she dropped the Count to the ground, and opened the olive wood coffer. There she placed his heart, his greedy heart, a ruby of untold wealth. With a laugh, the woman spit on Count Graf's body, and left him lying in a creeping pool of crimson on the bedchamber floor.

FIFTH CIRCLE: WRATH AND SLOTH

WRATH

OBADIAH SAT PERCHED WITH the book on his knees, his wings tucked close, as Azubah guided their boat through the swampy waters of the River Styx. All around, wrathful souls fought each other using all manner of weaponry to kill what could not be killed.

"I suppose you want one of these maggots for your record keeping?" the demon asked, stopping the boat near a cluster of dueling souls.

"Yes, that one will do." Obadiah pointed to a hooded brawler.

Azubah latched onto the hood and hauling the figure to the boat, heaved the person aboard. The hood fell away to reveal—

"A woman!" Obadiah gasped.

"Even women nurture the fires of wrath," she hissed. Her hair was slick with the greasy waters of the swamp, but even coated with green slime she was beautiful. Her almond eyes bore into Obadiah hinting at her readiness for a confrontation. She nervously looked in every direction, surveying the boat, the River Styx, and the battles around them. Her attention returned to the angel and the demon and her lips sneered into a smile. "What do you want with me?"

Obadiah could hear the rage contained in her voice. Her fury surrounded them in an invisible cloud, inciting him to a tenseness he'd never experienced. He didn't like this feeling. "Your battle is not with us, woman. Your wrath continues to consume you even in death."

The woman laughed wickedly, and then, sadly. "My wrath consumed me in life, why should it not follow me to my grave?"

Azubah gave her a shake as she sat on the bottom of the boat. "Tell this angel your story, and be quick about it."

"What are you talking about?" she asked.

"Suriel has commanded that I record random stories from each circle. You are that random story," Obadiah said, and shook off the clinging sensation of rage that engulfed him enough to open his book and begin writing.

A BOXFUL OF DRAGONS
91 BC CH'ANG-AN, CHINA

Yang Lu-shan melted into the arms of Hui-fei as he trailed soft kisses over her neck and shoulders. Never had she felt so safe and loved as she had within his arms. She looked into his eyes and smiled. The smile he gave her in return lit up his entire face. She sighed a breathless sigh, entwining her fingers in his long, black hair. His calloused hands removed her *qipao*, and dropped the loose, silken garment onto the wood floor. Gradually, she eased her way beneath his strong frame and allowed him to part her soft thighs. Hui-fei murmured words of love and endearments into her ears, as he caressed her body and filled her sacred cloud with his jade-hard white tiger. Her hips rose to meet his every thrust, and waves of pleasure wafted over her, as Hui-fei resisted his urges. Only until she had orgasmed several times, did Hui-fei shudder with his own release, gathering her yin essence into himself. Yang lay in his arms, in pure bliss, her breasts heaving with each breath.

"I miss you when you are gone," she whispered, face upon his chest.

"As I miss you, my little green dragon," he teased, playing with her long ebony tresses.

Yang sighed. If only she could be his wife. If only they could live in love forever, but her if only's were never to be. Her station would not permit the love of a fisherman. She risked much by allowing herself to love this man, but love she did.

Hui-fei sat up in the bed. Yang moved to let him stand. "Where are you going?"

"I forgot I must meet with your uncle. I'm to deliver a fresh load of fish to the temple tomorrow." Hui-fei gathered his robes and put them on.

Yang lay back among the cushions, caressing her own thigh. "Will you be back later?"

Hui-fei leaned over and kissed her on the forehead. "Not until tomorrow night. I love you, blossom."

Yang smiled. "Tomorrow night then, my great white tiger."

He mimicked a roar and slipped through the door and into the night.

Hui-fei hurried over the path that led to the street, staying to the shadows. Soon he made his way to the other side of town, and crept through the darkness of another garden. He picked a pebble from the ground and tossed it against the wood shutter of a closed window.

The shutter opened a crack and a beautiful oval face peered through. "Who is it?"

Hui-fei smiled. "Hui-fei. Were you expecting another lover?" He laughed softly.

Chao Li Eng feigned insult, but then laughed. She knew that her lover trusted her. She had given him her virginity and loved no other but him—and would die loving no other than him, so sweet was their love. "Come to the back door . . . my mother has gone to her sister's. The servants are asleep, and Chung Fao is with the cook in the stable." She giggled girlishly, covering her mouth with her hand. But, then she was but a girl plucked from the vine, fresh and vibrant, free with her love to the man she believed she could convince her mother to allow her to wed. Hui-fei knew better, but held his tongue.

Hui-fei smiled, and hurried to the back door.

• • •

How it was Yang Lu-shan's little servant girl, Maiko, stumbled upon the knowledge that Chao Li Eng had wooed Hui-Fei into her bed of deceit, Yang Lu-shan didn't know. The little maid, sent to fetch baubles from the market as a reward for a job well done, returned not with her little gifts as expected, but in tears with the news that she knew she must deliver to her mistress. Maiko was just a few years younger than Chao Li Eng and didn't know very much about the other girl other than she once was a good student. After Yang sent the girl to her bedchamber to lie down and rest, she cried bitter tears of her own. How could Hui-fei deceive her so? Promise her love, promise her loyalty—and then lie in the arms of a mere girl! Yang curled herself into a ball, grasping the silken coverlets on her bed, crying mournfully as her heart broke within her breast. How could she live without him? How could she go on? Without Hui-fei's love she would surely perish.

There was no reason to exist but for his embrace. Yang sobbed. She had to find a way to keep Hui-fei from straying—to love only her.

• • •

When Emperor Wu was struck ill, his cousin Yang Lu-shan was certain his illness was a result of black magic. That her cousin was ill didn't concern her; what *did* concern her was finding and hiring the powerful shaman responsible before Wu's shamans found him. Yang wanted to know by what method the shaman had cast his spells for she was in need of retaliation against a bitch of a girl: Chao Li Eng. Yang paid a servant in Wu's household to learn all he could and report to her; and he had.

She now found herself dressed as a peasant woman walking through the narrow roads between fishermen's huts near the Wei River. The shaman, Ming-Yuan, was seated outside of his son's hut smoking a long, slender jade pipe.

Yang bowed respectfully and flashed a radiant smile. The old man was noticeably smitten. "You are Ming-Yuan?" she asked.

"Yes."

Yang lowered her voice. "Are you a shaman?"

The old man removed the pipe from his mouth and glanced around at the busy street, a frown on his face. "What if I am?"

Yang moved aside her overjacket and pulled a purse from the inner folds of her robe. "I have gold." She hefted the weight of the purse in her palm.

Ming-Yuan's eyes grew wide and his frown gave way to a surprised smile. "Come inside. Would you care for tea?"

"Very much so," Yang said, following behind the old man.

Inside the hut was neat and orderly. A young girl prepared tea for her grandfather and guest and then made herself scarce. Yang leaned nearer to the shaman. "I'm Yang Lu-shan, cousin to Emperor Wu."

"I know nothing of–"

Yang held up a hand. "I don't care about Wu. He's an idiot and should've died a long time ago. I'm not here about that. I don't care about what you know or might have seen where the emperor is concerned. I *do* care about the power you possess. I need a spell, magic, to eliminate a girl who mistakenly believes she's a woman: Chao Li Eng."

Ming-Yuan smiled thinly. "Jealousy?"

"Revenge."

"Ah, death's companion and friend," the old man said, and chuckled.

He set his cracked cup on the low table between them.

"My lover, Hui-fei, left my embrace to enjoy the favors of Chao Li Eng. She's but a child, giggling and fawning over him. She's so captivated him that nothing I do can persuade him to return to me." Yang seethed with anger, her fists balled tightly in her lap.

Ming-Yuan nodded knowingly. "Men are weak in the ways of love. Like a dog we go to many mates."

"Well, *this* dog promised himself only to me. *Then*, Chao *stole* him with her persistent flirtations. I want her gone, then my Hui-fei will return to me."

"Are you so sure?" Ming-Yuan said.

Yang scowled. "Of course, I'm sure." She set the purse on the table. "Will you do it?"

Ming-Yuan opened the purse and eyed the coins inside. "I'm your humble servant."

"Servants I have plenty. Shamans I have none."

"You have one now."

"It seems, I do," Yang said.

Ming-Yuan stood and rummaged through a cupboard. He returned with a box possessing a clasp shaped like a dragon. "In this box lies the power to solve your woes, but–" he held up a finger, "you must heed my instructions or calamity will befall you."

"I will heed your words."

"Good." Ming-Yuan unclasped the box. He removed three palm-sized porcelain figures in the form of a well-dressed woman and laid them side-by-side on the table. Then, he closed the box, clasping it. Closing his old eyes, he folded his hands atop the box, and sighed.

Yang stretched a hand to touch the dolls. Ming-Yuan opened his eyes abruptly. "No! Wait!" he said. "There is much to learn first."

"I'm sorry," Yang said, folding her hands gracefully in her lap; but, then her anger returned and she began to fidget with her fingers, twisting and wringing them. *I want her dead, the little whore!* were the only words that rolled through her mind in constant repetition.

"Take these three manikins and bury them in the yard of Chao Li Eng. In three days, the woman will fall ill and die. When she has joined her ancestors, return to me with three bags of gold."

"More gold?" Yang Lu-shan felt as if the shaman was taking advantage of her royal status.

"Is this deed not worth more gold? Do you not want your lover returned to your arms?"

"Yes, but–"

"Three bags of gold then." Ming-Yuan held up three fingers.

Yang grimaced as she nodded in acknowledgement, agreeing to his terms.

"If you fail to return with my gold, there will be consequences most dire."

Yang now felt like the old man was trying to manipulate her, but she only smiled. "Never fear, I'll deliver your payment, *if* Chao dies as you say."

"She'll die, have no doubts about this."

Yang stood, slipping the three porcelain manikins into her robes.

"In three days, then," Ming-Yuan said, showing her out of the hut.

"Three days." Yang walked away from the shaman and through the dusty road.

• • •

She paid a boy to bury the three manikins as close to Chao Li Eng's window as possible. The boy did even better and buried the figures below the floorboards of Chao's bedchamber. In three days, her rival was dead as promised.

Hui-fei made a hasty return to Yang's arms—faster than she dared imagine. He seemed totally devoid of grief for Chao; which made Yang rethink Hui-fei's worth. If a man could be so thoughtless and cold, without any mourning, what were his true motives behind his love? Yang grew angry thinking about how Hui-fei had been lured from her bed by the younger Chao. Hui-fei was a peasant, a fisherman, raised from his common status by her own generosity. Her rich rewards were ignored when Chao offered more gold and younger flesh.

Perhaps Hui-fei loved neither woman, but only loved what they bestowed upon him. Yang chewed absently on the end of her pen, as she wrote a letter to Wu. Perhaps, Wu would be interested in learning the name of the shaman responsible for his illness. Ming-Yuan's death would alleviate Yang's debt of the remaining gold owed the old man. She dipped her pen into the ink and began writing.

• • •

"Did Chao give you this fine attire before her demise?" Yang asked as she poured tea for her lover. The man was flustered, his cup shaking in his usually steady hands. He wasn't a good liar. From the expression on his face, Hui-fei obviously didn't know hat Yang knew about his relationship with the young Chao. "No? Who then? How does a fisherman buy such silks?" Her rage grew and with it the volume of her voice.

Servants accustomed to Yang's fits of rage scurried from view. Hui-fei sheepishly looked at his feet. He mumbled something incoherent.

"I can't hear what you said."

Hui-fei sighed. "Tou Wan gave me these robes."

"Tou Wan?" Yang shouted, realizing that Hui-fei had found his way into yet another wealthy woman's bed. Tou Wan was a much older, married woman. It wasn't for attraction Hui-fei was sleeping with Tou Wan! She had a face like a horse! "For services rendered?"

Hui-fei shrugged, and then immediately regretted his action.

"You think my love such a petty thing? You simply roll from one silken coverlet to another? Are we women *nothing* to you? You're nothing but a whore!" Yang slammed her porcelain cup onto the polished wood floor and it burst into a hundred white shards. "*Get out of my sight!*"

Hui-fei tried to reason with her. "But, Yang—"

"*Out!*"

A servant appeared from the shadows to usher the rejected lover away. Yang paced the room in a state of anger, jealousy, devastation, and hurt pride. How dare he spurn her *again*? And she had Chao *killed* for his affections! Affections that amounted to nothing but the consumption of her wealth. Yang let out a wail. She had that poor girl killed for that snake! Chao wasn't to blame: Hui-fei had broke Chao's heart just as much as he'd broken hers! He cared nothing for her, or any woman, only for their coins and gifts. She was a fool! Yang sat in a silken puddle and rested her face in her hands. *And*, she still owed that greedy shaman three bags of gold! She wasn't going to pay. Hui-fei didn't love her and she wasn't paying any more gold.

The house rocked as if an earthquake was underfoot. Screams echoed through the walls as servants ran to rescue priceless goods from ruin. Yang Lu-shan remained seated, clutching the rosewood table before her. The sky grew black like soot and a strong wind blew through the courtyard. Yang, unsteadily, made her way to the door and peered outside.

A giant dragon flew through the air, so high it looked like a black bat, but down it came, and landed on muscular haunches directly before her trembling form.

"You are Yang Lu-shan?" it asked, in a voice rumbling like thunder.

Yang, too scared to speak, nodded. The dragon seemed familiar.

The dragon's taloned hand shot forward, seizing Yang's torso, bringing her screeching and screaming before its reptilian face. Smoke curled in wispy tendrils from nostrils, circling around its enormous face. As the dragon stretched cavernous jaws, Yang realized where she'd seen this dragon. It looked exactly like the clasp on Ming-Yuan's box of black magic.

There will be consequences most dire.

The shaman's words raced through Yang's mind as the dragon coughed, consuming her in a rage of fire.

SLOTH

Obadiah watched Yang Lu-shan drift away, randomly joining the first fray she encountered. He looked hopefully toward Azubah.

"You've still got work to do here," the dismal demon said, pointing toward a mass of bubbles breaking the surface of the sludgy swamp. "The slothful."

Obadiah nodded. "Ah, yes. Can you reach in there and pull me out a subject?"

Azubah impatiently rolled his black eyes. "Sometimes to do Heaven's work, one must dirty his hands."

The angel smiled. "Is that a proverb?"

The demon laughed. "If it was it most surely was edited."

Obadiah sat waiting, but realized the demon wasn't moving. "Oh, you can't be serious? You don't mean for *me* to muck about in *there*?"

Azubah intently studied his dirty hooves. He polished talons on the hair of his thigh. "*Lazy hands make a man poor, but diligent hands bring wealth* or, in your case, diligent hands bring you closer to getting out of these miry pits."

"*Proverbs* 10:4. Impressive."

"Oh, don't think me ignorant simply because I was on the losing side. I had a role in Heaven before the fall."

The angel shifted uncomfortably in his seat. Sensitive topics of conversation were best avoided. Rolling up his sleeve, he stuck his arm into the water, and pulled a sputtering specimen of sloth from the slime. The woman, rather heavy set and coated in mud, gurgled a hello.

Azubah looked at the woman with distaste. "Woman, tell this angel the story of your miserable life so we might travel on. No questions! Speak!"

The woman looked dazed, but spewing mud from her jowls, she began her narration.

THE BREAD OF IDLENESS

Bobbie Sue pulled her TV tray closer, wedging it around her bulk, and scooted crispy peas around with her fork. Around the little tin square, she chased the elusive green orbs, occasionally spearing a couple with prongs, but mostly spearing soft silver.

The TV blared jingles of persuasion: buy this, buy that; promises of cleaner homes and luxurious hair woven into every tune. Already in a disagreeable mood, she snapped her head toward the sound of jingling keys as her husband, Herbert, came through the opening door. The smile on his face melted into a frown as he met her glaring eyes across the room.

TV dinners again. "Hello Honey," he said, avoiding the stacks of unwashed dishes and the clutter of newspapers, boxes and cans overflowing the trashcan.

"Hello yourself. You're late. Your dinner *was* warm, but now you'll need to reheat it in the oven. I left it on."

Herbert sighed. "I'll make a new one. The last time I heated one of those tinplates, the vegetables were burned to crisps."

"Suit yourself."

Herbert retrieved a boxed supper and slid it, boxless, into the cavernous oven. A gust of heat swallowed it, reminding him of Bobbie Sue's wide-open mouth.

"What did you do today?" He made small talk out of a sense of civility.

"Watched my shows. Ssh! The Jack Benny show's on!"

Herbert opened a cupboard in search of bread, the refrain from *Old Mother Hubbard* repeating in his head. "You go to the store today, love?"

"I *told you* I was watching my shows!"

"All day?"

"Herbert!"

"Yes, dear." His voice was a resigned, pathetic thing.

A mouse scampered from the laundry room. He watched it run into the pantry with no fear of broom or big, heavy shoes.

"The Arlingtons are expecting another baby." He tried again.

"Pff! Bother! More work to do!" Bobbie Sue waved an irritated hand.

"Mrs. Arlington said that when you've got four, a fifth one hardly adds any work."

"There should be a law against overpopulation. Five kids! Good grief!" Bobbie Sue said, fork waving.

"You ever think about it?"

"Think about *what*, Herbert? Gosh darn! I missed what they said!"

"Having a baby."

Bobbie Sue's peals of laughter abruptly stopped. "Are you kidding me?"

"No, I'm serious. Might be nice."

"*Nice?* Are you crazy? Diapers and bottles, and laundry and no sleep? Nice?" Bobbie Sue set her fork onto the TV tray with a clang of metal against metal. "You need more work to do? Come get this tray and then do the dishes. That should take care of your restlessness."

Herbert sighed and scraped the rest of the baked apples from the metal grooves. "When's your show over?"

"Sssh!"

Herbert wished he had a cigarette. He really needed one. Light it up and smoke his troubles away. *Puff, puff.* Light it up and *puff puff* his wife away. Guilt overcame his thoughts. He traced the rippled lines of Bobbie Sue's blue and white checkered peddle pushers, maybe if she took up gardening like her mother she'd shed a few pounds. The way she heaved when she walked, no wonder she was eternally tired. Her mother was thin as a rail, working from sun up to sun down. Why didn't she pass that work ethic on to her daughter? Herbert filled the white sink with sudsy water and sunk his arms to the elbows in the bubbles.

Through the window he waved a frothy hand at Mrs. Arlington and her three girls pinning wash on the line in tidy, coordinated swathes of color. He glanced wearily at the unwashed, unironed heaps of laundry in overflowing baskets on the floor. Bobbie Sue's laughter from the living room soon gave way to deep snores.

Herbert washed the last dish and placed it on the drain board. He dried his hands on the "On Friday we rake the yard" dishtowel, and sighed again.

The evening air was warm as he opened the screen door, careful not to let it slam and stir the slumbering beast on the divan. Sitting on the wood porch step, he watched a few boys, glove and ball in hands, rushing home in the twilight. The flapping of Mrs. Arlington's drying wash sounded like a flock of flying birds upon the wind. He ran his hands over his balding pate and pushed up from the step, returning to the desolate interior of his home.

The new issue of *Life* sat atop the counter and he scooped it and his eyeglasses into one hand and tiptoed across the hall toward the bedroom. The glow of the television cast eerie shadows over the dim room, drapes still open on the rising moon.

The magazine hit the floor in a flurry of rustling pages. Eyeglasses clinked on the wood at his feet. Herbert flipped the light switch, illuminating the room in a wash of electric light to make sure his eyes weren't deceiving him.

Not prone to cursing, Herbert let out a long, shrill whistle followed by a drawn out, "Well, I'll be damned–"

Bobbie Sue—or what remained of her—was seated on the couch. Gingham pants stretched over ample legs with feet on the ground, remaining upright as if viewing the many shows she habitually watched. Half of her rotund torso, shirt tucked into said pants, also was positioned before the television set.

Herbert moved closer, slowly touching a single finger to the scorched frame of wire, burnt wood, and charred upholstery behind the cooked torso, that once was the back of the couch. It was hot! He snatched his finger with his other hand.

The room reeked of burnt meat, sickening sweet and acrid to his nostrils. He bent over, peering beneath the smoking divan searching for Bobbie Sue's missing parts. Nope, nothing under there.

Gone. Flesh, muscles, bone. All of it. Burnt to cinders. Yet, only the area encircling her upper body was burnt. The seat and lower frame of the couch was undisturbed.

"Can't be—to burn bone—the fire would have to be so intense, the house would be gone!" Herbert retrieved the fallen TV tray from the floor and righted it. She must have knocked it over while she—while she—combusted.

Tilting his head, Herbert examined the scene. How could a woman who moved at a snail's pace, cause enough friction to spontaneously burst into flame?

There was no other way to say it. Herbert, dazed, shuffled to the phone and picked up the receiver. "Hello, Mabel? Can you connect me to Sheriff Donald?" His mind was a flood of emotion: sorrow, relief, confusion. Sure he'd wished to be free of the commitment he'd made for a lifetime, but not in this way. Not in death. Poor Bobbie Sue! But how—? There was no logic in her combustion. While he waited for the sheriff, Herbert opened a window. He breathed deeply, cleansing his mind and lungs of the ghastly odor and scene. The night breeze shifted and stirred the ashes of his wife over her seated legs—forever locked in her idleness.

SIXTH CIRCLE: HERETICS

OBADIAH STEPPED CAUTIOUSLY FROM the boat, clutching the rope railing around the rickety dock. The River Styx ran in two directions surrounding the walled city of Dis. Patrolling the walls were a legion of black-winged angels, fallen troops of Lucifer.

Azubah paused, surveying the city. "Do you remember when I warned you that things would get worse?"

Obadiah shuddered. "Yes."

"Welcome to Dis."

The angel tightened his grip on his book, holding it against his chest. "The sixth circle is Hell to heretics."

Obadiah followed in Azubah's wake through the iron gate that clanked open, the soldiers on guard expecting their arrival. They traveled into the outer regions of the city: a graveyard of tombs engulfed by raging fires. In and out of these crypts of anguish ran those charged with heresy.

Azubah looked at the frightened angel with something between a smirk and concern. "Stay here."

Obadiah needed not be told twice.

The demon walked through the flames and led out a man by a chain around his smoldering neck. The man cowered behind the demon, covering his sooty face with charred hands. "Foul heretic, despised by God and man, this angel wishes to hear your pathetic story to satisfy the census established by the Angel of Death."

"Wha—wha—what?"

"Speak or I'll cast you back into the flames of your tomb!" Azubah's voice echoed loud.

The man quaked in his stead, but turned to the angel and began his account.

A PAPAL DECLARATION OF INCREDULOUS PROPORTIONS

My name's Baldwin Chase and I've a pathetic tale to tell. A heretic. That's what the monks called me. Why you ask? Why, indeed! A dafter tale you'll not find.

My tale begins in Worchester, with a woman. Don't *all* tales begin *somewhere* with a *woman*? This tale begins with a dairywoman what that sells cheese and milk and cream, named Abigail Dee. Abby was a beauty: dark hair, dark eyes, skin the color of the milk she peddled. A clearer voice you'll not find on any girl, lest she be an angel; and you being an angel should know about that.

Well, Abby was married at a young age to Henry Dee, an old, miserly man who killed, or outlived, depending on whose view you take, three wives. He was a nasty man of poor hygiene and a sour disposition. Poor Abby Dee was denied the rewards of youth and when she failed to produce a son—why he needed more when he had ten living sons by his three dead wives—God rest their souls—is beyond my knowledge! But, the poor girl having to lie nightly beneath this beast of an impotent man finally couldn't bear the injustice of her marriage and turned to the arms of a lover for solace and a child: *my* arms to be exact.

Now, the day came that my sweet Abby was with child. Old man Dee was delighted and heaped baubles upon my Abby. All of his attention still couldn't win her love, and she continued to visit me whenever her carnal urges got the best of her. Our affair went undiscovered until the day she birthed her child, our child to be sure, for the old bugger couldn't pluck the maidenhead from my Abby so soft was his manly long-purple.

The child, a boy, was born with a dark layer of hair covering the whole of him. Where pink shells of fingernails and toenails should've been found, thick talons of yellow sprouted instead. As if these weren't enough, the infant boasted a row of sharpened teeth that tore Abby's teat when she brought him to suck.

Henry Dee cursed the babe and his bride, and accused her of witchery most foul. All manners of sin he laid at her feet invoking her to name her collaborators and reveal her familiars. Abby denied all until that wretched man had his own wife tied to a rack and stretched for half a day.

Abigail declared that she had a lover who was a werewolf, a being most magnificent with strength and unsurpassable sexual prowess. She told of copulation with her lycan lover in his human state, and on her knees, serving him in his canine form.

Such a spectacle Abby's tale was! Another session on the rack, and my poor Abby let loose my name. A monk and a crowd of n'er do-wells dragged me from my shop where I was mending pots. Covered in soot and sweating I was. The monk bellowed, his fat gut shaking, that I was sweating from my fornication with Succubi. I found this amusing and said so.

This outraged the fetid father, who pointed his sausage of a finger at me and declared I was a werewolf. Astounded, I laughed from the hilarity of his claim. I told the pious monk that I didn't believe in such a beast as half a man and half a wolf and that he could provide no proof that one existed nor that I was this beast he accused me of being.

I was immediately led to the same dungeon in which my poor Abby was housed, and I suffered her fate upon the rack. Three days of stretching did I suffer and not one word of confession could the fat monk and his minions stretch from me. My hands and feet they abused and crushed, but still I refused to admit that I was a werewolf.

Finally, all tortures save death itself exhausted, the monk declared that because of my denial of the existence of werewolves, I was proclaiming a papal decree, from four years earlier, a lie. The existence of witches and werewolves was a truth most certain and my persistent denial branded me a heretic.

And so, for the crime of Heresy, the monk and his mob sentenced me to burn and burn I did. And here, I burn still, flailing and writhing in these tombs of fire, never to be extinguished for all eternity.

I've but one request of you, angel. If ever you come across a werewolf in your travels, please send him here that I might lay eyes upon him, for even as I burn and burn again, I still don't believe in such a thing as a man that is also a wolf.

SEVENTH CIRCLE: VIOLENCE

OUTER RING: VIOLENCE AGAINST PEOPLE

OBADIAH AND AZUBAH PASSED through a corridor illuminated by flickering torches. The stench of fetid meat wafted to their nostrils. Both grimaced. A stink Obadiah couldn't identify encircled him, but before he could question the source, the corridor opened upon a river bubbling as if boiling liquid in a cauldron.

"The River *Phlegethon.*"

Obadiah scowled, eyebrows knit tight. "Is it—blood?"

"Very perceptive," the demon said. "And over there, centaurs, guards of the outer ring which corrals the sinners punished for violence against humanity.

The angel eyed the patrolling centaurs suspiciously.

"Don't expect these swine to cooperate. Some may, some may not."

"I'm not without my methods of coercion," Obadiah said.

Azubah's face registered surprise.

"Don't think me helpless, demon. Suriel wouldn't have sent me if he feared me incapable of my task." Obadiah looked around. "Come, we waste time. That one will do." He pointed to a tall man, partially immersed, delicately licking the crimson blood from long, white fingers. Behind him, clutching his arm, was a lovely woman lapping the blood from the river, uninterested in who might be watching her feast. Obadiah noted the peculiar behavior of the two in his book and waited for the man's story.

THE TERROR

When the Terror first began it was a good thing. The country was cleared of the *nuevo riche* clinging to his ankles demanding recognition. One bitch changed everything. *Madame Guillotine*. She ended the life of the living and the dead, respecting not the *la différence*. Weeded them out—the lurkers, the admirers, and the ones with noble blood who fancied themselves his equal. How could anything rival four hundred years of existence? And he was a duke as well. Duke Etienne de Montclair. Four hundred years and a duke were a hard combination to best. But, there were those who tried. And, they *bored* him immensely. It wasn't that he didn't have time to tolerate their annoyances. He had all the time in the world. It was just that after ten, twenty, thirty years of the same repetitious games involving the same boorish individuals that he discovered he simply failed to be amused.

The one thing that kept him feeling alive, needed, was Anne's mortal family. They didn't know he existed, but he watched from afar, forever fulfilling his promise to her. Anne was his mortal lover so many centuries ago. She knew what he was, what he was capable of, but she didn't fear him. No, she loved him with abandon. She died a happy, old woman in his arms clinging to his promise of protection for her family. There had been Isabella, another Anne, Sophie, Babette with her two sons and five daughters all more beautiful than the last; and now, Marie. Marie, who so resembled Anne.

When this liberation, this freedom nonsense began, he reasoned it would burn ferociously: burning itself out quickly. Instead, he watched, dismayed, as the nobility and not so noble of France were carted through the streets like animals to the slaughter—that quick flash of silver releasing more blood than even he ever hoped to see. Rivers of blood. All in the name of freedom. *Viva la France*! At least, he never dressed it up and called it by a name it wasn't. Murder was murder. When would it all end?

He cocked his head inquisitively as if to study a fine doll through a cloudy shop window. He watched her sleeping—deep, ragged breaths—exhausted from sleep deprivation. Her flesh was the color of morning cream trickling from a white porcelain pitcher. Dark purple bruises colored her cheeks, her neck and breasts. The jagged rip in the coarse linen shift revealed more cruel bruises across her thighs. She slept deeply.

This was the first night since her imprisonment that she slept unmolested, without being mauled by the peasant swine who abused her for their carnal desires. He waited and watched torn between his promise to Anne to remain at a distance, and the promise to Anne to protect her family. The swine wouldn't be disturbing Marie again. He relieved them, quite permanently, of their duties.

Her nose tipped exactly like her so many great grandmother's had. Marie was Anne incarnate. Even the tangled golden hair was Anne's. So many generations between them hadn't diminished the resemblance. He went crazy with anger when he learned Marie had been seized. The abduction was in the morning, while he slept. His faithful servants were waiting for him to awake so they could inform him of the news. Several of his servants died trying to defend her. He was wise to place his own men in her employment. He could depend on them for information and the protection of Marie. And, they proved loyal until their bloody ends. Broken and bleeding, the wounded and dying were brought to him. He gave them the choice: death, or life as he lived. The results varied. Descendants of his servants from his days of mortality, they were aware of *what* he was. Some of them longed for life; some had no such yearnings. But, they knew the truth and remained loyal.

And, they knew of his promise to a beautiful woman named Anne, and of his love for Marie. Because they loved him, his servants loved Marie. But, their sacrifices couldn't stop the fiends who dragged her away under the bright sun.

And now, she slept.

He was faced with a dilemma. She was weak, battered, sick. He doubted she possessed the strength to stand on her own legs. He didn't have much time until the guards were discovered missing from their posts. He could carry her, but that would slow them down. Or, he could infuse her with his blood and give her strength.

If he did this, she'd want more. Blood such as his, pure and noble, old and strong, could not be denied. Anne never mentioned her feelings on his methods of protection. She didn't directly tell him to deny his blood to her children; but, somehow, because of her own choice, he believed she wouldn't approve.

Marie was the last of Anne's line. Without his blood, he feared he'd soon be without Marie, and this was unacceptable. A failure. A breach of his promise to his beloved. Marie must live. Must escape.

With a quick movement, he sank his fangs into his own arm and tore the veins. Blood spurted, turning the white lace at his cuff pink then crimson. He cupped Marie's golden head and tilting it back, let his blood gush between her lips. She sputtered and fought against the vile taste; but, then, eyes open, eyes locked onto his, suckled at his flesh like a hungry babe.

He pulled his arm from her lips and used a handkerchief to tie off the flow. Blood dribbled from each side of Marie's open mouth, her eyes wild, as she stared at him as if she knew *who* he was.

"Don't be afraid. I've come to take you from this hell," the duke said.

"I'm still thirsty," Marie said with a voice as sweet as a girl's. But, was she still a girl?

At nineteen, she could be either girl or woman. He'd known both at the same age. Some still giggles and pink blushing, hands fluttering to hide shy smiles. Some who moved with a seductive sway, hypnotizing men with the grace of their walk. The ones who knew which glance, what look, what flutter of the eyelash signaled to a man that she was wanton and willing to lie lithely beneath him in an embrace of passion. Was Marie just a girl?

"You may drink later," he said. "For now, we must not tarry. We must leave."

Marie understood his urgency. She stood. "How did you get in?"

"Not important. The question is: how do we get out?" Duke de Montclair grasped the iron bars, pulling them from the floor. She slipped out and he followed.

His blood coursed within her, strong and bold. She looked over her shoulder, listening with senses growing more acute by the minute.

Someone was stirring in one of the filthy cells as they crept past. Ragged, wretched forms of humanity slept on flea-ridden rags, lice-infested straw, shivering against the chill of the night. The cold stone floor was worn from years of use. How many feet had trod these corridors? So many entered only to leave in two pieces, cut down by the blade. The duke stopped, listening. He counted three distinct hearts beating up somewhere past the spiral staircase. Whoever was there was quiet, except for the thud of their boots as they patrolled. Marie glowed with newfound defiance. His blood gave her boldness.

"There are guards approaching," he said.

"You should kill them and let these people go free!"

He shook his head. "Kill them, yes, certainly. As for the others—these people are none of my concern. I have who I came for."

"Who am I to you? I've never made your acquaintance. Why am I more important than these other innocents?"

"It's a long story for which we don't have time. Once out of here I'll willingly tell you everything. For now, we must hurry." The duke motioned for Marie to move into the shadows. Ducking into a niche in the wall, he waited for the bodies that accompanied the three beating hearts to pass.

One hand—quick—darted from the gloom of the stone wall, clutching the nearest man's neck. *Crack.* The man fell over. Duke de Montclair remained undetected. The other two stopped, looking back at their fallen friend.

"Jean Pierre?" they said in unison, kneeling, shaking their fallen friend. Jean Pierre was sprawled, his neck bent at an unnatural angle.

With a forward leap, the duke appeared from his hiding place and powerfully smashed the skulls of the other two guards. Marie came from the shadows and stood over the corpses, delicately dipping a finger into the pooling blood seeping over the stone floor. Bringing the blood-drenched finger to her lips she sucked the ruby nectar and smiled.

"No time. Come." The duke knew that escape against two or three poorly trained guards was possible, but even with his supernatural strength, escape against a throng of sword-wielding, ax-swinging guards would be near impossible. He also kept in mind that their tool of destruction cared not that he was a creature of the night—his head stayed off permanently just like any mortal's did.

Down the winding stairs they circled round and round, until they reached the ground floor. Screams could be heard. Marie bristled and stopped.

"They're not our concern," he said, pulling her toward the rear of the prison fortress.

This corridor reeked of death. A small door used to remove bodies lay in the dark, dank recesses of the corner of the fortress. The duke pulled Marie along. Her hand flew to her nose. The door opened into a shallow pit, filled with lime-covered corpses. They fell onto the rigid, foul-smelling carcasses.

"Come," he said, extending a hand and jerking her from the pit.

A lone guard leaned against an exterior wall trying to fight slumber. His head was bowed, shoulders sagging. It was so quiet, that de Montclair could hear the man's tired breathing. Marie stood staring into the pit of death, revulsion and anger rising. "This isn't democracy!"

The guard whirled around, suddenly revived, shock registering on his weary features.

"They'll pay for what they've done!" she hissed as she watched Montclair snap the neck of the surprised guard.

"Later," he whispered and pulled her by the hand through the courtyard bathed in pearlescent moonlight, toward the back gate. No fresh guard had replaced the earlier one he'd dispatched. He was relieved. "Come," he said again.

Marie followed in her bare feet over the cobbled streets, through the muck and sewage, until they came to a black carriage awaiting their coming.

"Home," he commanded and the driver drove them to the castle.

Marie gripped the leather seat anxiously, frowning. "Who are you?"

"A friend."

"Of whom?"

"Aren't you tired?" he asked.

"*Oui*, but answer my question."

"I'm a friend of your family."

"I've no family. I'm the end of the Caraveaux line."

"Yes, you are. I'm a friend of one of your ancestors that have gone on before."

"Who?"

"Anne Caraveaux, daughter of Madeline."

Marie smiled, and then laughed. "Impossible. The Anne you speak of has been dead for two hundred years." She waved a dismissive hand.

The duke shrugged and said nothing.

Marie finally relaxed on the seat, but continued staring at him. "What's your name?"

"Duke Etienne de Montclair."

"How do you know my family's lineage?"

"I told you earlier, that it's a very long story." He sighed. "Do you think I would've risked my life to free you if I meant you harm? Trust me."

"Trust you?" She balked. "I don't know who you are! I don't even know *what* you are! This feeling inside of me, this way that I feel, what poison have you given me?"

He laughed. "You speak correctly when you call it poison, *mon fleur.*"

Marie glared at him and was jostled forward as the carriage, at last, came to a stop. The door opened and a gloved hand extended to assist Marie out. Grudgingly, she seized the hand. "Where are we?"

"My home."

Marie observed the castle before her. It was ancient. Vines clung to the stones and crept farther than her eye could see in the moonlit night.

"Louis will show you to your chambers. Tomorrow we'll discuss everything."

"You'll tell me who you are?"

"But, I've told you. I'm Duke Etienne de Montclair."

Marie stood with a hand on her narrow hip. "And you knew a woman dead for two centuries?" She laughed.

"Tomorrow," he said and disappeared into the castle.

A servant stepped forward, indicating that Marie should follow. She sighed loudly, but followed the man up the grand staircase. He showed her to a dark chamber possessing not a single window. Frowning at the claustrophobic surroundings her eyes fell upon a wood box, very coffin-like. She watched, horrified, as the servant opened the lid to reveal a satin and lace interior. "Your bed, mademoiselle."

Marie shuddered. "What? Certainly you don't mean me to sleep in there!"

"It's a necessary precaution."

"For what?"

"Your transformation. Sunlight is very destructive to your existence."

"What *exactly* did the duke *do* to me?" Marie stooped and ran her hand along the ruffled pillow edge.

"That's not for me to say."

"Damn you then. I'll ask him in the morning."

"*Pardon moi*, but you'll sleep until the evening, as does the duke."

"Maybe I will, maybe I won't." She shrugged defiantly and waited for the servant to see himself out.

• • •

She did sleep until the evening. By the time she awoke, the sun had sunk below its ebony blanket and she made her way to the dining hall and to the table where the duke was seated.

"Wine?" he asked.

"*Merci*," she said, taking a drink. "Is this what you gave me when you refreshed me in my cell?"

"No, my pet, that was wine of a sterner stuff."

"Such as?"

"My blood."

Marie choked and sputtered. After calming herself, she frowned at the duke. "Blood?"

"Certainly you know the old legends about blood-drinking undead creatures staked in their graves at crossroads?"

"Well, of course," Marie said. "But what do legends have to do with me or you?"

"I am, we are, vampires, *mon cher*. Creatures of the night. Blood is our sustenance—the fresher the better. I hesitated in giving you the gift as your great many times over grandmother never desired to be as I was; but you—you were so weak, I feared you'd perish."

Marie laughed, setting her crystal goblet on the table. "And *that's* the story?"

"*Oui*. On the upside, you'll live as long as you want if you keep your head on your shoulders."

"So the *one* thing I have to do to stay alive, just happens to be the one thing these lunatics are calling for in the streets? *Off with her head!*" Marie rubbed her face and ran her hands through her hair. "I'm not inclined to believe any of this. I think you're a prankster, albeit a very handsome prankster."

At that moment a sleek black cat emerged from the shadows and leapt to the table. Without warning, Etienne seized the cat, twisted its snarling face, and sank his teeth into the feline neck.

Shrieking, Marie jumped to her feet, chair tumbling backward. Etienne drained the cat of all blood and slung its limp body into the great fireplace. Marie shrieked anew. Etienne smiled a blood-rimmed smile, before wiping his mouth on the back of his velvet sleeve. "Do you believe now?" He stood and made his way to the hysterical woman. Wrapping his arm around her lithe waist, he yanked her body to his. He smeared a bloody finger across her lips. "Does it make you hungry?"

"Stop it!"

"Does it make you thirst for what you tell yourself you don't want?"

"Stop it, I said, stop it!" Marie wrestled in his grip, his finger streaking blood across her porcelain cheek.

"You are what you are, *papillon*. Do not deny yourself what you must have. There's a fire in you—a strength—that Anne never possessed. You want what I've given you, that much I *know*."

Marie's face grew stone hard. "If it will help me destroy those that wished to destroy me, then, *oui*! I do want to be this *thing* that you've rebirthed me as."

"Oh, it can help you if that's what you want."

Marie's eyes flashed with anger. "I want to kill them all!"

Etienne laughed. "Then we have a busy night ahead of us, do we not?"

Marie smiled. "But where should we start?"

"We can start at the bottom and work our way up through the ranks, or we can start at the top and work down to the last man."

Marie relaxed in his grip. She nestled closer to this stranger, this monster, this demon. "I know where some of the leaders reside."

"The night is young, *mon cher*. Let us go!"

• • •

They descended upon the instigators of the terror like a creeping infection, blanketing the prisons and meeting rooms of the liberators like a devastating plague. All of France believed opposing parties, known enemies, were infiltrating the ranks and murdering them one-by-one, but the killers were nowhere to be found. As a precaution, those in charge rounded up a few suspects and sent them to the guillotine. As the leaders began to fear more and more for their lives, the bite of *Madame Guillotine* was felt less and less. Soon, Etienne and Marie found themselves without a cause for revenge. And, from there they traveled the world over until they met their end in another revolution in Russia: peasants angry at the mounting unexplained deaths pinned the blame on two newcomers who had a bit too much money. In the same roughshod manner Marie had been dragged from her home nearly two centuries earlier, they were stripped of their newly purchased mansion and without any further explanation were relieved of their heads.

Obadiah stopped writing and watched the elegant Frenchman.

"And so, *mon cher*, thus ended our own Reign of Terror."

"I see." Obadiah closed his book. "*Merci.*"

Etienne, with Marie at his side, bowed formally, and drifted into the river of blood once more.

MIDDLE RING: SUICIDES

As Obadiah followed Azubah, he pondered the fate of Etienne and Marie. "Those two seemed like they were *enjoying* their punishment."

"I noticed that. Odd turn of events," Azubah said. "I suppose there must be an exception to every punishment. Those two will be feasting on hot blood for eternity." Azubah's voice trailed away as they crossed a barrier dividing the middle ring from the outer ring of the seventh circle.

"What have we now?" Obadiah asked. All around them were groves of thorny bushes with no souls to be seen.

"Suicides."

"Hmmf." Obadiah shook his head.

"Not your favorite sinners, I take it?"

"A waste of a gift."

Azubah laughed. "An easy life you've had for eternity, Obadiah. Not all are as fortunate."

"Where are these sinners?"

"They're all around you. They're here—there. The bushes! Each thorny, woody bush is a soul lost in the crime of murdering oneself."

Obadiah stopped walking. "How do I communicate with a *bush*? I'm not Abraham."

"And these aren't burning. Watch me." Azubah reached to the nearest bush and cracked a branch off in his hand. A moan arose from the split. "You have a lot of snapping to do."

Obadiah frowned. He didn't want to be the tormentor of this lost soul, but without the breaking of the bush's branches, he couldn't obtain the necessary story. Reluctantly, he began to snap and explain. Snap and explain. Until the soul said, "You wouldn't believe me, even if I told you."

Azubah laughed mockingly. "Try us, sinner." And he grabbed double handfuls of branches, cracking them all at once. The sorrowful suicide sighed and began his tale.

WIEDERGANGER

Ahren Hauser lived an ordinary life. Every day he hauled sacks of grain into the mill and delivered sacks of flour to the owners of the milled grain. Unlucky in love, Ahren was often caught peeping into the windows of village women, and chased away by husbands and irate fathers. Some villagers believed Ahren was simple-minded, but the miller who had daily discourse with him claimed otherwise. Ahren set his heart on a beautiful girl named Greta. She had too many suitors to pay him any attention. Ahren, anonymously, lay wreaths of flowers at her door, and spent his extra earnings on little baubles and lengths of fabric to leave at Greta's home.

Greta, receiving these gifts, imagined they must be from a wealthy suitor who wished to remain anonymous as some sort of game. She decided that man must be the count's son. She found any excuse she could to be in the young man's path and finally she caught his attention and they were wed.

Ahren, in the meantime, was heartbroken; and more than that, he was in debt due to his lovesick purchases. For years he worked to pay what he owed, but his sorrow prevented his duties from being fulfilled. Finally, he was driven to such madness that he sought out a cunning woman and drank her ghastly poison—escaping his life of pain forever.

Or so he thought.

Three years after his burial, Greta heard what sounded like walking below her bedroom window. "Husband?" she whispered in the dark of the room. "Do you hear that?"

The count listened. Footsteps echoed against the cobbled stone of the courtyard beneath their window. He yanked open the bed curtains and donned his robe and sword. "Stay in the bed." He crossed the room and threw open the shutters.

There was no one to be seen.

This continued for three more nights. On the fourth night, after hearing the noise, Greta's maternal feelings of protection got the best of her, and she went across the hall to the nursery to look in on their children.

Her scream echoed through the house.

Count Rudolf ran through the hall toward the sound of his wife's terror. He grabbed the doorframe as he nearly slid past the open door. Greta cowered against the wall near the fireplace. Orange flames licked the logs, casting a pale glow over the room. Frau Klaus, the nursery maid, lay face up on the rug. Her shoes were gone and green-hose covered thick calves, which peeked from under a shredded brocade skirt. Hunched over the supine woman, was an animated body in the state of ghastly decomposition. Yet, it was alive.

The creature plunged hands into a jagged hole in Frau Klaus's abdomen. Looping globs of bowels coiled around blood-smeared arms as the abomination feasted on the woman's innards. A dark void filled the center of the man's eyes where pupils should be, and he went about his grisly mutilations without the slightest hint that he knew Greta and Rudolf were there.

Greta bit on the sleeve of her robe to keep herself from crying. Motionless, she clung to the wall, her eyes fixed on the cradle and small bed behind the creature. Rudolf could see the babes were unharmed. An inch at a time, he scooted closer to his wife and gently touched her shoulder. Her eyes locked with his and a slight smile told her the babes were alive and well.

A grunting noise broke their focus on one another. Rudolf looked to the slobbering beast of a man as Greta involuntarily whimpered.

Hand dripping with sticky crimson and globules of gore, the undead thing pointed at Greta and grunted again.

"What is it?" Rudolf said.

The creature, still squatting on its haunches, cocked his head studying Greta. He pointed again, more emphatically, blood droplets slinging across the floor from his arm. Greta's whimper grew louder, and she looked at her feet in an attempt to keep her emotions in check.

"Who are you and why do you defile my home?" Rudolf asked, anger in his tone.

The creature stood erect, the foul stench of death and the grave wafting through the air. He continued to grunt incoherently.

"Don't you see, Rudolf?" Greta hissed, recognizing the creature at last. "It's Ahren Hauser, the simpleton! He's returned from the dead a *Wiederganger!*"

"Nonsense! That's the stuff of fairytales told by old grandmother's and nothing more!"

"No, no, don't you believe what we're looking upon?"

Ahren's putrid body shuffled closer to the cradle. Greta bolted from her spot near the wall and ran to the cradle, snatching the sleeping infant into her arms and then to the small bed, slinging the toddler over her shoulder. The young boy awoke in sleepy confusion.

Ahren shambled toward her.

"No, Ahren! You go away now. Go on!" Greta commanded.

"What's that in his hand, and there, in his coat pockets?" Rudolf lunged forward in the path of Ahren, blocking the zombie from his wife and children.

"It's my music box. The one you left on my doorstep those many years ago."

Rudolf looked at Ahren, whose face registered a form of anger.

"And—look—the shell and silk fan you left with the Edelweiss–"

"I didn't leave any of those trinkets for you, Greta."

Ahren stopped his swaying and fidgeting.

"But, I thought–"

"I let you believe I left them. You were so damn fixated on me, and you're so beautiful. I didn't know who left all those baubles, but I figured they did me a favor."

"All these years you let me believe it was you?"

In a guttural, primal rumble, Ahren grunted: "Mine."

Greta frowned. "Did *you* leave those gifts for me, Ahren?"

The Wiederganger's shoulders slumped as if he suddenly remembered something sorrowful.

"You did, didn't you?" Greta said, compassion heavy in her tone. "I'm sorry, Ahren. I didn't know."

"Imfophodulhumf–" the creature said, slobbering profusely.

"I don't know what you're saying, but thank you." Greta moved toward the door, not breaking eye contact with the monstrosity.

Ahren dropped a severed arm to the floor with a *thud*, rocking from side-to-side, watching Greta. He lunged forward, grasping her arm with his foul hand.

Greta screamed; the children matched her horror with a chorus of wails. Rudolf drew his sword, brandishing it before the beastly man. "Let go of her, Ahren!"

An evil grin spread across the distorted face of the wronged man, and instead of relinquishing his grasp, he sprang onto Greta with animal-like ferocity and bit a mouthful of her arm flesh—spitting it defiantly into the face of Rudolf. Broken fingernails raked across Greta's face as she fought to protect her crying children.

Rudolf plunged his sword through the monster. Enraged by the blade, Ahren released Greta, who immediately scooped up the infants and ran screaming from the room.

Count Rudolf punched the man hard in his rotting face as Ahren slid from the blade, the stench of rotting guts permeating from the wound. Savagely, the zombie attacked Rudolf, tearing his flesh with teeth and fingernails. The floor turned into a pool of scarlet as the two fought— Ahren for revenge and Rudolf for survival.

A commotion came through the hall and into the room. Greta had brought help from the village, and a mob of men armed with all manner of weapons arrived.

Overpowering the zombie, they chained the reeking creature and carried him from the castle into a waiting cart. The throng made their way to a crossroad and there they hacked the foul abomination to pieces.

Rudolf, clutching his bleeding arm, threw a torch, handed to him by a man among the crowd, onto the chunks of rotting flesh and the others followed suit. They watched Ahren Hauser's remains burn to ash, and the ashes scatter in the wind. The remaining bones were kicked into a ditch and covered over. Rudolf thanked the men, promising rich rewards. Greta and the children stood on the road. He walked toward her, kicking something in the darkness. A soft tune danced merrily to their ears.

"My music box!" Greta said, voice near a whisper. She stooped, retrieving it from the dirt.

"I guess he came back for his gifts," Rudolf said.

"Or worse. He came back for *me*."

Rudolf gathered Greta in his arms. "Let's go home."

The air, pungent with the odor of burnt flesh and bone, encircled them and blew the last bits of Ahren Hauser into the cold night air.

INNER RING: VIOLENCE AGAINST GOD/ BLASPHEMERS

Obadiah shielded his eyes from the scorching sun, puzzled that he could see it at all this deep in Hell. A desert of flaming sand rose in fiery dunes around them, and Azubah spread his thick, leathery wings above their heads as a shield. "Yours won't do us much good here," Azubah said, pulliing a compass from his belt.

With flaming tails, great bursts of fire streaked from the sky, crashing to the ground. The souls of the punished lay sprawled on the sand, fire pelting them from above and engulfing them from below.

"There's a man, there, seize him–" Obadiah said with haste.

"Why so many men, angel? Have you a fondness for women? Women sin as well and as much as men. Look around you—there are many."

"Very well, a woman then. It makes no difference to me."

Azubah braved the fireballs and snatched a suffering soul from the sand. She gave a startled yelp, but sighed from relief for the momentary reprieve. "This is Obadiah, sent by Suriel, the Angel of Death. He's collecting the tales of woe from the belly of Hell. You've been chosen to relay your life's story."

The woman smiled. Somehow, even though her face was sooty, and her flesh cracked and burnt, she smiled with seduction. Obadiah fiddled with his quill uncomfortably, as the woman revealed her tale.

TO DANCE AMIDST THE SHOWERS

Jezreel twirled beneath a veil of silvery gauze, around and round. The drums beat wildly and men beat the earth with their palms as her whirling continued. Sweat glistened over her bronze flesh, naked save for a belt of beads. She waved the veil through the air in a ribbon of silver, letting it settle over the shoulders of the man of her choosing.

The man, a soldier, stood from his place in the dirt and extended his hand for hers. The other men broke into applause—ribald comments filled the air as Jezreel and the soldier, Shemach, made their way into a nearby tent. They didn't close the flap for this was a rite for all of the men to enjoy.

Thick incense curled like beckoning fingers through the night air, wafting from the tent, tickling the noses of the spectators. Jezreel's glistening body was anointed with fragranced oils, their spicy pungency warming both the senses and the flesh. Shemach tugged his robe over his head, casting it aside, revealing a taut, muscle-rippled body. Jezreel laid upon a pile of goat pelts, scattered over with red rose petals, long legs akimbo, ebony tresses scintillating in the illumination of the oil lamps. The primal grunting and breathing that followed elicited more cheers from the spectators.

Shemach left a gold piece for the priestess before leaving the tent, another man rushed in to take the soldier's place.

• • •

When dawn broke, Jezreel awoke, sore and tired, asleep in a sticky puddle of the night's fornications. She stretched and waited for her maid, Hagarsh, to bring her morning meal. After last night, certainly, the great god of the storms had put a babe in her belly. The strongest and most battle-tested of Baal's army were in attendance at the fertility rite. Jezreel rubbed her back and aching thighs. If she bore a child, Great Baal would honor her people with an abundance of crops and all would be fed.

Hagarsh opened the flap letting the rays of the morning sun into the dim tent. "Already awake, priestess? I've brought you honey and bread. Come—after your long night you must be hungry."

Jezreel laughed. "I could eat an entire altar of meat!"

Hagarsh poured golden honey over the flat bread on Jezreel's plate. "And here, I've poured you a sweet drink of ass's milk and honey, good for the spirit and for the palette."

"You spoil me, Hagarsh."

"And shouldn't the handmaiden of a god be spoiled?"

Jezreel swung her legs in front of her and curled around the tray of food. "I'm full of a child, I know it."

Hagarsh pulled the top goat pelt from under Jezreel's legs. She grimaced. "If this pelt's any indication of the seeds planted in you, I'd say you're full of more than just one child."

"Twins?" Jezreel said, ignoring the double meaning to the servant's words. She spread the bread around in the honey. "That certainly would be a blessing."

Hagarsh tossed the pelt outside.

"What's all that noise?"

The sounds of hammering filled the air, ringing through the morning with thunderous repetition. Hagarsh scowled. "Noah."

"Noah? Ham's father?"

"The one. He's insane. He's building this huge *thing*. He calls it an ark. Says that it will float on water and in between hammering he claims *his* god is going to destroy the rest of us."

Jezreel burst out laughing. "Poor Ham."

"Poor all of us."

"He'll never finish," Jezreel said. "Besides his boat is too far from water. How will he get it there?"

"He won't." Hagarsh said. "He's crazy."

"Let's talk about something else. I'm in too pleasant of a mood to worry about a foolish old man and his inferior gods."

"Ssh," Hagarsh hissed. She looked around worriedly.

"What? What's wrong?"

"Hold your tongue. The god of Noah is a spiteful, vengeful god. Why seek trouble?"

Jezreel laughed again, even louder. "What's this god's name?"

"Yahweh," Hagarsh whispered.

"And is he *your* god too?"

"No! You know I serve Baal above all others!"

"So you would serve this god of Noah's as well?" Jezreel held out her arms as Hagarsh poured water over her hands to wash them.

"No—I–"

"You're afraid of this Yahweh?"

Hagarsh feigned a smile. "Of course not. What god could match the powers of Baal?"

Jezreel's eyebrows rose in suspicion. "Well, I don't believe this Yahweh exists. Except in the mumblings of an old man who's obviously crazy." She waved a dismissive hand. "I'd like my bath now."

Hagarsh smiled and took away the tray of empty dishes. "I'll be back with the water." She left the tent, leaving the flap open.

Jezreel listened to the tap-tap-tapping of Noah's hammer. If she continued listening to this noise, she'd go as insane as Noah. Not waiting for Hagarsh or her bath, she stomped from the tent, naked save for her belt and went directly to Noah's place of construction. To her surprise, not only Noah, but all of his sons were occupied with hammering. Beneath a nearby tree, Noah's wife sat making a list on a clay tablet, not paying Jezreel any heed.

"Noah!" Jezreel shouted over the hammering. "Noah!" The hammers slowed, then stopped. "Thanks be to Baal. You must *stop* this noise." Jezreel stood, hands on her hips, full breasts bobbing.

Noah looked her over like one does a slave at market and ignoring her, resumed hammering. Ire rising in her gullet, Jezreel shouted again. "Noah!"

The old man stopped hammering, and wiped his brow with his sleeve. "Look at you, you harlot of Baal. Who are you to tell me to do anything?"

Jezreel felt her face flush with rage.

"You come to me, a whore, fresh from your bed of fornication, the seed of man streaming over your naked thighs like water. Whore. Be gone, I have much work to finish."

"Work? Building this—this–" Jezreel waved her arms at the monster of a boat before her. "This boat, a boat that will never float even if you could get it to water!"

Noah pointed to the sky. "Yahweh will bring the waters to me. And in doing so, you and your worshippers of false gods will perish beneath the waves of his wrath."

Jezreel rolled her eyes. "Baal is the god of storms, old man. Your Yahweh doesn't exist. A feeble god created by a feeble-minded fool." Exasperated, she stomped to her tent, not waiting to hear what else Noah had to say.

Hargarsh came in with a jug of water and a pot of oil and perfume.

"When do I return to the temple? I fear I'll go as crazy as that old man if I have to continue listening to his hammering."

"Not until time enough for a babe to be born, remember, priestess. But I'll bring you anything your heart desires to make you as comfortable as possible." Hargarsh moved the jug over and indicated Jezreel should stand outside the tent. Tenderly, the maid washed the woman and anointed her with oils. Jezreel relaxed under Hagarsh's ministrations, but could still hear Noah's hammering.

"I'm going to scream."

Hargarsh laughed. "I shall bring musicians to play and banish the hammering from your mind."

Jezreel clapped with happiness. "Oh yes. And, I will dance!"

• • •

9 Months Later

Jezreel awoke with a start. The earth rumbled and quaked. Noah finally ceased his hammering, and she finally had peace. At times her tent was so quiet, she swore she heard the babe stirring within her. Hargarsh still believed there were twins in her womb.

Throwing back her furs, Jezreel wobbled her round body to the tent door and went outside. The ground jumped and vibrated. Long lines of animals of all kinds, some she'd never seen before, were going straight to Noah's boat. "Baal's balls! What now?"

Hargarsh came around the tent. "Would you look at that? Some of these beasts I've seen, but what devilry has made these others?"

Jezreel laughed, but then grew quiet. "How does he command them?"

"It's that Yahweh."

"Oh, piss, Hargarsh, we've been over this before. Yahweh is no god and even if he were Baal would have dominion over this lesser deity."

"Then have Baal send these creatures back to where they came from!" Hargarsh shivered.

"Baal has more important things to do: his child is coming." Jezreel placed a hand on her bulging belly and stroked the kicking babe. "His son will be here before nightfall."

Hargarsh smiled. "I must fetch the high priest."

"Bring me a pitcher of water before you leave. I'm exceedingly thirsty."

"I'll go now." Hargarsh made her way to the well with the jug, careful to avoid the lines of roaring, cawing, braying animals. *What were these beasts?* A shudder of fear washed over her as the servant hurried to return to the priestess. "Now into the tent with you," she said, returning with Jezreel's water. "The water's nice and cool."

"Thank you, Hargarsh." Jezreel sat on her pelts, strumming an instrument of shell.

"I'm going to get the high priest. You rest. You'll need your strength to bring Baal's son into the world." The old woman patted Jezreel and rushed away.

Jezreel was restless. She didn't want to lie down. Instead she paced outside the tent watching the parade of animals making their way into the gaping doorway of Noah's monstrosity of a sailing vessel. "It'll never float, and now, with all those beasts inside, how will he ever get it to water?"

The babe was kicking hard. Jezreel wanted the child out. She was miserable and the pangs of labor were crashing upon her. "Walk. Just walk. Walking helps," Jezreel said aloud.

She slowly walked alongside a gray donkey, until she reached Noah's boat. Noah was nowhere to be seen. Jezreel sat on a stump and watched the animals. There were no trees for as far as she could see. Noah and his sons had used them for this crazy ark.

A thunderous clap smacked in the sky; Jezreel jumped. *Boom! Boom!* More thunder followed closely with great white jolts of lightning. Pain ripped through her and she cried out, clutching her side. She was certain the thunder was Baal's announcement that he was in attendance for his son's birth. *Where was Hargarsh?* Something wet hit her face. Rain was pouring from the sky. The animals moved faster and finally she could see the end of the line.

Ham came from the ark, chasing the stragglers inside; and then, ignoring her shouts of pain, he pulled the big door shut. Jezreel held to the stump, squatting over the grass. The rain rushed in torrents over her feet, gathering in a growing puddle and over the barren ground. Soon, the waters rose above her ankles, but Jezreel was concerned about other things. The baby was coming. Wet hair plastered over her face, she grit her teeth, pushing out the babe.

In a slither of blood and fluid, a baby, small and shriveled, blue and lifeless, fell into the rising waters. Jezreel reached for the boy, but before she could grasp its ankle, another pain shot through her. Baal be praised, there *were* twins in her womb. One was dead, but the other still might live. "Hargarsh! Where are you?"

She looked upward and spied Noah and his sons aboard the boat's deck, watching as she gave birth. "Help me!" she shouted, water at her knees, her dead infant floating around her, secured by his umbilical cord. She screamed in pain. The flesh of her woman parts rent and she reached between bloody legs and pulled forth the horned half child of Baal.

The body of a male babe with the head of a black calf, the monster mewed in her arms, rolling black watery eyes against the pummeling rains. Jezreel looked at her infant and horrified, began to scream. "Baal! Great lord, what is this?"

Noah leaned over the deck, looking upon her as she scrambled to stand on the stump, waters rising, her abomination of a child grasped in her arms. "Mock me now, harlot. Even as the waters rise, you still call for your false god. Look at the monster in your hands: demon! Whore. Yahweh will destroy you and all the fornicators that dwell on this earth. He'll wash it clean!"

Jezreel began treading water, her bastard child cast away. The thunder rolled and the waters washed in mighty waves as if on the ocean shore, pummeling her. She clung to the side of the ark, beating upon the walls. Loss of blood and exhaustion wore her down, until she clutched the crack of the massive door with her fingernails, desperate to hang on. Terror consumed her as her eyes scanned the waters for a sign of something solid on which to stand. There was nothing. The waters had covered everything. Carcasses of drowned animals floated beside her. Corpses of dead people bumped against her, piling against the side of Noah's boat.

"Let me in! Open the door!" she shouted, but her shouts faded to whispers as her strength was no more. Her fingers slipped and the waves engulfed her. Weakly, Jezreel called upon Baal for deliverance.

But none came.

EIGHTH CIRCLE: SINS OF FRAUD

THOSE GUILTY OF DELIBERATE, knowing evil. Located within a circle named Malebolge, it is divided into ten ditches with a bridge crossing to each ditch.

DITCH 1: SEDUCERS

Obadiah cupped a hand to his brow, keeping the swirling dust from his eyes as he overlooked the great gorge known as Malebolge. Within the gorge were ten ditches. They would have to cross a bridge to get to each ditch. Azubah muttered to himself, obviously disgruntled.

"What is it?" Obadiah asked.

"I want you to realize that I don't descend lower than where we've been."

"You've never gone beyond this point?"

Azubah scowled. "Oh, I've been there. *Twice.*"

"Hmm," Obadiah said. "Do you not wish to continue? I can request another guide. Though I must admit your expertise has been very useful."

The demon looked insulted. "I never said I wasn't continuing. I just wanted you to be aware that the last two circles contain the vilest of sinners. I avoid these levels."

"Azubah," Obadiah said. "You're a *demon.*"

"That's quite apparent." Azubah gestured up and down, indicating his body proclaimed his demon status. "But, I'm guilty of only being on the wrong side of a battle, other than that, I had a spotless record."

"I see."

"These souls are guilty of wretchedly evil acts that even I find repugnant. That's not to say there aren't other demons that don't relish their crimes."

"Just not you."

"Right. Not me."

Obadiah chewed his lip. "How do we get into the gorge?"

"The cliff."

"I was afraid you were going to say that." Obadiah sighed and tucked his long robe into the breeches underneath. "Lead on."

It took some time to scale the cliff. When they arrived in the circle of Malebolge, they were dusty and disheveled.

"It would've been easier if you flew us down here." Azubah brushed dust from his body.

"Can't. My wings don't work this far from Heaven without a permit. Do we take one of those bridges?" He pointed to ten bridges in various states of disrepair. They approached the first bridge.

"This bridge will take us to the seducers. Don't be fooled by beauty or silver tongues, angel. Everyone here deserves their punishment."

"I'll remember that." Obadiah walked behind the demon guide, across the wobbly bridge, to the ditch on the other side. Before them two lines of those punished for acts of seduction trudged in opposite directions as they were lashed with whips by hoards of demon soldiers.

"I'm grabbing the first soul we can. The demon masters don't take kindly to visitors."

"Of course." Obadiah sat on a pile of wood, probably intended for bridge repair, and waited for Azubah.

The demon snatched a middle-aged woman with dyed blonde hair from the line and hauled her, protesting, to Obadiah, explaining what was going on along the way in order to save time.

The woman put a hand upon an ample hip, and batted singed lashes. "So yer the angel fella wantin' to know my story?"

"That would be me, yes."

"Well, git yerself comfortable, 'cause this is one tale I know you ain't never heard before."

THE INJUN MEDICINE OF CUT-NOSE

Lyla King draped her shapely arm over the rumbling top of the piano.

She listened to the vibrating music echo from within the wood cabinet as Professor pounded away at the keys.

"Don't cha have a customer, Lyla?" Professor asked, still tickling the ivories.

"Course I do. He's waiting in my room. He wanted whiskey, but it's so hot up there, and I walked by your piana and felt the cool air blowin' through and had to stay awhile."

"What's the real reason?" he shouted over the din of his own playing.

"Ah, got ole Harry Bradford up there. *Bastard.*"

"He's a mean one, alright. Thought Madame Violet weren't gonna 'llow him in here no more."

Lyla shrugged. "All Violet cares about is gold. Every throw is another dollar. She ain't about to turn out more money."

Professor played one handed as he pulled his pocket watch by the fob. "You better scoot. Old Bradford's bound to get pissed waitin'."

Lyla sighed and patted Professor on the back before ascending the staircase. She passed Lily on the stairs.

The sassy Creole flipped raven locks over her shoulder. "Who you got?"

"Bradford," Lyla hissed.

"Oh, hell, honey. He's gonna wear yer backside out. That man wants it in the ass more than any man I ever knowed."

Lyla rolled her eyes. "Last time I had Bradford, the bastard put me out of business for a week. 'Bout ripped me in two."

Lily looked at the whiskey in Lyla's hand. "Better drink as much of that as you can. Deaden the pain."

"Yeah, well, if I don't come out by mornin', come make sure I ain't dead," Lyla said, sauntering through the hot hall toward her room. She opened the door.

Bradford lay on the bed, his stiff pecker standing up in his hand. "There you are, girl. What took you so long?"

Lyla closed the door, and sat the whiskey and glasses on her dry sink. "Packed house. You know how it is." She filled his glass. "Whiskey?"

He reached for the glass. As he did, he knocked his pile of dirty clothes from the bed. Lyla retrieved them, slinging them into a nearby chair. A small, beaded pouch fell to the floor.

She picked it up. "Where'd you git this?"

Gulping his liquor, he shrugged. "Off a dead Injun woman. She didn't need it no more."

"This is Pawnee." The words slipped from her mouth faster than she could think 'em.

"How you know what type Injun made that?" Bradford said.

"You see a lot of folks in my line of work. You learn stuff."

Bradford eyed her suspiciously. "Where'd you git that black hair from, girl? You Mexican? Madame Violet told me you were a white girl. Told her I didn't want no Mexican cunt."

"Born and raised in America." Lyla laughed, her heart pounding inside. She opened a window a crack and wiped the perspiration from her brow. "More whiskey?"

Bradford held out his glass. She filled it. He gulped the liquor, and tossed the glass into the corner. It shattered. Lyla frowned. Before she could say anything, Bradford clapped a beefy paw around her arm and yanked her to the bed. His whiskey-heavy breath pelted her with pungent puffs. "I betcha part Injun."

Lyla squirmed beneath him, turning her head away from his flying spittle. "What makes you think something like that, Harry?" She laughed, hoping she was persuasive.

"A hunch."

"Harry, you can't go around claiming people are Injun based on a half-drunk hunch." She laughed again. "Now we gonna lay it, or you got another idea?"

Bradford leaned his forearm over her chest, pinning her to the bed with his girth. He ripped her shift from her in shreds, throwing the fabric to the floor. "I think you *are* Injun. You know what I *do* to Injun girls?"

"Can't be any worse than what you do to white girls, now, Harry. Come on, lemme up." Lyla tried to diffuse the drunken man.

"Oh, no siree. You ain't foolin' me no more, girl. I always knowed something was off 'bout you." Harry mounted her while he rambled, and started huffing away.

Lyla let her mind wander the forested mountains surrounding the cabin of her childhood; that peaceful place before her trapper father drown and her mother died with a baby stuck half way in and half way out. She almost forgot, but not quite, that beastly Harry had his pocked prick stuffed inside her. "Ow!" She snapped to her senses at the sharp stick of what was a knife. "Harry!" The bastard was tauntingly pressing a knife blade against her leg, point in her flesh. "What the hell?"

"I'm gonna cut you, whore. Gonna cut you wide open like I did the Injun woman I took that beaded bag from."

"Now, Harry–"

"Yer an Injun. I know it."

"I am not!" Slowly, Lyla blindly reached for the beaded pouch on the chair beside the bed. It was a shaman's pouch. The poor woman who was wearing it, that Harry killed, must have needed protection. She wondered why it had failed her. Lyla clutched the bag. She felt the silky beads cool against her hot hand. Harry jabbed her again, harder. She felt blood trickle over her leg. She gripped the pouch and chanted a few words.

Harry froze. "Whatcha sayin'?"

"*Ah-wa-ee-cha-naw-wee.*"

Bradford sat back on his haunches, rage twisting his ugly features. "Uh-huh. I knowed it." Before he could finish his sentence, the window came crashing inward, glass shattering. A huge, lumbering figure tore the thin curtains away from his body with a fury of snorts.

"What in the name of–" Harry sprang from the bed quite agilely for a man who'd consumed as much whiskey has he had, but then fell on his face.

Standing before them was a misshapen, monstrosity of a man. Bulging muscles covered with dirt, grime and a layer of black hair, formed the man's legs, torso and arms; but on his shoulders rested a huge, horned head of a buffalo with strange human eyes as blue as sapphires. An odor of death and decomposition clung to the beast, and Bradford gagged at the smell. The creature snorted and bellowed.

Lyla called his name: "Cut-nose!"

Bradford dropped his knife and made for the door on his hands and knees, his swollen member shrinking on the way.

Cut-nose blasted a ghastly roar. Lyla's hands flew over her ears as she cowered on the bed against the wall. The abomination bounded across the room, grabbing Bradford by the shoulders, pulling him to his stinking body. With massive hands, Cut-nose broke Harry's back across his lifted knee and then seeing the cast off knife, sliced the moaning man's penis from his crotch. Lyla knew what Cut-nose would do next. Fearful of the creature, she held out the beaded pouch. Gently, the buffalo-man gathered it up and undid the leather laces. Cut-nose turned it upside down, spilling a hard, shriveled piece of flesh onto the floor: a dried-up, severed penis.

He put Bradford's hunk of flesh into the pouch and handed it, blood-smeared, back to Lyla. The creature grunted something incoherent, before leaping through the busted window into the night. Harry

Bradford lay on the floor bleeding, babbling like a madman in a pool of piss and blood.

Lyla slipped the protective pouch around her neck as Madame Violet burst through the door. "What the hell's happening in here?"

Lyla trembled, feigning terror and pointed to the destroyed wall and window. Violet, hands on hips, knit her brows, and called for Linus, the hired jack-of-all-trades. "Git this man to the doctor, and when he's done with him, tell the doctor to come check Lyla. She's my best girl. Get a move on! Time's money, man!" With a motherly embrace, she pulled a gown over Lyla's head, and walked her from the room. Lyla locked eyes with Bradford, and gave him a little smile.

• • •

Obadiah stopped writing, strangely perplexed. "Cut-nose didn't kill you?"

"No."

"This wasn't the story of your death?"

"Of course not, honey. Who wants to hear that sad tale? I died alone in a Denver brothel with a bottle of whiskey in my hand, fat, old and with too much rouge. Not exactly a fittin' tale for yer book there." She pointed to the book. She smiled, licked her lips, and laughed.

Obadiah thanked her and off she walked to face the whips for the rest of eternity.

DITCH 2: FLATTERERS

Azubah led the way, his walking stick thumping over the rotting wood bridge, his hooves occasionally wedging into a hole. A terrible scent bombarded the pair as they reached the center of the bridge. Each looked at the other and cupped hands over noses. The ditch was full of human excrement. Azubah was the first to step from the bridge. "Mind you stay to the path," he cautioned.

Obadiah let his gaze drift over the ground to each side of the path. More excrement covered the land. "You won't have to tell me twice." Before them they beheld men and women sunk waist deep in great globs of excrement. "Perhaps we should just speak with a soul near the path?"

Azubah nodded. "An excellent suggestion."

Near the path, a woman wailed, her face and hair streaked with liquid dung. She sniffed when she noticed the angel and the demon. Azubah detailed their assignment. She attempted to stave her sniffling nose by wiping it on her arm, but instead smeared more foul crap all over. At last Obadiah ripped a scrap from his robe and, with pity, gave it to the woman. She cleaned her face as best as she could and got on with her story.

CEAD MILE FAILTE

(*Kaid Mee-la Fall-che*: 100,000 Welcomes)
1500 Leinster, Ireland

"I'm warning you, Bran O'Keill! Brigid Flannegan doesn't want yer heart, she's after yer money, plain and true." Gwyndolyn thumped her fist on the table, dishes jumped. Bran's eyebrows rose disapprovingly. He continued eating his breakfast without reply. "Aren't you going to say anything?"

He set his spoon on his bowl, pausing to take a deep breath before answering his over-protective, though genuinely loving, sister. "You've nothing to fear from Brigid. She's a hard worker and when she's my wife she'll help ease your responsibilities."

Gwyndolyn pushed her chair away from the table. "So that's it, then? You'll ignore all that I've told you? Mark my words, that woman will be your ruin!"

Bran laughed. "The only thing she'll be is my *wife*."

"Not if I can do anything about it!"

Bran stood, facing his defiant sister. "Remember who is lord of this manor, sister."

"Aye, I know who runs this roost. It's that silver-tongued devil with scarlet hair that promises the moon and stars and all manner of things she can't produce. She doesn't love you, you fool. Can you not see through her pretty words and womanly wiles?"

"That's enough." Bran crossed the room to the fireplace, turning his back on his sister.

Gwyndolyn thought a few words, but held her tongue. She watched her brother's broad shoulders bend toward the embers as he poked the logs. Brigid Flannegan wouldn't be mistress of this house, not as long as Gwyndolyn had breath to breathe. She threw down her napkin and stomped from the great hall into the corridor, leading to the outside courtyard. On her way, she passed a servant ushering the bitch herself, Brigid Flannegan, inside.

Brigid tossed handfuls of copious tresses behind her shoulders. "*Cead mile failte,*" she said, a smile curling pink full lips.

Gwyndolyn admired the woman's beauty. It was easy to see why Bran was smitten, but she knew the strumpet bore a bastard to the Earl of Dunsbury and paid with the Earl's money to hush wagging tongues. Bran refused to listen, dismissing it as gossip, nothing but jealousy from old maids. She smiled in return, but narrowed her eyes and spoke quietly: "Don't be so sure you're as welcome here as you claim to welcome me."

Brigid flashed another smile. "Oh, I'll be welcome within my own home. For this house that we're in, will most certainly be mine and I the mistress of it."

Gwyndolyn gathered her skirts in a rage, marched through the corridor, pushing doors open in a fury, and into the sun-lit courtyard. It was quiet save for a groom and a waiting carriage. As she stood there deciding what her next strategy might be, her brother emerged from the house with Brigid on his arm.

"Good day, sister. We'll be traveling to Lord Tartington's for the afternoon. Brigid tells me you already bid one another good morning."

Gwyndolyn eyed the red-haired harlot with suspicion. "Aye, brother, that we did."

Brigid smiled. She patted Bran's arm. "I was telling Gwynny what a handsome brother she has and how we're fortunate to be in your good blessings."

Bran blushed.

"Aye, you did," Gwyndolyn said. "And I remarked how it was a very lucky thing indeed for a girl with such expensive whims to have snared a fish as fine as you."

Bran frowned at his sister. "Such sharp words."

Brigid laughed musically, a twinkle in her eyes. "Oh, Bran, she jests for no words so sharp could come from one so soft."

Gwyndolyn smiled at the two-edged words of Bran's betrothed. "Have a pleasant outing," she said and sent the groom to fetch her own carriage. She felt the need to get away from the manor. To think. To scheme. To find a way to save her brother from this devil in a woman's skin. She knew where she needed to go, and she knew what she needed to do. It was a risky plan, but a necessary one.

After she watched Bran's carriage rumble through the gate, Gwyndolyn went inside the manor house, and selected a gold platter from the cupboard. With this tucked under one arm, she returned to the courtyard in time to greet her driver. "Take me to the fork near the bridge that crosses the River Boyne." Off the carriage jolted and bounced, the horses swift, the road narrow. It didn't take long to follow the winding country road to the river. Gwyndolyn observed her reflection in the gleaming platter as the minutes passed. With a bump, she was jostled forward as the carriage came to an abrupt halt.

"The fork, mistress," the driver called, stopping the carriage.

She looked from the window into the lush valley that held the rushing waters of the river.

The driver assisted her from the carriage, and waited silently for further instructions. Gwyndolyn smiled at him. "Stay here. I'll return when I'm finished." She gathered her skirts into one hand, and the platter in the other and walked alone, into the valley, and to the gurgling river that flowed between the forest of emerald green.

The ways of the old ones were strong in these parts and when Gwyndolyn's mother had been alive she'd taken great care in her daughter's instruction in the old gods and goddesses. The fat priests in their robes of brown might promise holy works, but those steeped in the old ways were accustomed to actions, not mere words. If you wanted something, you went straight to the source. Stopping Brigid Flannegan was no easy task. Her brother was bent on bringing about his own destruction at the hand of this strumpet. If Gwyndolyn's mother were still alive, she knew that she'd be here on the bank of the river doing exactly what she was doing now.

Gwyndolyn tossed the gleaming gold platter into the rushing waters. It landed with a loud splash. She bunched her skirts beneath her and settled upon a flat stone to wait for Boannan, that goddess of ancient Eire. If Boannan couldn't rid Bran of Brigid, no one could.

The waters parted as if pulled back like the Red Sea in the monk's tale of Moses, and a woman that shone like the sun stood upon the wet, bare ground. "I've heard the heart of a daughter calling me from my slumber," she said, in a voice as clear as the waters dancing in a towering wall to the sides of her.

Gwyndolyn bowed, her nose brushing the swaying grasses and peaty moss. "I called you, oh beautiful and healing Boannan."

The goddess looked Gwyndolyn over, and then smiled radiantly. "I knew your mother."

"Aye, it was my mother who taught me your ways. I've never summoned you before. But, now I need your help if you would find it within your heart to grant me your favor."

The goddess's face was full of compassion. "Tell me your need."

"My brother, Bran, won't listen to caution when it comes to his betrothed. He's flattered by her forked tongue and heeds nothing I tell him. She wants to marry him not for love, but for his money."

Boannan frowned. "Is this so unusual? Marriages are oft arranged out of necessity's sake, not out of love for each other. How is this woman different from all of those?"

Gwyndolyn nodded in agreement. "What you say is correct, but in those cases the couples involved know the way of things and don't assume that love is given. Bran believes that Brigid loves him because she has told him so. She doesn't love him at all. She only loves his wealth. He isn't the first nobleman that Brigid has tried to secure for herself."

Boannan pondered these words. "Deception is vile. Deception where love is concerned is even fouler. You're a wise sister to try to save your brother from this whore. Because you love your brother, and your heart is pure, I will help you." She stretched forth her hands and a silver urn materialized. "Take this. Make it a gift to this flatterer."

Gwyndolyn scowled. "A gift? For Brigid?"

Boannan smiled. "Behold the urn, daughter. It will tell you much."

Gwyndolyn accepted the urn. On one side, a beautiful woman's face was embossed. On the other, the woman's face was twisted, distorted, hideous to behold.

"Heed my instructions. Make this a present unto your brother. When he touches it, his ears will begin to heal. He will begin to hear the lies in her words."

"But you said this was a gift for Brigid."

"Oh, but it is. Does not this woman covet all things of worth that are your brother's? Won't your brother bow to her desires and make her a gift of the thing she wants?"

Gwyndolyn smiled. Now she understood.

"Once Bran gifts it to Brigid, the urn will give her what she truly deserves. You must tell her that the goddess Boannan will give her all that she desires."

Gwyndolyn nodded.

"When the urn has done its job, return it to me."

"Aye, I will, goddess." She turned to leave, but Boannan stopped her.

"Don't you wish to ask something for yourself?"

"No, Boannan. My brother's happiness is gift enough for me."

"You are a wise sister," the goddess said, and as she spoke, the waters crashed around her and she disappeared beneath the churning waves.

Gwyndolyn returned home and did as Boannan bid her. In two days, Brigid passed her in the hall, the polished silver urn tightly in her grasp.

"See what Bran has given me?"

"A family heirloom." Gwyndolyn feigned admiration. "Did he tell you of its magical properties?"

Brigid's eyes widened. "No!"

"Oh, he must have forgotten. The urn grants your deepest desires."

Brigid grew excited. "How does it work?"

"You only have to hold it and make a wish."

Brigid beamed. She held the urn before her, closing her eyes. Gwyndolyn flinched as Brigid's face was suddenly peppered with pockmarks and wrinkles.

"Did it work?" Brigid asked.

"I think so," Gwyndolyn said and waved farewell, as Brigid rushed outside to her waiting carriage. The driver showed obvious shock, but said nothing as his station dictated.

Brigid returned home and ran to her mirror to see the results of her wish. She screamed. Immediately, she grabbed the urn. She must have done something wrong. She'd try again. "I want to be tall, thin, beautiful and young!"

At once, her spine twisted and bent, her nose grew pointy and crooked, her beautiful mane of scarlet locks grew gray, wiry and sparse. The skin on her face sagged and yellowed and her once white teeth grew black and broken.

"What witchery is this?" Brigid shouted, shaking the urn. Although she wanted to cast blame upon Gwyndolyn, she couldn't as it had been Bran who had given it to her. Instead, she decided to sell it and use the money to hire a witch to restore her beauty.

When she took it to market to sell, she was accused of thievery and thrown into a dank cell. "Please! Will not someone send a message to Lord Bran that his betrothed is locked within this dungeon?"

The jailers found her amusing, but didn't deliver her message. They knew she was a crazy old hag, probably a witch to boot.

• • •

Bran waited, arms crossed, on the step overlooking the courtyard. His face was a map of sorrow. Gwyndolyn came from behind and wrapped a gentle arm around her brother. "Brigid still hasn't returned?"

"No."

"I saw her leaving with the silver urn I gave you."

"I was a fool to give it to her. It was a gift from you, but I can't deny her anything. Anything she asks, I give to her. I'm sorry I gave your gift away."

Gwyndolyn hugged him. "You love her. It's natural. But, ruefully, I must admit that I'm sorry you gave her the silver urn. I fear she only wanted riches and when she finally obtained something of great value, she showed her true colors and departed, never to return."

Bran's shoulders sagged.

"We'll find you a true love, one whose heart is pure," Gwyndolyn said.

Bran went inside and shut the door. A messenger arrived at the gates as Gwyndolyn was turning to follow her brother. In his arms he bore the silver urn. "The sheriff sends this to Lord Bran. He bids me tell you that an old hag was caught trying to sell it at market. She confessed that it was Lord Bran's."

Gwyndolyn accepted the urn and thanked the man. Bran must never know the message delivered, nor could he know that the urn had been returned. She called for her carriage.

As before, the driver waited at the fork while Gwyndolyn walked to the water. With a word of thanks, she tossed the urn into the ripples. She smiled as it sank, and with it, all of the evil words and deeds of Brigid Flannegan.

DITCH 3: PAYING FOR HOLY OFFICE

Crossing the next bridge was a better experience. Obadiah and Azubah were both relieved to breath fresh air again, though the overtone to any air found in Hell possessed a sulfuric tang. The bridge crossed onto a span of jagged rocks. Cold and barren. Gray and pocked everywhere with holes out of which legs waved in protest against the abuse heaped upon the bottoms of their feet. Demons with flaming torches repeatedly burned the soles of the flailing sinners, whose heads were deeply buried within the confines of the stone.

"I suppose we must yank someone from their hole," Obadiah said, watching Azubah's reaction.

"Lucky someone," Azubah said, and approached the nearest demon to explain their task. He returned with a fat, bald man who began wringing his hands more frantically the closer he got to Obadiah.

"This *monster* tells me I must relate my life story to you," the man said, voice hoarse from constant shrieking. He hopped from one bare foot to the other to relieve the pain of his charred soles. "I'd really rather not."

"Speak!" Azubah said, a low growl following his order.

The man flinched and scooted closer to the angel. "I'm an evil man."

"Yes, we realize this. Hence your being in Hell." Obadiah tapped his pen upon his book, anxious to continue. "We appreciate your cooperation. You may sit, if you'd like." He pointed to a rock, and the man sat, shoulders slumping, resigned to his duty of relating his tale.

BEC DE CORBIN
(CROW'S BEAK)

The end of Father Giovanni Cavalcanti's quill grew dull, so he pulled a knife from his robes and shaved it to a point. With fantasies of clinking gold from full parish coffers and loftier appointments occupying his mind, he repeatedly dunked the nib into the ink.

Father Giaus laughed. "Lost in thought, brother?"

Giovanni blinked his attention back to the task at hand. He yawned. "What I wouldn't give for a change of pace around here!"

"Come now, brother. What better past time could one have than to translate the words of our God?"

Giovanni laughed. "Translations. Prayers for the sick and dying. Confessions. It's an endless cycle. If I have to listen to one more blathering idiot tearfully confess the latest buggering of farm animals I might lose my mind."

Giaus frowned, but then a smile curled his lips. "Ah, it's excitement you crave?"

"That and more. The slow cogs of advancement within the church frustrate me. I'm an old man humbled for years in this same poverty-stricken parish. What I crave is a permanent move. Advancement. Change of game and scenery. Away from here."

"Greed."

"Probably so."

Father Giaus tapped the end of his feather against his cap. "Well, you won't get any of *that* around here."

"Ten years of laborious translation confirms that."

Giaus stood and crossed the cavernous room, footsteps echoing on the stone floor, and closed the door. He sidled over to Giovanni's table. "I have some information."

"About?"

"A man, a Cardinal, who might be able to help you. He once offered me something more than what I have now, but I wasn't interested in his offer." Giaus studied Giovanni. "You, on the other hand, just might be."

Giovanni smiled. "Why so secretive?" He nodded toward the closed door.

"Cardinal Bruno Scala is a dealmaker."

"What do you mean?"

Giaus sighed. "You don't believe men rise through the ranks based on works alone, do you?"

"Of course not."

"Well, your family is wealthy, are they not?" Giaus's voice trailed away.

A knowing expression crept over Giovanni's face. "This Scala, he can help me become a bishop or, an archbishop?"

"Maybe more. He has the Pope's ear."

"How do *you* know this?" Giovanni couldn't help but be a bit suspicious.

"Not important. What's important to remember is—if Scala gives you what you want, you don't forget who pointed you in his direction."

"Why don't *you* pay him then?"

"Alas, my family are simple farmers, not nobles like your stock," Giaus said. "I've already risen much higher in life than my station dictates. No big cities or fancy robes for me."

Giovanni laughed. "Well, if Scala can fulfill my desires, perhaps a lengthy stay at my lavish residence will be your reward?"

Giaus rapped the table with his finger. "Stay at your residence? I'll be doing the work for the both of us once you're gone." He grimaced and made his way to his table. "I'll write you a letter of introduction. How you get to Milan is your own business."

• • •

Milan, Italy

The marble halls of Milan differed vastly from the humble stone monastery he called home. Red velvet drapes held cold drafts at the windows. Fires blazed in hearths and wine was served in etched crystal goblets.

Behind a heaping platter of roast fowl, Cardinal Bruno Scala feasted, greasy fingers waving, lips smacking between words. He paused to pick meat from his teeth, and then he sized up Father Giovanni. "What do you bring for an offering?"

"Offering?"

"This appointment you desire is also desired by others," Scala said, following his statement with a gulp of wine. His glass hit the table with a clink.

"I have gold."

"That's a start. What else have you?"

"What more is there than gold?"

"What would you give for this appointment?" Scala stopped eating and waited for Giovanni's response.

"What would I give? I'd give my life! My soul! One more day of talking about herb gardens and parchment thickness and I'll go mad!"

Scala laughed heartily and wiped his fingers on a napkin. "Well, now, gold, your soul, and your life. That ups the payment now, doesn't it?"

Giovanni laughed along with the cardinal.

"Here, sit, sit! There's enough food here for an entire monastery. You look hungry. What do they feed you in the country?"

Giovanni sat beside the cardinal while a servant prepared his plate. He tried not to seem too famished as he shoveled the rich foods into his mouth.

Scala removed a rolled document from his robes and called for ink and a pen. Giovanni dipped bread into the salty sauce on his plate, while, curious, tried to read the upside down writing on the parchment. "Sign here," he said, holding the pen out to Giovanni.

Giovanni wiped his hands on his napkin and took the pen. "What's this?"

"Our agreement for your new appointment."

Giovanni smiled and scribbled his signature on the line near Scala's pointing finger. He never imagined it could be so simple. Scala rolled the document and wrapped a ribbon around it; then, he returned it to his voluminous robes. "Tomorrow you shall be a new man, Padre. Riches and glory shall be yours."

Giovanni's head rang with delirious rapture. Everything happened so quickly, so easily. There must be an abundance of archbishop positions, or maybe, he scratched his head while listening to Scala drone on, just *maybe* there was a catch. He realized he now owed Scala his uncompromising loyalty in Vatican politics and intrigue, perhaps *that* was the reason Scala was so quick to inter him in a choice position. Scala needed men willing to play by his rules. Well, for riches and power, Giovanni would gladly back Scala in whatever scheme he hatched.

• • •

Years rolled into decades and finally the day came when Giovanni's mortal coil was near expiration. Padre Scala had passed away many years ago in his villa by the sea and he, himself, had succeeded the cardinal in his position. Giovanni sent for a priest to hear his final confession in his bedchamber, as he was old, frail, and found it difficult to walk.

A knock rapped at the door.

"Come in, it's not latched." Giovanni called from his chair before the fire.

A black-robed figure entered, stooped and with a walking stick gripped beneath the robe's sleeve. The door closed behind the man with a *click*.

Giovanni's eyes failed him; all he could see was the blackness of the cowl and robe. Still, he waved him over. "Come, come, the fire's warm. Sit, *fratello*, sit."

The bent form of the priest hobbled to the chair. Giovanni watched as the black-gloved hands reached upward and lowered the blanketing cowl.

He gasped. "Y—you!"

"*Ciao, vecchio amico.*" Sitting in the chair, swathed in the layers of the black robe, was a gnarled creature, red and covered with boils. Long, black fingernails curled from knobby fingers, and the face that stared back at Giovanni was familiar.

"Is it really you, Scala?"

"In the flesh."

"But, you're–"

"Dead?"

"No! A monster!"

Scala laughed. "No more than always, Padre Giovanni. I just wear my *true* face now, that's all. It wouldn't do to roam through life with this–"

He waved to his face. "Visage, now would it?"

"But why?" Confusion rang in Giovanni's voice.

"Why am I here or why am I alive?" Scala said, another baritone chuckle escaping his black lips.

"Yes!" Giovanni clutched his robes fearfully.

Scala, or the demon-monstrosity that once was Scala, reached into his robes and pulled forth an old, battered document, rolled and sealed. His bony hands broke the wax and unfurled the parchment as he smoothed it flat upon the small table before them. "I've come to collect my payment."

"Payment?"

"For your position as Archbishop of Milan, and subsequently, cardinal. The one you've held so luxuriously for decades." Scala's eyes narrowed into a seething glare. "You promised me your life, *your soul*, if you recall the terms of our agreement."

Giovanni frowned. "Surely, you jest."

"Surely not!" Scala ran his finger over the paragraphs on the document. He read aloud: *What would I give? I'd give my life! My soul!* Do you recognize those words, Cardinal Giovanni?"

"No? Should I? What do they mean?"

"That was your answer when I asked you, those many years ago, what you'd give for the position you held, before holding my office."

"But, that was just an expression!"

Scala laughed and stood, leaning heavily against his walking stick. "One should be careful of one's expressions." He pulled a gleaming silver stiletto, long and sleek, from his robes.

"W—w—hat are you doing?" Giovanni said, withdrawing as far as he could into his chair. His mind begged his frail legs to run, but they failed to move. Instead, the old man pissed himself from fright. He held up his cross. "Get behind me, you foul demon!"

Scala laughed. "Oh, you're in much too deep for that. Remember the wine? The gold? The villas? The *women*? Look around you, cardinal. Behold, the fruits of your harvest—the abundance of your sins! You who have preyed on the weak using your power and office to obtain wealth and status. How many poor peasants have you trampled? How many girls defiled and boys buggered to satiate the desires of your flesh? You're a scavenger seeking your riches from the destruction of others. How many went hungry while you dined? You'd do anything to be powerful, anything to be rich! And now, I'm here to scavenge your payment as promised those many years ago."

Giovanni's body quaked. He clutched his chest as pains shot through his rasping heart. Scala touched the hard, cold blade to Giovanni's wrinkled flesh, and slashed the old man's throat.

Crimson blood gushed from beneath his feeble fingers, coursing in a stream over the heavy cross on his chest, as a look of terror gripped his face. Scala wiped the blood-smeared stiletto upon the document, and then dropped the blade onto the table with a tinkling sound.

"Debt collected, old friend." The demon Scala turned his back on the dying man and let himself out.

DITCH 4: SORCERERS

Azubah stepped from the bridge, followed by Obadiah. "Sorcerers," the demon grumbled. "We'll have to watch this specimen closely. These are the tricksters of Hell—always a ruse up their sleeves."

"I'll be careful, Azubah. You don't need to worry about me."

"Worry? I'd find it amusing if one of these bastards sucked you into their web of illusions. Then we'd be done with all this bother and I could return to my post."

Obadiah smiled and shook his head. His thoughts were cut short when Azubah suddenly stopped walking. "There they are," the demon said, pointing.

All around, sitting on rocks and craggy ledges, were the sorcerers of the circle. Still clad in all manners of velvets and satins, their luxurious robes revealed many a king's sorcerer—and the ragged, tattered of the masses revealed the poor man's soothsayers. But, it wasn't the costuming that caught the angel's attention. It was the unnatural state of the bodies before him. The heads of the damned were twisted around so they faced over their backs. Yet, their limbs remained forward facing so each body walked clumsily. Every now and then a scream could be heard as a sorcerer plunged over the ledge beneath the bridge into an even deeper section of the ditch.

Obadiah grimaced, which failed to go unnoticed by Azubah

"Pleasant, isn't it?" the demon said.

"Hardly. I choose that one, that crone there, and let's be done with this circle!"

Azubah seized the shrieking hag by her long black hair and set her upon a rock, back and face toward the angel to recount her tale.

IT ALL COMES UNDONE

The old woman pulled her ragged gown closer as she stirred a pot of stew for the stranger.

"I thank you for your gracious hospitality, my lady," the man, who was quite old himself, said.

"Zorah's my name and we can't have you freezing to death in the forest. Not any place to be in this cold. What takes you through these parts?"

The old man warmed his trembling hands before the fire. "I once lived near here."

The hag clucked over the stew. "You should know better then, these woods are rife with thieves."

"And witches, I hear," the old man said with a chuckle.

Zorah ladled steaming stew into a wood bowl and passed it to the man. "What do *you* know of witches?"

The man looked over his spoon, sheepishly. "I've heard stories."

Zorah cackled a laugh. "I have a story to tell about witches—that is—" she poked him with a skeletal finger, "If you want to hear it?"

"Yes, yes, tell me." The man blew on the hot vegetables in his bowl.

Zorah settled into her chair, pulling a goat pelt over her legs. With a smile curling wrinkled lips, she began her tale: "Years ago before the great Arthur was king, before the chaos of Mordred began, while Arthur was but a boy, his sister, Morgan Le Fey lay with the great sorcerer, Merlin, and was got with child. Neither Morgan nor Merlin trusted the other despite their romance. So, when Morgan delivered the babe, a girl, Merlin snatched the child and ran away with her.

Before Morgan could wonder where the sorcerer had gone with the baby, the pangs of labor were upon her once more and she birthed another child, also a girl. And *this* babe, Morgan gave to her servant and bid her spirit the girl away to Scotland to be reared by a faithful friend."

"What happened to the other girl, the one Merlin stole?" the old man asked.

"Merlin took her to a loyal knight's household to be raised in Wales. This girl had no knowledge of her true parentage, but the girl in the North was told of her parents, but *not* that she had a *sister*. Well, years passed and Merlin and Morgan confessed their misdeeds to one another, but felt it would cause naught but heartache if they meddled in the lives of their grown daughters with such knowledge after so many years."

The old man sat his bowl on the hearth.

Zorah put her bowl atop his, and continued her story. "Merlin's girl was known as Adeline the Witch of the West; while, Morgan's child, was called the Witch of the North. The Witch of the North coveted the comfortable castle of her cousin King Arthur, and so she acknowledged his Christ and Arthur welcomed her to Camelot. In the meantime, Adeline the Witch of the West came from Wales to serve an assistant to Merlin, who she knew not was her father."

"Complicated little family," the old man said.

"Aye, it was, it was." Zorah laughed, but continued. "It came to pass that Adeline fell in love with a priest who lived in Camelot. The Witch of the North and Adeline never got along. Adeline was free to practice her craft under Merlin's tutelage, but the Witch of the North had to pretend to turn her back on sorcery in order to please the king. The priest was a holy man and refused to yield to Adeline's charms, but the Witch of the North discovered a way to destroy Adeline, whom she grew to detest more each day."

"And, Adeline, still didn't know she had a sister?" the old man asked.

"No, and the Witch of the North doesn't know either. She just hates Adeline and is jealous that the woman can practice sorcery while Arthur has banned her from the arts."

"I see."

Zorah gestured with wrinkled hands. "Well, the Witch of the North went to Arthur and confessed the misdeeds of Adeline and the wayward priest. Arthur believed his cousin and ordered the priest burned for fornication. Adeline confronted the Witch of the North, certain it was her lies that caused the death of her beloved, but platonic, priest. They argued profusely, but before Adeline could use any incantations, The Witch of the North ran Adeline through with a sword. Morgan, her mother, burst through the doors shrieking, that the women were twin sisters."

"Too late!" the man gasped.

"Indeed. And, it failed to change matters anyway, as the one still abhorred the other, and Adeline was skewered on the end of the Witch of the North's sword." Zorah laughed as if the tale were very amusing.

The old man frowned. "What happened to the Witch of the North?"

Zorah smiled wickedly. "She persuaded Arthur that eleven of his priests also had carnal knowledge of that slut witch Adeline and they were all burned upon a huge fire."

The old man grew very somber. "And then?"

"No *and then*. The Witch of the North lived to be a very old woman who continued her magicks once she was free of that bumbling nit of a cousin of a king."

The old man squinted in the dim room, suspiciously. "I don't believe it. How could she just get away with her sins like that?"

"Don't believe it?" Zorah cackled, angrily.

"How do you know of this tale?" the old man asked.

Zorah poked the air with her finger. "*I am the Witch of the North!* I'm the one who killed my sister Adeline and turned the mind of Arthur, killing those wretched priests, and here I am—old and alive—safe in my cottage in the woods!"

The old man's face grew a shade darker and he leapt from his chair, sliding his sword from his robes with a hiss. Before the startled witch could reply, he lunged forward and ran her through with his sword.

"I am Lancelot, crone! And no more will you live while innocents lie in their graves unpardoned! In the end, all sins must be accounted for, Zorah, Witch of the North!"

Zorah collapsed against the stone hearth, blood seeping from her wrinkled mouth, as Lancelot gathered his belongings and left the cottage in the woods.

DITCH 5: CORRUPT POLITICIANS

"Here they come," Azubah said, his lips smacking with distaste.

"Who?"

"Them." Azubah pointed to a horde of terrifying demons approaching the bridge.

"Who are they?" Obadiah hadn't seen such demons before. Instead of leathery red flesh like his guide's, these huge beasts were black and ashy gray. Their wings were nothing more than nubs on their ridge-y backs, and they boasted long, reptilian tails.

"*The Malebranche.*"

"Evil claws?"

"They're the demons that guard the boiling lake of pitch, that we should be seeing, just about—now." As Azubah spoke, the pair crossed over a hump on the bridge and as they made their way to land, could now see a huge expanse of bubbling, black tar. Around the lake stood massive demon brutes with all manner of sharp implements. As a condemned soul surfaced from the boiling mire, one of the black demons would poke and prod him or her until the soul sunk below the pitch again.

The Malebranche stopped in front of Azubah, faces grim. "Lucifer sent a memo yesterday mentioning that we should expect you," the leader of the bunch said. "Get what you need and get out, there was a series of car bombings in the Middle East and we're expecting half a dozen politicians here at any moment."

Azubah bowed. "You won't even know we're here."

"But I *do* know you're here, and I want you gone A.S.A.P."

"Yes, my lord." Azubah groveled beneath the penetrating stare of the demon. Then, he glared at Obadiah, who flinched.

Obadiah knew the demon couldn't be happy about the display of humility he underwent in front of him. They cleared the cluster of demons, as Obadiah cleared his throat. "Sorry about back there."

Azubah frowned. "Don't apologize. I don't want your pity. We all have a cross to bear."

Obadiah's eyebrows arched in surprise. "Still, I–"

Azubah had picked up a long-handled hook from a pile of discarded weaponry. "Angel, stop talking."

Obadiah sucked in a breath.

Azubah slung the hook into the tarry lake and pulled on whatever it snared. "Help me pull this bastard to shore."

The angel sat his book and pen on a flat stone, and seized the end of the hook, putting his back into assisting Azubah. Like a cork from a bottle, a man was sucked from the sticky tar and plopped with a pop, dripping and sticky, onto the shore.

Azubah sneered. "It's *him*."

"Who's him?" Obadiah walked closer for a better view. He saw who it was. "Oh, *him*!"

The *him* was a former president of the United States: Michael Webb. One of the most despicable leaders to ever hold office. An American who took the lessons of Stalin and Hussein to heart when it came to eradicating his own people for his own twisted personal gain.

Azubah kicked the man in the backside. "Stand up!" The tar-coated man struggled to his feet. "This is a census-taker. Tell him your mortal tale."

"You both know who I am," the man answered, his voice haughty.

"Maybe so, but Suriel says we record stories, so we record stories.

Now, start talking." Azubah knocked the man in the back of the head.

"Perhaps I don't care about your census."

Obadiah looked over the edge of his book at the gooey former president.

"Then maybe I'll have to get one of *them*–" Azubah thumbed over his shoulder toward the hoard of *Malebranche* demons, "to persuade you to grace us with your honored tale."

Michael Webb eyed the demons with fear, and hastily changed his tune. "No, that won't be necessary. I'll tell you anything you want to know."

JUDAS RENEWED

"Yeah, yeah, yeah. I don't care how much it costs." Burton Wylie paused. "Listen; just make sure the Fentanyle derivative is released into the subway system at precisely 5:25 pm Eastern time. We want the two attacks simultaneously choreographed." He thumbed through a pile of folders atop the president's desk. He looked at his watch. "Okay. You got it: 5:25. The anthrax assault will hit the D.C. metro-rail, red, orange and green line, at the same time. Of course, we've taken precautions for the team. Don't let me down, Hugh." Burton hung up the phone.

"Thanks, Burton." Michael Webb, President of the United States, looked up with a charming smile as Burton scowled and stood, moving from the president's chair. "You ready for the impending chaos?"

"As I'll ever be," Burton said. "You better hope that private army of terrorists and assorted scum you've hired is ready to do the job they're being paid to do."

"Everything's in place. They'll do their job. They've been promised too much not to." Webb stared out the window absently. "We've got exactly two hours to settle our nerves."

"I sure hope this works. My nerves won't be settled until the whole operation is completed. Nothing like this has ever happened in the United States before. I guess it's about time *someone* tried to overthrow the government and seize power for themselves."

Webb laughed maliciously. "Oh, it'll work, Burton. God damn, it has to work. Besides, I've got people everywhere. This has been a long time coming. You know that. Now relax."

Burton moved to the couch and flipped the television channels, while

Webb worked at his desk, and the hands of the clock raced around the face much too quickly.

"Okay, Burton. Five minutes and counting."

Burton flipped to CNN and settled into the couch for what would be a long night.

"You have all the documentation necessary to establish martial law once this goes down?" Webb asked.

"Yes, Mr. President."

"And the arrest and execution orders for the names on our list? The necessary individual has been contacted to expedite the process?"

"Yes, and yes, every last political opponent clogging up the pipes is on that list, sir."

"Excellent. After tonight, we should be rid of every ass slowing down our agenda. The American people will turn to us for protection against the *terrorists*. We'll dole out the vaccines and there won't be anything we can't do in their eyes. Voila! Super heroes!"

Burton uncrossed and re-crossed his legs. "5:28, sir."

"I imagine it'll be a few minutes until the media coverage is coordinated enough to begin. Would you like a drink?" Webb walked to the mini bar camouflaged as an antique cabinet.

"No, sir, not right now."

The regular programming broke away abruptly to a nervous reporter standing in front of a hospital. The journalist was fidgeting with her earpiece. She got a sudden deer in the headlights type of expression as she realized she was on the air. "Ten minutes ago the patients and staff at Lincoln Memorial Hospital began streaming from the facility and collapsing. All over town, commuters on the Metrorail encountered the same gas—whatever it is—that's been released into the hospital's ventilation system. Reports are still coming in as to which lines have been affected. Whatever we're dealing with is highly toxic." Sirens blared behind the reporter. People were visibly dead and dying in the background.

"Oh, god," the journalist said, as an orderly stumbled, falling and writhing at her feet. The camera swung the other way. Before the reporter could continue her broadcast, the channel returned to the anchor, sitting at his desk. A new screen shot of the gray, dirty streets of New York City flashed onto the set. Cops and emergency workers were unconscious in the midst of heaped citizens.

"At 5:25 pm the subway system of New York City was attacked by lethal gases. There's no way to confirm how many are dead, but early estimates put the numbers into the thousands."

Webb hit the mute button on the remote. "The attack on the west coast should be along shortly."

Burton stood and crossed the room to the mini-bar. "I believe I'll have that drink now."

• • •

By midnight, seven additional attacks across the country targeted major cities. The death toll mounted until numbers were close to a million. By the next day, the staggering estimates continued to rise, and Michael Webb's plan fell into place. By the following night, over 100 men and women were rounded up and executed in a secret location and the military—who waged its own little war among the ranks of loyal Webb followers and true patriots—had assumed control of every state and its infrastructure. Webb's people were, indeed, everywhere. No one asked where the missing politicians had gone; no one cared. The country was in a state of mass confusion and complete panic. Multiple biological agents were pumped into the air. Webb's team of scientists stood by with truckloads of vaccines waiting to be administered upon the president's orders. The attacks continued until no hospital, no public transportation service, and no public building were safe. Runs were made on sporting goods stores and Army-Navy surplus stores for gas masks and other ventilation equipment. In the end, people remained indoors, panicking, sealing windows with plastic, and boarding their homes expecting the worst.

The Red Cross, supplied by Webb's scientists, moved in with vaccines against the biological agents. The government was doing everything it could to combat the *terrorists* and protect the citizens. Then, a period of relative calm settled over the nation as the attacks finally came to an abrupt halt.

Burton knocked on the door. "Mr. President?" An inaudible reply. "I need to speak with you. It's urgent."

Webb threw on his bathrobe. Terror gripped his chest. Almost everyone who knew anything that could connect him to the plot had been eliminated. And then, the handful of individuals doing the eliminating had been eliminated as well. But, he wasn't delusional. Many high-ranking individuals had been involved and executed. He was prepared for problems somewhere. It was inevitable. Webb checked his desk drawer. His loaded gun was there. He'd take himself out before he let anyone else do it.

He jerked open the door.

"Sorry to disturb you," Burton said, and pushed past the president. He grabbed the television and slid a silver disc into the DVD player.

"What's this?"

Burton scowled. "Footage from a Red Cross clinic in New Jersey." The grainy black and white security camera shots came into view on the set. People were dropping to the floor, clawing at their necks, frothing at the mouths.

"Anthrax?" Webb asked. The attacks were supposed to be over.

"No, the *vaccines*. Wait. It's not over."

After a few minutes the seemingly dead people flailed and stumbled but made their way to their feet where they promptly attacked anyone in their line of vision. A huge, shrieking brawl erupted into a bloodbath of gore and carnage.

"—the Hell?"

"Precisely, Mr. President. Hell is what seems to have erupted. The vaccines are tainted. The military has given the order to shoot on sight anyone behaving in this manner. The biggest concern is that most of the *military* is behaving in this manner, as they were the first ones vaccinated." Burton pointed to the wriggling mass of humanity on the television screen.

Webb sat on the couch. Hard. "This wasn't supposed to happen."

"Military scientists believe the vaccines may have been tampered with by terrorists. *Real terrorists.* Another biological agent might have been substituted for the vaccines."

Webb buried his hands in his hair. "No. No. No. This wasn't the plan!"

"Sir, *the plan* has gone terribly awry. We're no longer on the established course as dictated by your plan. Terrorists—*foreign terrorists*—have used this opportunity to strike further vulnerability into the country."

"But how?"

"The U.S. completely turned their back on any conventions devised by the International Biological and Toxin Weapons Convention. There were safeguards established to prevent this sort of thing that got ignored," Burton said.

"Thanks. A lot of good all that does us now."

"We need to hold a press conference to deal with this new issue. People need to remain indoors *away* from the affected individuals and you need to advise *against* getting vaccinated."

Webb rubbed his eyes. "How many dead, or sick, or whatever the hell's happening, related to the vaccines?"

"No way to estimate. It's anarchy out there. Sheer chaos. Doctors, nurses, police, and the military, received the first wave of vaccines." Burton flipped open the blinds. The street in front of the White House was jammed with cars and people clinging to the fence around the perimeter. Intermittent gunfire was heard as Marines shot people who refused to let go of the fence.

Webb eyed the madness fearfully. Clearly, he'd lost control. "Okay, let's do the conference."

Burton got on the phone.

• • •

An hour later, Webb walked to the podium: blue oxford, sleeves rolled to the elbow, no tie, a look of exhaustion draining his features. He rattled off everything he'd been coached to say. A noise from the back of the room disrupted the conference. Chairs flying. Shrieks. Shouts. The sound of people screaming as they were trampled, and shoved aside. A handful of men, clothes rent and faces smeared with blood and gore, leapt beyond the FBI agents in their sunglasses and pressed suits and made a line straight to the president.

Gunfire. More screams.

President Webb went down in the shuffle, his cries for help drowned by the grunting of the creatures and the chaos of the room. A Marine open-fired on another three or four slobbering attackers. One clutched the gnawed leg of a woman; red pump still perched upon the foot. Blood splattered his face and chest.

It became very clear to President Webb that he and his country of fiendish infected zombies had reached a point of no return. He looked across the noisy melee hoping to find a clear path to exit. He searched the shrieking masses for Burton. Horrified, he watched a reporter go under three or four lurching monstrosities.

"Burton!" Webb shouted, defending himself with a flagpole against the onslaught of crazed monsters. Burton disappeared beneath a mound of moaning infected people.

"God damn zombies!" Webb screamed. There was no way out of this mob. All exits were blocked. He turned as a man, a former FBI agent, clasped an iron hand on his shoulders, and pulled Webb to his snapping jaws. The lunatic sank his teeth into the muscle of Webb's neck, snapping tendons and with a powerful twist, cracked Webb's neck.

DITCH 6: HYPOCRITES

They crossed over the next bridge. Before them, wandering very slowly, were souls condemned for hypocrisy. Knees buckling, soul after soul would end up, face in the dust, before staggering to wobbly feet. Each hypocrite was eternally bound into a cloak weighted with lead. Under the heavy weight, very step was a constant struggleAzubah stepped on the trailing cloak of a young man, fair of face, but weary from centuries of laborious walking.

"What's your name, sinner?" Obadiah asked the man at the end of Azubah's hoof.

"Richard Conn. Father Richard Conn."

"Oh, for the love of Peter. *Another priest*? They really should add a whole circle for the lot of you," Obadiah said.

"The angel is gathering information for Heaven's census. You will provide your revolting story for his book." Azubah passed over all formalities and got right to the point.

The priest looked from the demon to the angel, and with a shrug, and a very tired voice, began his narration.

BETWIXT THE HILLS A SONG COMES CALLIN'

Father Conn carried his noon meal in a scrap of cloth, his prayer book in his other hand. He wandered far to find a serene spot. Too long amongst poverty, hunger, and disease, he longed for some place sparkling, fresh and untouched. And so, he wandered through the forest and over the emerald hills. Until at last, he came to a cave, not more than a tunnel between two mounds that barely qualified as hills. Claw-like roots extended into the pithy corridor, but Conn pushed them aside, and entered the cramped space to see where it might lead. Call it adventure. Call it wanderlust. His curiosity got the best of him.

Dark and dank the cave spiraled downward, and he felt his way along the damp wall with the security that the exit was not too far behind. At last he broke into a brilliant light and fancied himself on the other side of the hill. A sapphire pond shimmered into view, and resting peacefully along its banks were the most beautiful women Father Conn had ever seen.

The nearest beauty looked startled when Conn wandered to her, asking her name.

"Who are you and from where do you come?" she said.

"I'm Father Conn of the Monastery at Connacht."

A frown marred her perfect face. "I don't know you." She glanced at the other women who shook their pretty heads in the negative.

"That's fine. We can talk while I eat my meal." Father Conn held up his bundle of food. He settled upon a mossy rock, untying his package, when the cluster of women began to leave. "Come back! Where are you going?" He retied his food and followed them. They moved quite fast, tiny feet seeming to glide over rocks and rills, carrying them to a grove of yew trees surrounding tidy cottages.

In the center were a slender man and a woman, both of whom had flesh that sparkled in the sun as if they'd been dusted with diamond powder. The man stood. Father Conn gasped, retreating out of fright.

The man unfurled wings of violet hues behind him and smiled. "Did I frighten you, mortal?"

Conn sucked in a sharp breath and looked around. He pointed to his own chest, questioningly.

"Of course it's you. There are no other mortals here in my realm today. How did you come to be here?"

Conn opened his mouth, but no words came forth.

The woman laughed a tinkling laugh of happiness. "Don't be frightened. This is my brother, Bodhrai, Prince of the Fairies, and I'm Te'a. Come, sit, tell us how you happened upon our realm."

Father Conn shuffled to the chair that suddenly appeared next to Te'a. Bodhrai continued to smile, though Conn felt the man considered him amusing in a patronizing manner. Finding his voice, Conn said: "I came by way of a cave, a tunnel really, in between two small hills."

Te'a placed a perfect hand on Conn's knee. She leaned toward him invitingly, whispering, "We don't have many visitors from Inis Fail. Bodhrai has his lovers, but he jealously protects them from the rest of us. We're so curious about the other side. Stay and dance with me!"

"Te'a that's not true. Ainea is free to go wherever she chooses," Bodhrai said.

Te'a glared at her brother, her thin eyebrows fading into a wrinkle. "*She* is *your* plaything. *He* shall be *mine*!"

Bodhrai laughed and waved a dismissive hand. "Do what you will. I've other matters to attend." He started over a path, a flock of winged women following behind.

Te'a's happy expression returned as abruptly as it had faded. "Dance with me, Conn." She clapped her hands sharply and musicians materialized from the surrounding trees and filled the air with music. Her gossamer robes floated like shimmering wisps of light, and she held Conn's hand, twirling him in his rough robes of earth brown. Father Conn never remembered feeling so light, and when he looked to the ground, he gasped to see that neither his feet nor those of the fairy princess touched anything but air.

"Will you stay with me?" Te'a cooed in his ear as she led him into a cottage, and to a pile of silken cushions strewn upon the floor. Her hands caressed and undressed him, laying him down, ivory thighs embracing him as she broke his lifelong vow of celibacy, and stole his virginity.

Hours faded into days and Conn knew he must return to the monastery. Explaining poverty and hunger, concepts Te'a had never known, he found himself laden with gifts with which to feed the starving masses. He left by way of the tunnel, promising to return.

• • •

Every month, Conn returned to his fairy lover, and every month the wayward priest grew more fearful of discovery. He wasn't afraid his sins would be found out; rather he was frightened others would discover the source of his newfound wealth. Conn wasn't feeding the starving or giving the money to the church. Instead, he purchased a fine manor and was living the life of a nobleman with nary a care. He lied and told the others at the monastery that the property belonged to his brother and no more questions were asked. In the woods, on his way home from the fairy realm, he devised a scheme to ensure his fairy connections—and lover—would never be discovered.

• • •

"No more will you seek the assistance of these demons you call Sidhe-folk! They're monsters! Vile devils from the pits of Hell sent by Beelzebub to defile you, debase you, and steal your eternal souls!" Father Conn bellowed from the platform, high above the crowd.

"This girl, Ainea O'Shea, is guilty of cavorting with demons. She's taken a lover from among their evil kind! Today Father God will cleanse her mortal soul with the purifying fires: to burn the flesh is to save the soul!"

Ainea O'Shea whimpered, tied to the stake, her mouth gagged to prohibit her from revealing Conn's sins. She knew he visited the fairy realm and that he had a lover in the fairy princess—sister of her own lover, Bodhrai. The leaping tongues of fire licked her flesh, burning her until only a charred mound of meat and blackened bone clung to the iron shackles in the fire. And, Father Conn felt satisfied, knowing his secrets were safe.

• • •

Bodhrai, the Prince of the Fairies, waited for his lover. Three moons passed and still she didn't come. His heart bursting with heartache and mind racing with worry, he sent out a scout to bring her to him. The fairy scout returned with news most brutal: Ainea was no more.

"Who did this foul thing?" Bodhrai shouted.

"It was Conn, the servant of the god who died on a wooden cross," the scout answered.

"Te'a!"

The sister of the prince flew to his bidding, disturbed at the rage in his velvety voice. The tale was told. Te'a wept tears of pearls that gathered at her feet and rolled into the lush grass. *How could Conn do something so vile?*

"He must be punished," Bodhrai said.

"But–"

"Sister! He's taken a life! And for what? Because of his greed! He hoards the riches you bestow upon him and feeds not a single starving mouth!"

Te'a shook her head, confused, bewildered. "No, that can't be true!"

"Lies! He's a master of lies! It's not for the warmth of your embrace, the perfume of your breasts or the love of your heart that he comes. He's like all men: treacherous, vile and full of deceit. He only wants the wealth you provide."

"I love him, brother."

"As I loved Ainea."

Te'a hung her head, her white-gold tresses spilling over her saddened face; and she wandered into the grove of yews, her wails of lament a woeful dirge.

• • •

Conn wound his way into the forest, growing nearer to the hills and his cave. Owls hooted in the treetops, and the moon hung heavy like a lustrous pearl. His thoughts raced to the coffers of jewels hidden in his manor. A smile crept over his face. *What riches would Te'a reward him with tonight?*

A branch cracked. Something lashed through the darkness, the rapid whipping sound rushing past his head. The ground was yanked from beneath as he soared through the night, a stinging sensation biting at his ankles, tearing at his flesh. His brown robe hung upside down, covering his face like a bag, exposing his nakedness to the cold night air.

All around him the trees filled with the buzzing of a million bees, but a voice penetrated the blackness and Conn realized it wasn't bees that engulfed him.

"Ow!" Conn shouted. "Ouch! What is it? Who's there?" He called into the humming forest, but all that replied were the roaring buzzes and a million tiny needle pricks sticking his body.

"Father Conn of Connacht, for the destruction of the life of the woman called Ainea O'Shea, I sentence you to death." It was Bodhrai.

"Te'a? Are you there?" Conn said, frantic, hands flailing in the air.

"My sister is not among us. To honor her love for you, I granted her wish to remain in our realm while we carried out your sentence," Bodhrai said.

"Sentence? You can't pass judgment here. This isn't your realm, your world," Conn argued.

Tiny, tinkling laughs filled his ears like the sound of miniature bells. Bodhrai laughed mockingly, louder than the rest. "I'm the Prince of the Fairies. Do not believe that your mortal realm is beyond my powers."

The needle pricks continued. Conn realized they were the jabbing of hundreds of tiny swords—tiny, but many. Conn swatted at his limbs, face, torso, as if chasing flies, and soon his hands dripped with the sticky warmth of his own blood. Together, they were dicing him with their teeny blades—small, but deadly sharp. Slivers of sharpened silver flashed in the white of the moon, a pearl that glistened white as bright as the tears Te'a cried for the loss of her beloved.

• • •

When the monks found Father Conn all that remained of the priest were bones swinging from a rope lashed to an oaken bough, and a pile of what looked like silver needles with odd golden nubs resembling tiny hilts. The ground below the dangling skeleton was muddied with crimson blood. With no brother to be found, his property was given to the church, and the monies raised from the sale, fed a long line of starving mouths.

DITCH 7: THIEVES

The unlikely traveling companions crossed the swaying bridge, glad to feel solid ground beneath their feet again. A massive centaur stood guard in the tower before them. The beast stared furiously, his face a man's though his lower half was a stout warhorse.

"What do you want, demon?" the centaur shouted.

Azubah cleared his throat while casting a nervous glance at Obadiah. "Oh, mighty Cacus, guardian of Ditch 7, we come by order of Suriel–"

"What's that meddling angel of death want with my ditch?"

Obadiah started to speak, but Azubah shook his head, cutting the angel off before he began. He scowled, answering the centaur: "This angel is taking part of the census team and is gathering random stories of the inhabitants of Hell. We need to speak with one soul from your ditch and then we'll be on our way."

The clattering of hooves upon stone echoed to their ears as Cacus made his way to ground level to open the gate. The iron chains clanked noisily: an occasional screech of metal sending chills over Obadiah's arms.

Once inside the gate, Cacus emerged, hands on his waist. "Pick your soul and be gone with you."

"Thank you," Obadiah and Azubah answered in unison.

Cacus eyed Obadiah with disgust and flipped his tail testily as he went to shut the gate.

All around, in a state of chaos and noise, condemned souls ran from enormous serpents that lashed out and bit them. The traveling duo beheld the bitten instantly turn to ashes, and then within seconds rise again as new bodies or transformed into serpents giving chase to other thieves.

Obadiah watched in amazement. "Seems like an odd punishment."

"We're not here to analyze, angel. Pick your victim."

The angel laughed. "Victims, now are they?" He let his vision fall upon a middle-aged man, whose blackened teeth were visible as he screamed at the top of his lungs. "He'll do."

Azubah waited for the screeching man to run by and then snatched him from his feet by his tattered coat. The man continued running in air, and then realizing his predicament, held still, dangling in the demon's grasp.

"What's this all about then?" the man asked.

Azubah provided the usual explanation. The man smiled wickedly and said, "You're gonna love this . . . "

ASHES TO ASHES, DUST TO DUST

Black Bill Cooper backed his wagon to the mound of earth piled over the new grave; a lantern hanging from a branch provided faint light, but enough by which to dig. Before long the pile of dirt had moved to the end of the grave. *Thud.* Shovel hit wood. He pulled a crowbar from his heavy apron and wedged it under the coffin lid, pulling the wood and nails away from the coffin.

"Ah, now, there 'e is. And, what a dandy 'e be." Black Bill snatched the cuff links from the body's shirtsleeves, and plucked the mother of pearl buttons from the waistcoat. The gold watch he popped into his pocket and the dead man's hat he plopped firmly onto his own greasy head. Then he pulled the rigid corpse to standing and propped it against the grave's wall until he could fasten a rope around the deceased's torso like some dry log of firewood.

Black Bill crawled out of the damp hole and began the slow process of dragging the body from the grave. He dumped the dead man into his handcart and quickly refilled the empty grave.

Piles of burlap and straw covered the corpse as Black Bill wound his way through the back alleys, in between screeching cats and catcalling whores, until he came to a shady niche and knocked on the door.

It opened just a crack. "What ya want?"

"Got a delivery."

The eyes looked to the cart and the door opened all of the way. The man in the shadows stood to the side, waving Bill inside. He rolled his wagon right into the narrow flat, and dumped the cadaver onto the floor without ceremony. While Bill scooped the straw and burlap into the cart, the man with no name, but lots of coins, counted quite a few into a pile on a nearby table. Bill deposited the coins into his purse and tipped the dead man's hat to the body ghoul and rolled his way outside.

That made twenty-six. Twenty-six bodies. One more and he'd have passage to America to live with his cousin David in New York City. They were going West to buy a farm and start a new life.

The next day, he canvassed the cemeteries watching for processions, surveying for fresh graves. He watched a man in black, a priest perhaps, leaving some swell's crypt through an iron door beneath a large P in bronze script. The lock and chain swung freely on the handle. The man forgot to lock it. Black Bill grinned from rotted tooth to rotted tooth, rubbing his dirty palms in anticipation of the potential loot. He waited behind a hedge for the sun to set and the moon to light his path.

No shovel necessary for this job. Lantern in hand, he crept inside of the stone crypt and through a narrow corridor. Niches in the walls boasted coffins dating to the late 1700s, but the prize awaited in the chamber at the end of the tunnel: a coffin of bronze and draped with roses of all hues. He hung the lantern from a fixture on the wall.

"Maybe it's a woman," he said aloud, thinking that if she were beautiful he may have another use for her before he delivered her to his usual customer. There were no rules against having his jollies with the pretty pussies of the dead.

Bill lifted the casket lid with a creak. White lace billowed out; long golden tresses covered the pillow beneath. He let out a low whistle, and pawed hurriedly at his trousers.

His dirty hands showed even grimier next to the snow white of the young woman's burial gown—presumably the wedding gown she'd never get to wear—as he hiked the silken fabric around her waist, and then—

His hand flew over his mouth, stifling a shout.

From the waist down, the woman's body was white and wet like the gelatinous mass of a maggot.

"My god! What foul creature are you?" He gasped, fighting the urge to retch.

A slim hand clasped around his with the strength of an iron shackle. Startled, Bill looked to the woman's face, her eyelids opened. He screamed. She smiled and then laughed.

"What are you?" Bill said, clawing at the hand latched onto his own. "Let me go!"

She sat up, dragging her gigantic maggot half with her. With the other hand she reached out and seized his flaccid member. "Aw, change your mind?"

"Let me go!" he shrieked.

"Why should I?"

"You're—a—monster!"

She laughed again, but then her eyes glowed green and her lovely face distorted, twisting into an ugliness Bill had never imagined. "And so are you, robber of the dead, defiler of corpses!"

Bill slung a leg over the side of the coffin in an attempt to get away, but now the monstrosity reached over and clasped him on the shoulder, pulling him closer. He could smell her foul breath: death and decay was its fragrance.

"You wanted me, now I want you." Her fingers grew to taloned claws and bit into his flesh like blades. From out of her mouth curled a slimy proboscis, waving in the air, hungry and snapping. A dangerous rounded tip emerged from the folds, boasting rows of sharp hooks ready to bury within his flesh. Fangs emerged around this lashing elongation and her eyes glistened green then red.

Black Bill began to shriek.

The proboscis was sucked back within the depths of her mouth, her mouth spreading into a sick smile. "Ssh, they'll hear you–" her voice was sing-songy, a taunting childhood chorus that tormented him and teased him. She pulled him closer until his ear was next to her mouth. Her putrid, fetid breath was sticky hot against his neck and then her razor nails cut into his jugular as she twisted the bone there with a loud crack.

Black Bill went limp, but something was wrong. "I'm nnn—not dead."

She cackled a laugh and smiled in delight. "Oh now, *that* wouldn't be any fun at all."

"I can't feel my body!"

She sunk her teeth into the flesh of his arm and ripped a chunk of bloody meat from his bone. "That's probably a good thing." The rubbery proboscis slithered from her throat and poked and prodded its way into the hole in his limb, snaking under the flesh.

Bill shrieked and screeched, but couldn't do anything except lay on top the white satin pillow atop the laces and silks of the monster beneath him, and watch as she slowly ate his flesh—until the white satins turned crimson and the dim light of his lantern flickered away with his life.

DITCH 8: FRAUDULENT ADVISORS

The next bridge was easier to cross as it was made entirely of stone. Arriving upon the other side it became evident to the demon and the angel as to why. Standing as still as pillars, reminiscent of Lot's wife without the salt, the souls of fraudulent advisors were entirely consumed in flames. The sounds of crackling fire, anguished shouts and tortured moans drifted over the breeze that served to stir the licking tongues.

"At least I don't have to chase someone this time," Azubah said, shrugging. He reached into the fiery pillar of the closest burning soul and yanked a naked man into the air. Charred flesh came away in a greasy mess in Azubah's hands as he dropped the man to the ground. The burned man lay in a crumpled heap, panting, watery eyes darting about, looking for the cause of his deliverance. "Thank you," he muttered between cracked lips.

"Don't thank me just yet. Your reprieve is but for a duration while you tell us the story of your life. You'll have to return to your fire," Azubah spoke.

The man began to weep, but no tears flowed. His bloodied hands grasped the hem of Obadiah's robe. "Please, please take me away from here."

Obadiah was filled with both compassion and revulsion for the sinner. "I'm not in the position to release you from the punishment you secured for yourself in life."

The man gasped and wailed, but sitting up painfully, he started his unfortunate tale.

A PLACE TO REMEMBER
1645 MARY KING'S CLOSE, EDINBURGH, SCOTLAND

Up and down the lane, the houses were marked: *Plague.* The narrow road had been hit hard: 1,005 dead. Dr. Bruce MacAlister watched many waste away and die: whole families, multiple generations. People he'd treated for fifty years. All dying. Until Bruce had an idea.

On the outskirts of town lived a stooped, old cunning woman that some referred to as a witch, plain and simple. Dr. MacAlister scraped together all the gold he could and hauled it to the old crone's hut in a wood cart. He stopped before her ramshackle door.

The old hag hobbled out, ladle in hand. "What's this then?" she asked, surveying the handcart.

"Gold for ye services."

"And what services might those be, good doctor?"

Dr. MacAlister sat on the bench under the apple tree that was as stooped and crooked as the crone. "I want ye to give me a potion that'll keep those dwelling in Mary King's Close alive. Can that be done?"

The crone clicked her tongue in thought and then jabbed the air with her ladle. "Come back in three days time."

"Why three days?"

"The good lord found new life in three days, now don't ask me questions."

Dr. MacAlister, sufficiently upbraided, left. And returned in three days as instructed.

The old hag hauled her cauldron on the good doctor's handcart along with the doctor to the center of the main street in Mary King's Close. The curious inhabitants poured from their accursed dwellings, hovering in doorways and on stoops.

"This broth will cure you! This will keep you alive!" the doctor said and he ladled a spoonful into every mouth that wandered past, much as if he were administering Holy Communion.

After everyone had partaken, the bent hag smiled a wicked smile that the doctor noticed and, as a result, felt an unexplainable uneasiness in his gut. "Why do you smile, crone?"

"Ah, there's a *catch*."

"A catch to *what*? We paid you good gold."

"A catch to the potion, of course."

The doctor groaned. "And what would it be?"

"Well, ye asked me to keep them alive and that's been done . . . if they remain out of the sunlight."

"What?"

"And, they'll remain disease-ridden, just alive. T'were the best that I could do."

Dr. MacAlister blinked. "Are you telling me that those people will *never* die?"

"Not unless they go into the sunlight."

"But, if they don't?"

"Then, aye, they'll live as long as they choose."

After a few weeks it became evident that the inhabitants were riddled with plague, but living. Life continued as normal, only with business during the night as though it were day. And so Mary King's Close resumed life with these new rules.

1750, Mary King's Close, Edinburgh, Scotland

For nearly a century, the rest of Edinburgh avoided the inhabitants of Mary King's Close. Unknowing people who wandered into the streets, found it odd that everyone slept in the day, only to have the streets bustle at night with normal daytime activities. It mattered not what the hapless visitor thought, as anyone who stayed long caught the plague and ended up dead in a pit covered over with lime.

The city began to feel uneasy about the cursed inhabitants. Several clergymen were sent as near the Close as they dared venture in order to exorcise the apparent demonic activity with which the streets were rife. The legend had it that these plague ridden people were all over one hundred years old!

To check the spread of disease, Edinburgh sealed the Close, creating a maze of dead ends and a city within a city, sealed off from the sunlight forever. The rest of the city continued to grow around the sealed streets, until Mary King's Close became a type of basement to the city— closed off and forgotten.

• • •

In 2002, workmen repairing pipes broke through a layer of brick and debris below the city streets and discovered a thirty-foot, winding staircase made of wood and metal. With flashlights in hand, three workers made their way into the belly of Mary King's Close which had been forgotten.

They came at first to a larger home, with around twelve inhabitants coming and going from the residence as if it were as light as day. Nearby, on the street corner, a pocked man of undetermined age played a woeful dirge upon the bagpipes. Shutting off their flashlights, that were generating too much curiosity, the workers found that after a significant amount of time, their eyes adjusted to the dark. Slivers of light filtered into this underbelly of the city from the pipes and drains below the roads above.

Silently, they explored the streets, watching the match sellers and ragged-clothed people living their normal lives, until too many people began to notice the strangeness of the workmen's clothes and several men and boys gave chase. For a few moments they hid behind a roving herd of sheep. The plaintive mews covered their heavy breathing.

"These bastards smell like shit!" one of the workmen named Johnson whispered.

"Shut up! These buggers already know somethin's not right about us. Maybe if we stay hidden for a bit behind these bloody sheep, they'll forget about us," Ian replied.

"These sheep are fucking blind. Look. They got no eyes!" Johnson flashed his light at the face of the nearest sheep to reveal no sockets or eyes, just flat bone where all should be.

"Over there! There they are!" a voice cracked the silence, and the sound of running feet could be heard upon the cobbles. "Get them!"

Up the winding, rickety stairs the workers ran, jumping steps to make time. When a handful of the inhabitants chased them into the sunlight, the ghostly white, disease-scarred creatures threw up their hands defensively and burned to charred flesh before the workers' eyes.

Two of the workmen came down with the plague within hours, but they told of sights spectacular to modern eyes: an 18th century world undisturbed by time.

The City Chamber decided to send a representative into the Close to negotiate a tourist opportunity, but the plague-addled victims wanted no part in the outside world. Too long they'd lived beneath the streets, bodies adapting to the lack of light, until their eyes became an all-too Morlock way of functioning. The representative, fearing the close residents would seal themselves off from the world once more, didn't want to lose the tourism dollars that the city stood to gain. So, he incited the underground dwellers into a mass riot and they chased him to their doom in the sunlight above.

Ale and whisky flowed at pubs around Edinburgh celebrating the man who had generated new income for the city. He boasted plans for electric lighting, a new all-metal staircase, and travel brochures with a historical slant.

The tourists began arriving. And, one-by-one, they encountered Sweet Maggie who sold matches on the corner beneath a brownstone bathed in a glow of a gaslight. Her singing in the thick brogue of old lured many a man to her lips. So taken they were with her accurate portrayal of one of Mary King's Close's residents, that many stole a kiss from dim lips—only to carry the germs of a potent killer, an unrestrained strain of the Black Death, out into the world.

The Close was soon shut up again. A handful of ragtag residents crept from the shadows. The dirge of the pipes are still heard wafting through the streets of Edinburgh, from beneath the sewers and water pipes, in the dead of the night.

DITCH 9: SOWERS OF DISCORD

Obadiah tread close on Azubah's hooves. The irritated demon turned around to glare at the anxious angel. "Why do you walk so close?" he growled, vexed to his last nerve.

"This ditch is frightening."

"Moreso than the others?" Azubah laughed, but, he too, grimaced at the sounds of the demons wielding swords that chopped down the sowers of discord in their midst. Great bloody piles of entrails and gore dribbled over rocks and ledges, and blood ran like so many torrents of rain through the pathways carved by demon hooves.

As soon as the demons visited their carnage upon the lost souls, the bodies would reform; gelatinous at first, but slowly the solidity of flesh transformed severed piles into a body whole again.And then the wails and moans began anew as the demons cut the sowers of discord to bits once more.

"For the love of Peter, choose one and let's be done here!" Obadiah lamented, and Azubah plucked a man missing an arm from amidst the chaos, and quick-rattled the rules of the game.The man, a corpulent fellow in sumptuous robes, seemed happy for the reprieve, and picking at the frayed sleeve of his bloodied attire, began his narration.

GATE OF THE GODS

And they said to one another, Go to, let us make brick, and burn them thoroughly. And they had brick for stone, and bitumen had they for mortar. And they said, Go to, let us build us a city and a tower, whose top may reach unto heaven; and let us make us a name, lest we be scattered abroad upon the face of the whole earth.—Genesis 11:3-4

543 B.C., Babylon, Babylonia

Mighty Nebuchadnezzar II built his city, this Babylon, carved it from rock and sand from a throat-parching desert. Irrigation grew the gardens and canals brought the ships inland where priceless treasure hoards were unloaded from vast hulls of cargo ships and trader's vessels. The city was molded from bricks of clay and straw—baked under the sun that beat mercilessly upon the rising ziggurat upon which thousands of men labored, one layer at a time, slowly inching closer to the sky gods. Soon, only a few million bricks of clay would separate god from man.

The baked bricks shone a brilliant blue as the tower soared upward. Zanibur wiped the sweat from his brow. He added the final touches to a wall mural inside the chamber built for the fertility rites of the gods. The Rite of Consecration was about to begin even as he was finishing the murals. Already a beautiful maiden clothed in gauzy robes tinkling with the sounds of golden beads, was being anointed with perfumed oils upon a couch of gold. The priest chosen to host the god, pranced about, naked, save for a giant gold phallus strapped around his middle. His own member of flesh jutted rigid, looking small in comparison.

Zanibur's presence was tolerated only until he finished the scene. The priests were anxious to dedicate this complex story of the tower to the gods before further construction continued. The walls boomed with the music provided for the impending rite. Outside, musicians strummed strings and drummers imbued the tower with a lifebeat that coursed through the bricks of clay like a deep, pumping heart lost in the levels of bricks. Zanibur picked up his bucket of paints and brushes and left the chamber by way of a small corridor, but before anyone could see, he ducked into a tiny niche in the wall and pushed himself into the shadows. He'd watch this god rut with this virgin princess.

Two other priests began to chant, ritually undressing the woman who drank from a silver chalice, head lulled to one side. Potent were the herbs within her wine. The musicians outside played louder, frenzied, as if imitating a great storm: Baal's trademark. A brief squabble took place between the three priests; a pecking order established. Zanibur watched, his own member stiff within the working fingers of his hands as the three priests split the bronze thighs of the woman and rent her virgin seal three times over.

Sticky crimson smeared the woman's legs as she lay, breasts heaving, arms flailing rhythmically to the beat of the outside drums. The priests filed from the chamber leaving the woman, thrice blessed by Baal, naked on her couch.

Zanibur crept from his hiding place and through the corridor into the fertility chamber. The woman—that drugged receptacle of the seed of the gods—giggled as he loosed his robe and climbed atop her, sinking his own pole deep into her folds. The flashes of art danced around him, painted from his own brush, as he grunted and thrust inside the woman, finally exploding, his seed mingling with that of the gods. Quickly, he looked around, fetched his robe, and scurried from the chamber careful not to be seen. The sound of workmen stacking bricks, scraping mortar, filled the air that had recently been alive with the sounds of drums and the hum of strings.

His job was finished until the next chamber called for his art. He made his way down the plank to the ground level, winding around and round, in a seemingly forever spiral.

• • •

And the Lord came down to see the city and the tower, which the children of men builded. And the Lord said . . . Go to, let us go down, and there confound their language, that they might not understand one another's speech. —*Genesis* 11: 6-7

Zanibur watched the workers with their baskets of bricks, the stories of the tower rising into the clouds. So close they were to touching the gods.

Something akin to the tongue of the Hebrews echoed from the clouds like thunder. Zanibur knew the sound of the language, but didn't know the words. Confusion crossed the faces of the men. Zanibur set his bucket of paints on a platform of bricks and gazed into the haze of clouds. *That* wasn't the voice of *Baal*. Why was the *Hebrew* god shouting from Baal's sky?

Mass confusion broke out as workers stumbled into one another. Lighting flashed across the sky like skeletal fingers. Thunder rent the silence and laughter full of mockery reverberated from every corner of the vast blackness looming over them. All around, words, foreign and senseless, were uttered. Workers shook one another in frustration, unable to communicate with each other. Words, never before heard, were shouted from story to story, and the foundation of the tower began to sway and shake.

Zanibur watched in horror as the toppling tower tossed bricklayers from the tiers like children's toys. Broken bodies littered the vast expanse of ground at the base of the mighty building. One by one the levels of the ziggurat folded inward like a cake, falling one atop the other. Zanibur thought of the beautiful woman, legs spread and sticky sweet with the seed of so many mingled with the blood of her purity, lying naked on her couch of gold. He thought he could hear her screams of terror, as she must surely have met her death in the collapse.

When the earth ceased shaking, all that remained were piles of bricks and broken bodies, and scores of men babbling incoherently; renting their clothing, and heaping dirt upon their heads. Such was the demise of Bab-ili, the gate of the gods.

Zanibur lost his bucket of pigments and brushes, and made his way to his home amidst the fury of the Hebrew god and the flood of curious people seeking, frantically, this worker or that, who would be found, eventually, beneath the rubble of the mightiest ziggurat never finished: the Tower of Babel.

DITCH 10: LIARS

"My nose!" Azubah said, pinching his nostrils.

Obadiah laughed. "Me thinks the demon doth protest too much."

"Stop trying to be clever."

The angel smiled. "I thought me rather successful at my cleverness." He coughed, sputtering, as the air grew increasingly foul. "*What* is that stench?"

"Probably more shit."

Obadiah frowned. "Whenever you don't *know* the answer to my question, I get nervous."

They came over the bridge and surveyed the masses of writhing, flailing souls. The nearer they grew to land, the more they could see. Sweating, vomiting, wailing, and moaning bodies littered the ditch. All manner of foul disease plagued them; the stench of the consequences of the afflictions permeated the air.

"There's your answer." Azubah covered the lower half of his face with his leathery arm, nodding toward the bodies. They stopped and read a slipshod sign, haphazardly nailed to a broken fencepost: Liars.

"Charming," Obadiah said.

Azubah laughed. "Beginning to wonder what it was that you *did* to be given this assignment, aren't you?"

"Supposedly it was my orderly ways and tendency to do things efficiently."

The demon smiled, crooked teeth showing black against even blacker gums. "Wonder what job you would've been assigned if you were *bad* at what you do?"

"There. Get her! She looks a little less ill than the others. Bring her to me," Obadiah said, ignoring Azubah's comment.

The demon crossed the stony path to a woman seated on a rock, pulling a blue veil closer to her face. Obadiah watched the demon explain the situation and then lead her to him.

Azubah wore a surprised grin on his hideous visage. "You'll never guess who this is."

"Given the sheer number of souls condemned to Hell and the thousands of centuries we're dealing with, you're probably right."

"Mary Magdalene!" Azubah just about burst with excitement.

Obadiah scowled. "I'm quite certain Mary Magdalene is registered in Heaven. Purgatory at the very least."

"Nope. *We* got her. And, she's ready to tell her story." Azubah gave her a gentle push and she stepped closer to the angel. She was covered from head to foot in boils, flesh swollen and crusted. She looked altogether miserable, but smiled politely, arranging her robes to cover most of the putrid pustules.

"The demon speaks the truth. I am Mary Magdalene, wife of our savior, Jesus Christ."

"Wife?" Obadiah paused his quill above the paper.

"Yes. Wife and mother of his children. Some truths are buried deep in Hell for the sake of preserving falsehoods perceived as truth created throughout the ages for the perverse reasons of man."

"Are you trying to tell me that you've been banished to the tenth ditch of the eighth circle of Hell for *political reasons*?"

"The Catholic church did quite a number on the development of Christianity. One of those deliberate redirections was the history of Jesus's personal life. In order to justify their celibate priests, the Pope had all evidence of Jesus as a husband and father destroyed, covered up, and wove new tales into the void."

Obadiah's eyebrows arched inquisitively. "And you have the true accounting for this void, as you call it?"

"Yes. I *am* the void. When the Pope saw that teaching about Jesus's wife would cast our Lord in a human light, he wanted to remove that image. The clergy needed justification for the perversity of forcing men into celibate lives and needed to bury the real reason: that being a way to claim all the monies of any noblemen bound to the church by eliminating any potential legal heirs. So, if Jesus remained celibate, so should the priests and all others in the church."

"I see."

"In order to tarnish my image, I was cast down as a common whore.

A prostitute. Harlot. And to make matters seem somehow compassion- ate to an unfortunate like me, the Pope showed how Christ forgave and supped with sinners: moneychangers, thieves, and whores. What fate here in Hell do those men suffer who transformed me, a woman, from the wife of a god into a common whore?"

Obadiah looked at Azubah as if expecting an answer. Azubah shrugged and said, "I'd have to check the registry. I'm sure whatever it is, it's not nice."

Mary laughed. "I should hope their accommodations are less pleas- ant than my own."

Azubah waved an impatient hand. "We're not here to discuss the punishment of your pope. We're here to record your story."

Mary shifted uncomfortably on the rock. She attempted to stop the flow of a rivulet of pus from her cheek with a gathered wad of fabric from her sleeve. Obadiah winced.

"So, is there anything more you can tell us?" he asked.

Mary breathed heavily and reached her unoccupied hand into the folds of her robe, pulling forth a scroll. "On this scroll is the lineage of Jesus up until my death. I meticulously recorded each birth and death up until the year of our Lord, 1200."

"1200? Am I to believe you lived for so long?"

"I did. You've heard of the Knights Templar and their hidden trea- sure, have you not?"

"I have."

"The children of Jesus were that treasure and the knights guarded them well. So well that descendents of our savior exist even today among the ruling families of the world. Royal blood equals holy blood."

Obadiah rolled his eyes. "This sounds like a really bad novel."

"I assure you it's true. Why else would I be in Hell? My imprisonment here remains part of the ongoing conspiracy to taint the life of Christ."

"Uh-huh." Obadiah scrawled on the paper. "Go on."

"There were twelve children and from those twelve nations were born, kings were made. The knights fought and died to hide us, to keep the Catholic church from succeeding in its dastardly plan to annihilate the blood of Christ so that they might rule supreme. Are you Catholic, cherub?"

"The doctrines of men don't rule the throngs of angels in Heaven. We existed long before men came cowering naked from the garden and even longer still than the previous inhabitants of the Earth which emerged from the slime and muck of primordial ooze."

Mary nodded knowingly. "I could give you my scroll, but I've grown attached to it."

Obadiah squelched an image of the parchment sticking to her pus-covered flesh. "I'd like to read it."

"Maybe a quick glance." She handed it to him just as a massive, thorn-covered demon came from a rocky cave and toward the unusual cluster of angel, demon, and boil-engorged soul.

"What's this?" he barked.

Azubah pulled a letter of passage from his belt and handed it to the irate guardian. The thorny demon scanned the missive, returning it with a grunt.

Obadiah, scroll in hand, quill in the other, his book perched precariously on his knees, greeted the guardian of the ditch. "We're nearly finished with our interview of Mary Magdalene here, and then we'll be moving to the ninth circle. I hope we weren't too–"

"Mary Magdalene?" the thorny demon said, voice bellowing, annoyed.

"Yes," Obadiah looked at his entry and said. "She's nearly finished with her tale."

The demon boxed the woman's ear and dragged her by veil and hair, screaming to her feet. She yelped in pain. "This woman's name is Levitica. She died in 1955. Mary Magdalene! Hmpf!" He gave her a shove toward the cave. "I think that's the conclusion to her story. Lies! All of it! Did you expect to gain truths from a ditch full of liars?"

Just then Levitica leapt upon the thorn-covered demon, mouth frothing, a crazed look spreading across her features. She screamed and cursed and raked the demon's face with her fingernails. The thorny protrusions on the demon's body snagged ripe boils and pus flowed copiously over the demon and the woman.

Obadiah and Azubah stared at each other incredulously. Obadiah unrolled the scroll to read Mary's—or Levitica's—meticulous ancestry: It was blank.

"Tricked," he said, casting the scroll to the ground.

"Lied to," Azubah corrected

The big demon wrestled the insane woman to the ground and planted a huge foot atop her head. She shoved at his foot and kicked in the dirt. "Hold still, woman!" he said. "You want a story? I'll tell you Levitica's story. Lies! She's lived a life of lies and paid dearly for it."

Obadiah readied his pen. "We'd appreciate your help."

The demon gave the woman a jab in the arm with a pointy finger. "Hush your protests and let me tell your miserable biography so these two can be on their way."

She continued her shouts, writhing in the dirt. The demon rolled his eyes. "If you're quiet, I'll reduce your vomiting sentence for the day." She whimpered and lay still.

MADAME ZENIA'S HOUSE OF SPIRITS: CASH ONLY

Levitica Morris, also known as Madame Zenia, smoothed the red velvet tablecloth and rearranged the chairs around the table. A lamp of blue glass hung in the corner of the room, and a couple of wall sconces glowed gold within their amber glass. A whirling crystal ball perched on ornate legs sat on the table, along with a stacked pile of Tarot cards. Near the door sat a small stand that held a copper kettle with a handwritten sign that read: Cash Here.

She made her way to the front shop window and peered through the crack in the heavy purple, fringe-trimmed drapes. On the other side of the drapery sat a manikin dressed as a fortuneteller and a table that looked much like the one inside. The building originally was an old hardware store in the 1800s, and it retained brick walls and wood flooring. The big display window was perfect for drawing folks into the shop out of curiosity or a sense of adventure. The whole manikin get-up had a way of making people feel they were doing something entertaining.

Madame Zenia had a steady customer base and managed to attract new clients by word of mouth and by way of advertisements in local newspapers. She had a reputation for conjuring spirits and channeling the dead. The less adventurous of her customers relied heavily on her palm reading and tarot skills. She didn't mind; she charged by the half-hour no matter what service was required.

The little bell on the door tinkled, catching her attention. She smiled warmly. "Come in!"

An old lady, bundled in tweeds and wools, came in out of the cold wind, clutching her pillbox hat to her head. "Hello there."

Madame Zenia crossed to the woman and helped her with her coat, hanging it on a hook on the wall. "How can I help you today, Mrs. Talley?"

The woman, a regular, sat in one of the wood chairs facing the table with the crystal ball. "I need to speak with Anson again. I miss him so. I'm finding it hard to go on without him."

"That isn't unusual, Mrs. Talley. You were together for sixty-one years. Being by yourself must be a bewildering experience." Madame Zenia sat in her chair and rubbed the orb with her palms.

"Anson was so talkative the last time I was here. I thought that perhaps, he'd–"

"He'd come back and talk some more?" Madame Zenia offered.

"Oh, yes! I'd gladly come back every week just to talk to my dear Annie."

Madame Zenia continued caressing the crystal ball. "I'm sure he'll come. Let's see what happens."

Mrs. Talley hovered close to the ball that flashed a warm orange and then turned a cold blue. Fog stirred within the clear sphere, and she strained to make out what was forming inside.

"There he is!" Madame Zenia said, her voice cheerful and full of hope. "Hello Anson. Your wife's here and wants to talk."

The table vibrated and Mrs. Talley jumped out of surprise. "Oh!" she said, and then clutched her arms. "Is he doing that?"

"It's the spiritual energy. Happens all the time."

The old woman nodded. "Oh. Is he still there?"

"Yes. What would you like to tell him?"

Mrs. Talley began talking. And she talked. And she talked. Madame Zenia sat quietly, smiling and nodding, all the while rubbing the crystal orb, watching as the colors swirled and the ball hummed. "Mrs. Talley? I hate to interrupt you, but I just wanted to make you aware that it's been an hour and forty-five minutes. I charge by the half hour . . . I didn't know if you were on a budget?"

Mrs. Talley waved a hand. "What's money to me when I can talk with my Annie? Does he want to say anything to me?" She put a wad of folded bills on the table with a pat of her hand.

Madam Zenia smiled, warmly, as always. "Oh, yes he does." She went through a variety of shakes and quivers. Her head lulled to one side and then jerked to the other. Her whole body shook violently, and then she rolled her eyes into her head and lowered her voice: "Rebecca?"

Mrs. Talley's hand flew to her mouth. "I'm here, darling, I'm still here!"

"I miss you so much. It's lonely here without you. I hoped you'd come back so we could talk."

"Oh, I'll come back every day if you want me to!"

Madame Zenia rolled her head around on her shoulders, arching her back, raising then dropping her arms. "I've heard everything you've said. Those Willards are something else! Do you think the new Sunday school rooms will be built before the spring?"

Mrs. Talley started chatting again, but then looked at her watch and an expression of sorrow washed over her. "Oh, Annie," she said with a sigh. "I have to go. I've run out of money for today. I already used my grocery money to stay a little longer. I'll come back though, I promise!"

The fortuneteller had a slight seizure and collapsed, her head resting on the soft velvet of the table. She breathed heavily, obviously exhausted.

"Oh my! Are you alright?" Mrs. Talley asked, concern on her face. She touched Madame Zenia's arm in a motherly fashion.

"Y—yes. Just tired. Always tired after–"

"Here's the rest of what I owe you. I'll leave you to rest now, Madame Zenia. Thank you. Thank you so much!" Mrs. Talley plunked more money onto the tabletop and retrieved her coat from the wall hook. Then the little bell tinkled on the door, and she shut it sharply. The wind howled.

Madame Zenia sat up with a smile and counted the stack of bills. "Thank you, Mrs. Talley." She laughed and got up, going into a backroom through a black curtain to deposit the money into the safe. She returned to the main room, fingers fluttering over the crystal ball. "Little plump woman could do without a few groceries." The door opened amidst a tinkling, and Madame Zenia's head snapped to the sound, a smile on her face.

• • •

"I know you're ill, Judi. It's terrible. Maybe we can find a spirit to tell what lies in your future?" Madame Zenia said.

"I don't know. I've already spent more today than I should. I have to go to the pharmacy and buy my medicines."

"It's *your* decision, but if there's a spirit with information about your health, *I'd* want to find out."

"I don't know–"

Madame Zenia put her hands on the table and began to push her chair back in order to stand.

"Oh, wait. Okay. Let's do it. But not for too long . . . I don't have much money."

"It shouldn't take long. I'm sure you have a grandmother or an aunt that can find out as much information as possible."

"My grandmother. She died when I was ten."

"Well, let's look for her then, shall we?" Madame Zenia rubbed the crystal ball, chanting, humming, her whole body curled forward, her eyes fixated on the whirling mass of smoke contained inside of the orb.

Much the same scene conspired as did with Mrs. Talley. The conversation was drawn out as long as Madame Zenia could milk money from the sick woman, and then when she ran out of funds with which to pay, the fortuneteller concluded the session.

"But, I didn't find out anything about my future!"

"Your grandmother promised to find what she could."

The young woman looked perplexed. "That means I'll have to come back. I already used my medication money . . . now I'm going to have to spend sleepless nights in pain because I foolishly wasted what money I had."

Madame Zenia sighed. "Foolishly wasted? Your grandmother promised to find out *something*. *Something* is better than nothing. I tell you what. Come back next week and I'll give you your time half off. How's that sound?"

"I don't know. I'll have to see if I have the extra money. I don't even know if my grandmother will be able to find any information that will help me. What if all she tells me is something like *you'll eat breakfast tomorrow*?"

"Well, then at least we know you'll be alive to eat breakfast." Madame Zenia chuckled, but the young woman didn't join the laughter. "Come now, I don't mean to make light of the situation. It's a very grave health condition you have and I can see why you're deeply troubled, but next week your grandmother might have information. Think about it. Come in any time."

With a bothered sigh, the woman put her money on the table and said her goodbyes and left. Madame Zenia laughed all the way to the back room. She was just about to return to the main room to lock up for the night, when she heard the tinkling of the door bell. Thinking it was the young woman come back for something forgotten, she rushed through the curtain.

There was no one there.

Zenia went to the door and made sure it was shut properly, that the wind hadn't blown it open and closed again. It was securely shut. Then she checked in the small shoppe of herbs, potions, and books in the little room to the right. No one there either.

"Hmm," she said, but locked the door and pulled the shade on the door's window. She walked across the room, lifted the tablecloth, reached under and pulled the plug attached to the crystal ball from the electric socket on the floor. The bell on the front door sounded again.

Zenia or Levitica, now that she was off work, jumped from fright. The door hadn't opened, nor was there a window open to let in a breeze. The little bell just rang and rang as if someone was beating it with a stick. "Who's there?"

Silence as to be expected. Levitica frowned and double-checked the lock on the door. The bell stopped ringing. She turned to leave the room, when she suddenly gasped and backed into the wall, hands grasping for something to use as a weapon. "Who are you? What do you want?"

A man the shade of ashes sat in her chair at the table, the crystal ball glowing a shade of blood red. "Nice little set up you have here."

"What do you want?" she repeated.

"I want you to give the money back to those poor people that you keep robbing."

"What? I haven't stolen anything. What're you talking about?" Levitica fumbled with the lock on the door, but it wouldn't open. She pulled on the knob sweat slicking her palm.

"Oh, no? You steal from people every day. That's how you make your living, Madame Zenia . . . or should I call you Levitica?"

"I don't care what you call me. Why don't you leave?" She yanked on the knob again.

The man at the table sat calmly, hands folded on the table, face expressionless, eyes fixed on her. Sweat poured over her temples and her cheeks. She could feel rivulets of perspiration run down her cleavage and under her breasts.

"I'm not leaving without you."

"What?" Levitica ceased rattling the doorknob, as it had proved useless. The door wasn't budging.

"Come sit. Let's talk."

"Go away. I'm tired and I want to go home. How did you get in anyway? I must have left the back door open."

"Shouldn't you be more concerned about who I am and what I want?

What if I've come to steal your money and do you harm?" the man said, laughing, and then he stood and began to walk around the store.

Levitica gasped again. From the knees down, the man's legs faded into ghostly nothingness. He wasn't a man. He was a spirit: a real, live, honest to goodness spirit. She felt her eyes widen with surprise. "What *do* you want?"

The man flipped over a book, looked into an empty urn, and then poked a finger into the crack in the window drapes, peering into the dark display with the manikin and the table. He laughed. "Looks like you."

She frowned. "You haven't answered my question. I'm closed for the night. You'll have to come back tomorrow."

"You'd like that, wouldn't you? Then you could charge me more money."

"You haven't paid me any money. I don't even know how you got in."

"Quit the act. You and I both know that I'm dead. I realize you're quite surprised to actually be speaking with a real spirit since your business is founded on your spectacular acting abilities."

"I don't know what you're talking about," Levitica said.

"Of course you do, dear Madame Zenia." The man's voice dripped with sarcasm. "You know exactly what I'm talking about. What you're trying to figure out in that mean little brain of yours is what the hell I want with you and why I'm here. And from the look on your face, you're scared to death."

"I work with spirits every day."

"Oh, cut the crap. You're a fraud, lady. You bilk people out of money. You steal grocery money from old women, medication money from dying customers. You prey on the sad, the lonely, and the pathetic. You steal hope from everyone you meet."

"That's not true! I *give* them hope!" Levitica stomped her foot. "They come to me wanting to hear from a dead loved one, wanting a shred of hope to cling to about grave situations that they know there's no way out of, but they're willing to pay to hear that things will be better. Things will improve. It gives them something to live for, even if just for a little while."

"Is this how you live with your lies? Is this your flimsy justification?" The man floated to the chair he had vacated, and resumed sitting, shifting, as if crossing an invisible leg.

"It's not flimsy."

"And, why do you think I might be here tonight, Madame Zenia.

Why would a real ghost come to your little factory of deception? I don't have a dead husband to talk with, no shriveled grandmother to locate for information she probably doesn't have. Why would I waste my time here with you tonight?"

"The spirit realm has no time."

The man laughed loudly. "You seem certain about this."

"Why don't you just tell me and get on with it. Why are you tormenting me?"

A gentle breeze stirred the room and Levitica became aware of more spirits lingering in the shadows. She could only make out outlines; their faces were lost in blackness. She looked at the man, fear creeping into her voice. "Who are they?"

The man laughed again. The breeze began to increase in tempo. The velvet tablecloth billowed. The draperies around the display window flapped upward as if blown by a great wind. Books and papers spiraled in a torrent in the air. Levitica clung to the hat stand near the front door as if the object was heavy enough to provide her an anchor. Her hair whipped around her face in a frenzy, and her skirt wrapped around her legs. More spirits crowded into the small shop, closing in on her, forming a ring around her like some sort of ill-gotten childhood game.

The man stood. His face twisted into a visage of horror. Rotted flesh hung from decaying bone. One eye drooped from a maggot-ridden socket. His clothes transformed into rags that smelled of pungent earth. He reached forth a skeletal hand, moss and vegetation wrapped around exposed bone. "The grandmother found your information."

"What? Www—hat are you talking about? I made that up! There's no grandmother's spirit. She never went to find any information. I told that to the poor girl just to get her money!" Levitica shouted above the gale-force wind. The contents of the room lashed at her, bombarding her, hitting her with such force that her flesh was soon dotted with blue and purple bruises.

The spirits moved closer, arms stretched toward her, a low moan escaping long dead lips.

"Truth. Finally, our fortuneteller speaks the truth. Alas, too late now, Madame Zenia."

A wispy spirit of an elderly lady floated into the foreground, a look of disgust and contempt on her face. "I heard what you told my poor granddaughter. She only has a few months to live; yet you give her false hope and take her money besides! The little comfort she finds from her pain, you steal with your lies!"

"I was just trying to help!"

"As am I . . . no more will you plague the world with your false promises, your displays of bodily contact with the spirit realm. You've told your final lie!" The old woman sprang onto Levitica's torso, dead eyes sunken black in rotted sockets.

The ghosts swarmed the woman, shredding her clothing, ripping hair from her scalp in great handfuls, as the original ghost, the man in the suit, sat at the table, waving them onward.

"No!" Levitica screamed, fighting the non-corporeal forms. Her hands met no resistance, yet their slaps and bites and kicks were just as solid as any living human.

Ghostly hands seized her head, slamming it repeatedly against the thick planks of wood beneath her until the matte brown turned crimson and a puddle oozed in all directions under her body. She fought. Hard. Then with renewed determination she leapt to her feet, clutching the side of her head that was bleeding, and sprang into the display window, atop the wood platform there. The heavy drape wound itself around her as she laid hold of the manikin in its jeweled turban and velvet skirts, and slammed it through the old plate glass window. Shards of glass exploded in every direction, but the thick drape deflected most of the slivers. Carefully, Levitica disengaged from the heavy fabric and jumped through the jagged hole onto the sidewalk in front of her shop. The glass crunched under her feet as she started running.

Night swallowed the street and aside from a few parked cars, there wasn't much going on. Streetlights shone with their yellow-white halos over the sidewalk and trees. She continued to run until she saw a figure approaching. It was a high school boy clad in varsity letter jacket. He wore a menacing look on his youthful face and reached into his jacket, bringing out something that glinted silver in the lamplight. Levitica froze, one foot in mid-air. She sucked in a sharp breath and waited for him to threaten her. As he neared, he clicked a button and a comb popped from the hilt. He combed his greased hair, eyeing her like a delicious dinner. Then she saw it. He had no feet. He was another goddamn ghost! With a stifled scream, she choked out an audible grunt and ran right through him. Into the street. Running down the center. Instead of jaywalking she was jay running.

A cop car! Black and white. Headed toward her. Levitica waved her arms over her head and jumped up and down, shouting, "Help me! Help!" The car revved its engines and then, cold as arctic air, drove straight through her. The passing of the ghost car left her skin goose-pimpled, and her fingernails a blue color. She watched the car disappear into the black of the night . . . and saw that the horde of spirits from the shop were now following her, staggering, hovering, and floating along the sidewalk. Levitica ran. Two blocks. Over one. There it was: her house. She didn't have her pocketbook, left it at the store. She fumbled with a large stone in the front flowerbed and found the spare key. She stuck it in the lock. *Click.* It was open.

Once inside, Levitica's mind raced. A book. She must have a book that would tell how to get rid of ghosts. They were angry. Up to no good. And, quite frankly, she was afraid. They weren't like any ghosts she'd ever heard of. These spirits were pissed that she'd been defrauding her clients for years. They were ghosts on personal missions. She was the mission.

She found a flashlight and a book on hauntings and ran upstairs to the attic. Slipping into the cold, musty room, she closed the door and crept under the farthest rafter. Maybe they wouldn't find her up here.

Maybe—

There they were. The whole crowd of them. Old, young. The boy from the street. The two cops sans car. A disembodied head that floated between the other spirits as if looking for something: a body, perhaps. So many jumbled thoughts bombarded her mind.

Hands. Hands again.

"Let me go! Go away!" she shouted, smacking the dusty air with her flashlight. Her fists and arms and beam of battery-fueled light went right through them. Why was it they could hurt her, but she couldn't do anything to them. It wasn't fair!

One of them tugged the sash from her dress out of the belt loops and tossed it over the rafter. The others seized her legs, her calves, her hips and thrust her upward—into the noose that one of the evil bastards had tied there. And, they slipped her head through it. Shouting. Screaming. And they let her fall.

She swung there. Kicking. Holding onto the tightly drawn fabric. It would look like she killed herself. *She wasn't a suicide! It was a lie! A lie!*

The ghost of the man, who had first come to her, stood in the doorframe leading down the stairs, pale light illuminating the corridor behind him. He was smiling. Levitica reached for the rafter with her one hand, but it was too far. Her mind swam. Her neck ached. Her arms shook under the strain of holding on. Fingers slipping. Colors blending. *Can't breathe.*

The man in the suit began to laugh, as the ghosts filed out, leaving the fortuneteller swaying on the end of her sash, dust sparkling like diamonds in the gold-hue of her flashlight.

NINTH CIRCLE: TRAITORS

ZONE 1: TRAITORS TO THEIR KIN

FINALLY FINISHED WITH THE maze of bridges, Obadiah and Azubah crossed from the eighth circle into the final realm of Hell. Gone was the permeating heat of the previous circles and, instead, chilling wind growing ever colder took its place. The condemned might have preferred such heat to the barren, frozen wasteland that the ninth circle yielded.

A small way station of warped and weathered wood stood to the side of the path.

"Let's see if they have some cloaks in there," Azubah pointed to the hut and said. Smoke curled in gray loops like a mournful ribbon from the crumbling stone chimney.

"Sounds good to me." Obadiah opened the door for the demon. "Age before beauty."

Azubah laughed loudly. "Witty fellow, aren't you?"

"Laughter warms the heart, maybe the rest of us too."

Inside the tumbledown station they found a grotesquely deformed demon hunched over a single candle and a mug of black coffee. A wool blanket was pulled tightly around him. He sat in front of an iron potbelly stove, which radiated enough heat to keep the little room toasty. The demon squinted, looking at Azubah strangely.

"Azubah, demon of iniquity and unbridled sorrow?" the demon asked, a stubby paw-like hand waving in the air.

"That's me."

"Don't you remember me?" the coffee-drinking demon said.

Azubah cleared his throat. "I'm sorry. I don't. Should I?"

The demon latched onto his blanket tighter as a look of insult crossed his face. "*Should you*? We only dated for half a millennia. *Should you*? Of all the unfeeling things to say!"

Obadiah's eyebrows arched and a slight smile curled his lips. Azubah scowled, thinking hard. "Astrial?"

"Who else?" the demon, now revealed to be female, said, crossing her arms

"But, what happened? You used to be so—so–"

"Beautiful? I know. You know the saying: *pride goeth before the fall*. Well, you're looking at my fall, buddy. Isn't very pretty." She lowered her voice to a whisper. "FYI: It's not good to say you look as good as Lucifer did before the rebellion when Lucifer is standing behind you."

Azubah nodded. "Point taken. Bum deal for you."

"Now, what brings you to our little circle of joy?"

"I'm escorting Obadiah, this angel here, through Hell on as part of a census Suriel cooked up. We hoped you'd have some cloaks we could borrow. It's cold and rather unpleasant."

Astrial burst into laughter. "This is *Hell*. It's *supposed* to be unpleasant."

"Actually," Obadiah said. "It's a common misconception among humans that Hell is one big boiling lake of fire and brimstone. It's a little known fact that the inner circle of Hell is frozen solid."

"Huh? Fancy that! Stupid mortals. Cold always trumps hot in the Something-Very-Bad category."

Azubah laughed with her. "Well, I don't mean to be rude, but we're on a tight deadline here. About those cloaks?"

Astrial got off her stool and hobbled to a cupboard. She pulled out two blankets identical to the one draped around her shoulders. "I'm afraid these are all I have. They're itchy and plague-infested, but warm."

Azubah accepted the folded blankets, passing one to the angel. "Thank you. The blankets are better than the nothing we have now."

"You have to return them. I don't get supplies very often. This isn't a very busy region of Hell. Not many traveling this way."

"We understand. I'll make sure they get returned," Azubah said. He opened the door for Obadiah. "It was good to talk with you again."

Astrial sat on her stool. "You too. Mind your step in these parts."

"We will." Azubah shut the door.

The two clutched their blankets and pressed onward through a deep ravine. After walking for some time, Obadiah said, "So, you and the way station demon, were an item?"

"Don't start."

"No, I'm genuinely asking. We aren't allowed any of that up there." Obadiah pointed upward.

"Dating?"

Obadiah nodded.

"Not at all?" Disbelief simmered in Azubah's voice.

"We don't really have *those* kinds of feelings."

"Really?" Now the demon was intrigued.

"That's what got your kind in trouble after the rebellion, remember?"

Azubah looked puzzled. "Oh! You mean the Nephilim? Daughters of men and all that?"

"Yeah. Race of giants. Diseases. Genetic mutations in humans. Missing link. Yeah, *all that*."

The demon stopped walking. "That was a *long* time ago."

"Humans are still suffering the effects of that interbreeding."

"*Suffering* the effects? Reaping the *benefits* you mean! Without the blood of the Sons of God, humans would still be beating rocks together to start fire. Look at the pyramids in Egypt! Look at the advances of the Mayan! Of the Aztecs! Stonehenge! Easter Island! Mysteries still unsolved by mortals! Those effects *suffered* by mortals altered the fate of man, advanced him to stages of development and knowledge that would've taken three times the amount of time."

"Never looked at it from *that* perspective."

"We should move along if we're going to get you to Suriel in time," Azubah said.

They came to a ledge overlooking the deep ravine that was the circle. Arm-to-arm, giants stood guard. Visible from the waist up, their lower extremities faded into the gray haze of the mist that arose from the lower depths of the frigid ravine. Obadiah expected a confrontation, but if they noticed the arrival of the angel and demon escort, they didn't acknowledge them.

Azubah was visibly relieved at the lack of interrogation from the guardian giants. Quickly he surveyed their surroundings and located the massive stone stairway leading into the zones of the ninth circle. "There's our way down," he said, pointing to the stone steps.

Obadiah followed the black-taloned finger. The stone stairs were worn smooth from an eternity of use, and no handrails protected the sides. The steps were clearly made with the giant guardians in mind:

steep and huge. The sheer drop-off on either side of the staircase would be enough to make a mortal man fear for his life, if he still had one. Blanket drawn snug, he braced the blasts of frozen air and started slowly down, alongside Azubah, who was having a much more difficult time of maneuvering his gnarled hooves over the stone.

"I believe the air has grown colder still," Obadiah said as they neared the bottom.

"Cocytus is responsible for that."

"Who's Cocytus?"

Azubah grinned, emitting a shivering chuckle. "Not who. What. Cocytus is the frozen lake of ice that comprises the ninth circle. In the four zones, the worsening crimes result in more extensive immersion and subsequent frozenness."

"Have you ever been this far before?

The demon shook his head. "No. Generally speaking, this is a place only those that must go. I have no reason to come here. Well, until now."

Obadiah neared a sign made of rusty metal. The word CAINA was painted in fading red letters. Recognition of the word flashed in his mind. "Caina—for Cain."

Azubah smiled, impressed. "Very good. The ninth circle contains traitors with connections to the person betrayed. Caina imprisons those who betray their own kin. See them—there—the fog rises."

Obadiah beheld the masses of condemned souls wailing, rubbing their arms frantically trying to warm themselves, frozen from the waist down in the solid lake of ice.

The thin woolen blankets clutched by the pair failed to provide a shred of warmth, but they continued clinging to the rough fabric out of hope. Closest to the shore was a man, gaunt and blue-tinged, his upper body quaking so much his teeth loudly chattered.

"He'll do," Obadiah said.

Azubah slid and slipped to the man. The heat from the demon's hands flooded warmth over the man's body and loosened his lower limbs. The demon stared at his own hands, warm enough to melt ice, but not warm enough to keep him comfortable. He pulled the man over the ice and to the shore where the angel waited, quill in hand.

BROTHER'S KEEPER

Julian Deveraux kept a watchful eye on the pot. Sliding another log atop the flaming fire, he checked his leather bound book of potions—again. The iron pot was surrounded by a whirl of swirling smoke and its contents hissed and bubbled, emitting a horrendous stench. He grabbed a nearby wooden spoon, thrust it into the liquid and stirred. "That should do," he said to no one, but his cat meowed a response to its master's voice.

"Meow all you want, cat. This potion will pay for your supper. Old Man Pickering will be pleased with these results." He poured the foul mixture into a narrow-necked earthen jar and ground a cork into it.

On the way to Old Man Pickering's house, Julian passed his brother's bakery. Joan was kneading dough, flour dusting her fair face and ample bosom. He waved to her.

She smiled, returning his wave. "You coming in for a bite to eat, Julian?" she called into the street.

Julian entered the shop; carts of bread to be delivered lined the little room. "No, I'm off to Old Man Pickering's to deliver a remedy." She was beautiful. Beautiful and wed to his brother.

"Ssh. Mind you don't get caught with your bloody potions, brother. The priest is itching for another bonfire!"

He laughed. "It's naught but a relief for the old man's swollen joints, not enough cause to roast a man."

"That's what *you* think. Father Cassell is quick to light the bramble for a lot less than the magick in that crock."

Julian changed the subject. "Where's Kegan this fine morning?"

Joan wiped her nose on the back of her flour-covered hand, and rested both hands on wide hips. Her face lost all joy and vexation replaced all trace of happiness. "He didn't come home last night."

"No?"

"No. I've heard from Mistress Anna that he was at the tavern in the company of some wench named Edi. What sort of name is Edi? Slut." Joan punched the wad of dough in the wood trough before her.

"I'm sorry, Joan."

"Don't apologize for the bloody bastard, Julian. I shoulda married *you* when I had the chance."

"You were young," Julian offered.

"I was an idiot." Joan slapped and punched, pinched and pounded the dough. "And now, I pay for youth's transgressions."

"If I see him, I'll send him home."

"If I see him, I might kill him."

Julian smiled. He wished she would. But, then she'd hang and she still wouldn't be his. "Farewell, sweet sister."

Joan waved a hand and resumed punishing the dough for her wayward husband's infidelities.

Julian continued on to Old Man Pickering's hut, and gave him the corked crockery in exchange for two chickens in a poorly constructed wood cage. It was secure enough to hold the screeching birds until he could get them home to his coop. On his way home, he caught a glimpse of a groveling Kegan in the bakery and a furious Joan. Saddest excuse for blood a man could ever have. Julian sighed. Can't undo the past now.

• • •

That night, greasy bones cast on a cracked platter, Julian sat licking his fingers in contemplation. Joan was still the love of his life. There had been no other since she jilted him to marry his brother and live a life secure with a business and a home. Some said he should be angry for the manner in which he was treated those many years ago, but Julian loved Joan and watched in misery as his brother broke her heart anew every day.

The baker. Loved and needed by all. That was Kegan. Who was *he*? Julian was but a mistrusted warlock, a male witch, a sorcerer to those who required his services. His little hut was evidence of his waning business, for in this religious climate seeking assistance from a healer and a necromancer—a warlock and a sorcerer—was as dangerous as *being* the necromancer. And yet, he never starved.

When business was scarce, he hovered in graveyards asking the dead for directions to forgotten coins and buried treasures. The dead knew him well. Julian was more at home among the spirits than the living. Women and children skirted him in the streets, avoiding him, whispering that he was a conjurer of ghosts and the wicked. Fear held their tongues from confessing his existence to the priest.

The cat leapt upon the table and gnawed the bones, casting a wistful eye toward the silent man.

"If only there was a way to be rid of Kegan!"

The cat's ears twitched as it paused eating to stare at him, and then resumed chewing.

"Maybe the spirits can advise me." He pulled on his cloak and stomped to the cemetery at the edge of the village.

Torch in hand, he sat beneath a massive oak tree and called into the darkness. "Who walks tonight?" The rustle of wind cracked the branches and a low groan sounded. "Are you a friend?"

A laugh, full of sadistic sarcasm, rent the peace of the hallowed ground. It came from the far side of the fence, outside of the graveyard, next to the crossroads where the suicides and unholy were laid to perpetual unrest. "I have no friends, necromancer."

"Why's this?"

More laughter. "Who'd be a friend to a fiend, a killer? Who would call me comrade, friend or brother?"

Julian's mouth formed a silent o. "Why do you speak to me?"

"You're a man with a vexing situation. I'm a spirit with an awful solution."

"Go on," Julian said.

"Three days past I was laid to unrest in a shallow grave, clad in a shroud of rotting linen, full of holes and of poor weave. Ten men I strangled with my bare hands and so I was drawn and quartered and my body buried in this unhallowed earth."

"You mentioned a solution to my problem? How can you help me?"

"Eager bugger, you are." More grotesque laughter. "You got someone you want dead. I got someone I want dead. You're a necromancer. Put my soul in the body of your brother. I'll kill my intended victim and your brother will pay the price. In the end, I get what I want and you get what you desire: your brother, dead."

"That's not really what I desire. Just a means to an end."

"It's about a woman isn't it? It's always about a bloody woman."

Julian laughed this time. "You're very perceptive for a lunatic."

The spirit pounced against the iron fence. Julian jumped. "Do we have a pact?" the ghost said.

Julian grimaced. "It's a pact most foul."

"Did you expect a Sunday meal in the park?"

The spirit was right. Nothing about this decision was pleasant, but how could it be? He was killing his own brother. It might as well be his own hands squeezing the life from Kegan's neck. An image of Joan, flushed face and teary eyes came to mind. Beautiful Joan. "We have a pact."

The criminal clung to the fence, face painfully distorted, body oddly contorted as if not joined quite right. "Bring him here."

Julian nodded. "That shouldn't be difficult. I'll just buy him beer—a lot of it. And lead him here. He won't think anything of it because I'm his brother." A pang of guilt stabbed his heart. *I'm his brother.* Julian frowned. *And he's a bastard for the way he treats Joan. He doesn't deserve her. Beautiful Joan.* He turned his attention to the vexed spirit on the wrong side of the fence. "What's your name?"

"What's it matter? Do you want him dead or not?"

"You must have some sort of a name," Julian said.

"I'd be daft to give you such power, necromancer. With my name you can send me to the pits of Hell."

"I can do that without your name, spirit."

The ghost dwelled on this for a moment. His ashy gray face squinted, his expression perplexed and a bit fearful. "It's Otto Goethe."

"Otto Goethe."

"Don't go using it in some spell."

Julian laughed. "Why would I do that? I don't want any trouble. I want to get rid of that no good drunken brother of mine so I can marry his widow."

"All I promised was to kill the brother. I don't have anything to do with the marrying."

"Of course not." Julian smiled wryly. "Now, stay here. I'll go get Kegan."

Otto laughed this time. "*Stay here?* I've got nowhere else to go!"

Torch in hand, Julian left the darkness of the graveyard and made his way to the tavern where Kegan would be getting drunker than usual. Since he fought with Joan, Kegan was most certainly facing a beer.

As Julian approached The Red Boar's Inn, he could hear the raucous laughter and ribald singing floating into the village square. Peering between the half-closed shutters, he spotted Kegan toward the back, near the fireplace, a table full of empty mugs being cleared away by some saucy tart who didn't seem to mind that his brother had his hand up her skirt. Julian went inside and sat at his brother's table, shooing away the wench.

Keegan looked disagreeably at his brother. "Fancy seeing you here," he said, words slurred, spittle heavy, sloshing the swill that passed for beer.

Julian laughed good-naturedly. "Came for a pint."

Kegan chuckled, shaking his head.

"Can I buy you another?" Julian asked.

Kegan looked at him with vacant eyes rimmed in red, eyelids heavy.

"And where'd you come by money? Usually you're begging scraps from me wife just to feed yer belly."

Julian's pride stung. "I don't *beg*, Kegan."

"Sure looks like begging to me."

"Do you want that drink or not?"

"I want it," Kegan said, drool running over his chin.

Julian ordered beers for the both of them, but had no intention of drinking. Kegan would drink it for him.

Six drinks later and Kegan was barely able to sit straight and Julian was deprived of all his money, but it would be worth it to have the bastard dead and gone. Then, Joan would be free to marry him.

"Do you want me to walk you home?" Julian asked.

"Don't wanna go home to that bitch," Kegan replied.

"Joan?"

"That's the bitch," Kegan said. "Slut."

Rage stirred inside Julian. "Come on, let's go home. You can sleep it off at my place."

"That pig sty? That hut isn't good enough for a cow to live in."

Another blow to Julian's pride. "It's warm and keeps out the cold. I've got no complaints."

"You wouldn't. No friends but dead people." Kegan attempted to stand, weaving, wobbling, and scooped an arm around his brother's shoulders.

"Let's get you out of here," Julian said, and nearly carried, half-dragged, and half-steered his brother from the tavern.

It was dark out, but a thin mist clung to everything, visible in the bright light of the moon. Shadows crept eerily in shades of gray and ghostly whites, cast away from the stumbling form of Kegan and his ever-patient brother, Julian. They passed the lonely cemetery, the crooked crosses jutting from grassy mounds, the twisted trees growing from the fertilizer of rotting flesh, and rounded the corner of the iron fence to the burial site of the suicides and undesirables between the road and the grassy strip surrounding the graveyard.

A lone owl hooted mournfully in the black lace of the barren trees that sprang from the hard soil along the road. A wisp of even blacker clouds floated in an ebony tuft over the bone-white moon.

Kegan looked around. "We there yet?"

"Almost."

"Don't remember your hut being so far."

"You're drunk. Everything seems different." Julian impatiently looked for the ghostly manifestation of Otto. "Let's rest. You're heavy."

"Don't wanna rest. Not here. This is a bad place," Kegan said, at last realizing through his muddled mind where they were.

"Hog spit. Here. Sit on this log." Julian unloaded Kegan onto the hollow log. He stared into the shadows. *Where was that madman?* The owl screeched. Julian jumped. Kegan fell from the log. When Julian looked toward his brother, Otto loomed menacingly behind him.

"Beautiful night, necromancer," Otto said, his voice a throaty growl.

Kegan didn't, couldn't, hear the dead man.

"Most beautiful," Julian murmured.

"What did you say?" Kegan asked.

"Get on with it, Goethe!" Julian demanded.

The maniac laughed. "I've come up with a different plan."

"What? We had a pact!"

"Hear me out. I just want a little more time."

"Then I can't marry Joan!" Julian shrieked.

Kegan crawled around in the dirt. "What's that about Joan?"

"Nothing. It's nothing," Julian said.

Otto grew restless. "Only a few days. I'll fulfill my part of the bargain and your brother will take his own life, but first, I must kill the person who sent me to the gallows in the first place. *That* was part of our original pact."

"But you were going to do all of this quickly."

"And I still will. It's just that I've learned the man I want dead is in London on business, so it'll take longer than originally intended."

"How much longer?" Julian asked.

"Only a few days," Otto said, circling Kegan like an animal does prey.

"Alright," Julian said. He pulled a scrying mirror from his tattered robes and placed it on a flat portion of the grass. Hands cupped together he raised his arms above his head, mouthing an ancient chant created by sorcerers older than the Druids.

"What're you doing, Julian?" Kegan asked, groping the log. It moved loosely in the sandy soil, spinning. Kegan's grasp slipped and he fell on his face.

"Change places!" Julian suddenly shouted.

A violent seizure gripped Kegan's body and he thrashed wildly in the dirt. Legs rigid, arms flailing, he muttered incoherently and screamed intermittently. The apparition of Otto Goethe turned into a trail of curling fog as he dematerialized into a tendril of mist over Kegan Deveraux's mouth. Clawing at his throat, tongue lulling from a gaping mouth, Kegan fought the passage of the criminal spirit seeping inside of him. Kegan laid still, his eyes closed.

After a few minutes, his eyes opened; he blinked and moved his head from side-to-side as if adjusting his neck. Slowly and awkwardly, he sat up.

Julian observed all with an apprehensive frown. "Otto?"

A smile wickedly curled the face of Julian's brother. "At your service, necromancer."

Julian breathed a relieved sigh. "Where's the spirit of my brother?"

"Gone. Banished into limbo, neither dead nor alive until this mortal shell meets its destruction." Otto shook a foot, and then the other, testing them.

"When do you expect to be rid of this person with which you have dealings?"

"As soon as it can be arranged. In the meantime, you must show me to your brother's home so I can retire for the night." Otto stood, stretching his fingers as if they were unused and stiff.

An image of this beast ravishing Joan made Julian grit his teeth. He hadn't considered this. "You'll stay with me tonight. You're drunk."

"Nonsense. Just a bit of a buzz. Your brother couldn't hold his liquor, but Otto Goethe is not your brother."

Julian was all too aware of this already. "It's his body. Come on. We're going to my home. Let's go."

"This is about that wench? What's her name? Joan? Isn't it? You just don't want me sticking a stiff prick to the lady, do you? I'm her husband after all. I don't think our little Joan would be too surprised, unless your brother buggers arseholes of boys or something."

Julian scowled. "He didn't bugger boys and *you* aren't Joan's husband."

Otto looked at his arms and legs and smacked his chest. "Looks like her husband to me. What do we have in here?" He loosened the rope securing his trousers and peered inside. "Oh. There's nothing good in here. Poor wife Joan. I'll have to make do with what I've got, I suppose." He laughed raunchily.

Julian's face grew hot with fury and embarrassment. "Tie your belt. You'll not be sleeping with Joan tonight or any other. You'll rid yourself of this person you've discussed, and then you'll dispatch of Kegan's body promptly as agreed."

"Calm down, necromancer. I might be a lot of things, but a liar I've never been. You'll get yer fine wench in the end. Now take me to a bed so I can sleep off this ale your idiot of a brother drowns me with."

Julian led the way to his little hovel, and made a sleeping mat for Otto. Julian slept with one eye open watching the snoring carcass of his brother, while the cat hissed in the corner.

• • •

When daylight broke the gloom of night and slivered across the packed earth floor in shards of gold, Julian awoke, cat asleep on his shoulder.

Cat asleep on his shoulder.

Julian bolted from the low, rope-strung bed. *Otto was gone.* He ran from his hut toward the village. It wouldn't be hard for Otto to find Joan. All he had to do was ask where she was and feign a hangover. No one would question Kegan's usual state of drunkenness. *Joan!*

The necromancer ran to the bakery, but arrived much too late. A cluster of shrieking, sobbing women surrounded the little shoppe. Julian shoved past them into the warm room. The doughy loaves of rising bread lined the table, wading in puddles of thickening blood. The walls shone slick with crimson, splatters, spatters and streaks painted everything in a frenzied bloodbath. "Joan?" his voice squeaked from dry lips, barely audible.

A burned aroma drifted and snaked from the oven and Julian hesitated to open the iron door. Already from the scent of roasting meat, he knew what horrors awaited inside the oven. He slid the wood handle in place and yanked the door open: a ghastly plume of choking smoke billowed forth, heavy and black.

Mounds of Joan oozed from the baking tray, sizzling and burning upon the fire beneath. Julian vomited on his own feet. He slammed the door and shoved through the crowd gathered outside. *Where was Otto?*

The maniac couldn't have gotten far without a horse and there was only one horse for miles around and that belonged to their impoverished lord of the manor—aged and infirm upon the grassy hill. Julian asked around the village: *Where's Kegan? Has anyone seen my brother?*

Fingers pointed toward the manor.

"He went to borrow the lord's horse to hunt the lunatic who murdered Joan," the weaver said.

Julian didn't reply, but began to run for the manor.

• • •

The carnage witnessed there resembled that in the bakery. The elderly lord and his servants were slaughtered and the horse gone. Dead end. Julian stepped into the fresh air of the field around the lord's manor, threw his head back and angrily shouted, "Otto!" Then he followed the horse's hoof prints for as long as the wind allowed the indentions to remain. He stopped walking, tired and thirsty, at a tumbledown inn that contained only a handful of travelers.

In the back, eating a stew with an oversized wood spoon, Julian spied the body of his brother and the soul of Otto Goethe. He seized a meat knife from a table and stomped toward the man. Otto, or was it Kegan, looked up from his greasy food and smiled. "Come for stew?"

Julian hit the table with his knife-clenched fist. "You. Killed. Joan."

"An unfortunate accident."

"Accident? You deliberately killed her. You went straight from my hut to the bakery and butchered her!" Julian breathed heavily.

Otto didn't look Julian in the eyes, but continued eating. "Stew here's delicious."

Julian stuck the knife in his brother's back. Otto looked surprised and clawed for the hilt of the blade, grabbing and yanking it from his flesh with a painful gasp. Before Julian could think about what was happening, Otto plunged the knife into his chest. Julian gripped the wood handle, blood bubbling around it. Otto struggled to his feet as Julian sank to his knees.

"We had a pact," Julia gasped.

Otto tried to laugh, but pain prohibited sound, and instead, his face contorted silently. Both men slipped to the floor, the patrons of the inn gathering around in a fading image of mild concern and interest in whatever might lie in each man's purse.

• • •

Obadiah sighed. "Woeful tale, necromancer."

"Woeful indeed. I might've been in a better place but for my crimes against my brother," Julian Deveraux said, blowing into his blue-tinged hands. "If I might ask a question?"

"Yes?"

"Joan—is—she–"

"She's safe in the bosom of the Almighty," Obadiah said, his voice comforting.

"Thank you. Thank you." Julian stood facing Cocytus, resolved to his fate. "That's my tale." And then he resumed his place in the ice as before.

ZONE 2: TRAITORS TO THEIR COUNTRY

Obadiah followed Azubah along the hail pelted shores of Cocytus. They stopped in front of a gathering of lost souls immersed and frozen to their shoulders beneath deep depths of ice. A painted wood sign lay half covered by frost on the bank of the lake. Azubah picked it up and scraped the cold, wet stuff away.

"Place could use some maintenance," Obadiah said, stamping his feet for warmth.

Azubah failed to be amused. "ANTENORA."

"Is that the name of this zone?"

"Yes. Here we find traitors to their countries." Azubah flung the sign into the ice.

"There's a regal looking fellow–" Obadiah pointed, and Azubah again melted the man from his frigid prison.

A long, gold-trimmed, blue robe clung to the back of the bearded man's legs as he, with the help of the demon, carefully crossed the frozen lake to where Obadiah waited. A thin band of gold encircled the man's head and his countenance suggested more than just a man: he was a king.

"Your escort has explained the mission you're on," the man said, his voice a rich baritone. "This place is most unpleasant, so I'll be quick."

"I appreciate your concern for our well being–"

"Nebuchadnezzar, King of Babylonia."

Obadiah shot Azubah a surprised look. These Babylonians had a way of getting around. "We visited with one of your court artisans awhile back," he said to the king.

"Ah, my influence lives on."

"In Hell, perhaps, but many thousands of years have passed in the mortal world and your kingdom is located in the midst of a war-torn region, constantly plagued by misery and strife."

Nebuchadnezzar didn't look too happy to hear such details. "My buildings? My temples?"

"Little more than stone rubble. A few ziggurats exist in deteriorated conditions."

"My gardens?" A look of sorrow crossed the king's features.

"Gone. Swallowed by the desert. They survive only in myth and legends as one of the Seven Wonders of the World," Obadiah said.

"Gone? Gardens and buildings?"

"I'm afraid so. War continues to erode what precious little the elements spare."

Nebuchadnezzar squatted on his haunches, pulling his wet cape around him, desperate for warmth. He sighed loudly. "The vanity of kings–"

"Is not forgotten," Obadiah said with a slight laugh.

"Something remains then." The king chuckled. "But you came for my tale and so I shall tell it. This is a story you won't find in your Hebrew bible, nor will you find it anywhere else. This is a dastardly story of betrayal, science, and another world."

"I'm intrigued. Go on."

HE REVEALS DEEP AND HIDDEN THINGS: HE KNOWS WHAT LIES IN DARKNESS

543 B.C., Babylon, Babylonia

The lithe figure leaned a bulbous head inward, near the bowl laden with fruit, toward the center of the table. Long, skinny fingers, skeletal in appearance, seized upon a date and brought the fruit to its nose, sniffing. "What do you call this?"

"A date," Nebuchadnezzar said.

"What does it do?"

"You eat it."

"Eat it?" the creature, named Samfurati, asked, placing the date back into the fruit bowl.

"Yes. We put it into our mouths and it provides sustenance for our bodies."

Understanding flickered in the creature's eyes. "Our race hasn't *eaten* as your bodies require for centuries—in Earth years."

"Certainly you require some form of nourishment?" the king asked.

The thin alien blinked black eyes, and looked around the room. "We require energy."

Nebuchadnezzar looked puzzled.

"Something your race might not yet comprehend. Think of it as—oil—in a lamp. You light the wick with fire and the fire is fed by the fuel that is the oil," the being explained. "Only here, because your race is *primitive*, we have few options for our source of energy."

"Such as?"

"The easiest to come by is the life force of your people."

Nebuchadnezzar grunted, leaning back in his chair. "Is that why you would have me send people through the portal?"

"No, no. *That* is a matter entirely different."

The king could tell the alien wasn't going to reveal any further details at this point in the negotiations. "And what if I should refuse to give you people?"

The monstrous creature, flesh an opaque pink like the hairless flesh of a baby mouse, blinked watery black eyes. An expression of surprise crossed the being's face. "I didn't anticipate defiance."

"No one has defied you yet, but hear me, Samfurati. I am a *king*. I have defied many and won't hesitate to defy you if I think it necessary." The king slammed his fist on the table in a display of strength.

Samfurati's expression didn't change. "If our requests are met with defiance, we will level your cities and slaughter your people in ways your enemies could never imagine or inflict upon you. All of the dead from every battle you've ever fought will still not equal the mountain of carcasses we shall pile in Babylonia."

Nebuchadnezzar grimaced. Samfurati looked like a pink-skinned bag of bones— crushable—weak. He laughed. "If I do what you ask of me—send humans through the portal into your world—what will my kingdom get in return?"

Samfurati snorted a wet, nasally sound that must pass for laughter. "*You* and your *family* will be allowed to live. We will not come down to this world and enslave you. We will not make you grovel in the dirt like a cowled captive."

"You have a way with words, Samfurati," the king said, stroking the end of his squared beard. "But, the answer is: no."

"No?"

"No. You've come here, alone, and made these demands. So far, the only demonstration of strength or *powers* has been the strangulation of eight of my guards." The elder of the high council leaned to the king's ear and whispered. "Ten of my guards, then." Nebuchadnezzar looked at the elder, frowning.

"Did you not see the bodies of your men, king?" Samfurati asked.

"No."

"Bring them," the alien demanded.

Nebuchadnezzar waved a hand at the general standing to his left. "Do as he says."

Six guards opened the massive double doors to the chamber, and two lines of soldiers marched in, carrying a long rug between them. With expressions of disgust and revulsion, they placed the rug upon the floor in front of the dais where King Nebuchadnezzar sat. A mound of flesh, broken bones, and guts shimmied in a puddle of gelatinous gore on the rug saturated with the crimson blood of the men. Already the marble beneath and around the gruesome delivery was growing wet with the creeping expansion of blood.

The king's face grew hard as fury rose from his gullet. "What manner of beast are you?"

"We are determined to see our goals attained."

"This isn't gain, or honor. This is—is–"

"Is *your* fate and those of every living being in your kingdom if we aren't obeyed," Samfurati said, voice calm and deliberate, cold and hard.

Nebuchadnezzar shook his head. "I don't believe you have the power to destroy my kingdom and slaughter us all. That would take incredible manpower."

"So be it." Samfurati closed his eyes. His smooth face grew wrinkled as he concentrated. His knobby knuckled fingers gripped the wood arms of the chair and the floor began to rumble.

Thunder and lightening rent the sky and a dark cloud of black choked the sun. A roar of destruction slashed through the rain and the king's general ran to the balcony to determine where the sound originated. "My king!" he shouted.

Nebuchadnezzar leapt from his throne, his sandaled feet slapping stone as he ran to the general's side. A massive ziggurat still in construction swayed and quaked like a child's tower of building blocks.

"That tower is being consecrated to Baal," the general said. "The rites just ended. The priestess has received the seed of our god."

Nebuchadnezzar gripped the balcony, bronze knuckles whitening under his clenched hand. The tower teetered and then collapsed, slaves and stones scattering, the cacophony of death cries filling his ears. He turned his attention to Samfurati. "An earthquake!"

"You still don't believe?"

Through the open doors another monster resembling Samfurati entered, dragging one of the king's concubines. The woman struggled in the pink creature's clutches, shrieking. She babbled in some foreign tongue.

"She's been bewitched!" the general shouted.

The king looked from Samfurati to his concubine. The alien holding her in its clutches inhaled a great breath and blew it out into the face of the woman. She gasped, hands flying to her throat. She clawed at her neck and face. The alien let her fall to the marble floor where she writhed, turning paler and paler until at last, her body flipped and flailed. A great ripping sound was heard and then her flesh split down the middle and turned inside out, leaving her guts on the floor and her flesh in a tangle.

Nebuchadnezzar stood frozen. Around him, battle-hardened soldiers vomited profusely.

Quietly, in a voice barely audible, the king said: "What must I do?"

• • •

Nebuchadnezzar's council erected a massive statue of the king and proclaimed that everyone in the kingdom must worship it. In this fashion, the king began to weed out the captives, the slaves, and all the foreigners living in the king's realm. If the king had to sacrifice humans to these monsters at least he'd avoid sending his own countrymen to their deaths—for as long as he could anyway.

They'd need a different plan soon. They were running out of foreigners to send into the portals. They could always make war on a lesser kingdom for the sole purpose of seizing captives to use as fodder for the portal, but Nebuchadnezzar had his hands full. He still wasn't positive what the beings were using humans for, but his council believed the aliens were crossbreeding with the women. The women never returned from the portal, but the men did. Most came back muttering incoherently, obviously mad; they spoke of being forced to copulate with the females of Samfurati's race and then being allowed to return. The biggest and most handsome of the sacrificed males, however, never returned. The council believed these were being held as studs, great bulls in the alien breeding stables.

The king ran a hand over his face. It was time for another delivery to the portal. He made his way solemnly to the fiery opening. Samfurati had devised this wormhole to another place to resemble a furnace. Those sacrificed entered an illusion of flames and crossed to the other side unscathed, but the general populous didn't know this. The few that made it back were kept hidden away from prying eyes or questioning tongues.

Three men, Hebrews, were brought forward in chains. Nebuchadnezzar recognized the three as men from his foreign council:

ambassadors. They were foreign diplomats on good terms with the Babylonian government, but because of their dedication to their god, *Yahweh*, they refused to worship the idol. The three—Shadrach, Meshach, and Abednego—stood silently awaiting their death sentence.

"Have you anything to say?" the king asked.

Shadrach stepped forward. "It is better that we feed the tongues of fire than we should bow before your false idol."

The other two men nodded in agreement.

Nebuchadnezzar hated having to sacrifice three otherwise loyal and intelligent officials, but the memory of his concubine turned inside out like a cast off tunic of flesh and blood made him quiver with fear. "So be it."

The three men were led to the fiery furnace and cast inside. For a moment, Nebuchadnezzar could see Samfurati cross through the portal to receive the sacrificed men, and then they were gone.

The king peered into the flames. Visions of international disputes filled his head. He didn't need any other distractions while he must deal with the aliens. There must be criminals in the dungeons that could replace the three diplomats. He gave the order to the general at his side and shouted into the fire for Samfurati to return the three Hebrews. The wispy pink man appeared in the fire with the three men and shoved them through the portal. Not a blemish was found on the men. The crowds gasped in amazement.

The guards moved the crowd away. The people dispersed muttering and talking in hushed tones of all they had seen. When all were gone, the king had six prisoners brought forward in shackles and cast into the furnace.

"But, my king, those are Babylonians. I don't understand why you've exchanged your own subjects for these Hebrews," the general said, voice dismayed.

"Empty the prisons. Give the beasts the undesirables of our kingdom. Perhaps the gluttons will be satiated and they'll depart from us."

The general dared not defy the king and ordered the prisons be emptied and the prisoners thrust into the portal. For ten days and nights, every dungeon in the kingdom was cleared out and when that supply had been depleted, the king ordered all of the beggars and lepers be cast in as well.

Finally Samfurati appeared in the king's chambers. "What are you doing?"

"You want specimens? I'm giving them to you. Take them all. Keep them and be gone from us! Torture us no more! Take these that we've given you and leave our world!"

Samfurati snorkeled his mucousy snort, amused. "You give us your undesirables. Your discards. Your *trash*. Do you expect us to leave with these *imperfect*," Samfurati spit the word,

"—humans?"

"What *will* make you leave?" Nebuchadnezzar shouted.

Samfurati waved a slow, reed-thin arm toward the army barracks. "We'll leave if you give us your elite: fifty of your best warriors and fifty noble virgins untouched by human men."

Nebuchadnezzar felt the heat rise to his face. Rage shook him. "Monsters!"

"Your race may look upon us as such now, but in the future you'll thank us."

"Do it!" Nebuchadnezzar, shaking with fury, commanded the highest general of his court.

With a face of stony determination, the general issued the order and then stepped forward, kneeling before Samfurati.

"What are you doing, human?"

"I command all of my king's armies. I'm the finest of his warriors. I offer myself and my twelve daughters, all virgins, for the good of my country," the general said.

Nebuchadnezzar wept openly. "Nimrud, I would've spared you and yours."

"No, my king. If my brothers in arms are to be delivered to these beasts, then I shall go with them. This creature demands the finest, and who but your highest general is the finest?"

The king stumbled to his throne, tears blinding him. He could hear the shouts and cries of the men and women, mostly girls, being shoved into the portal thinking they were to die in the torturous flames of the fire: only to discover a fate far worse awaited them on the other side of the alien wormhole.

Samfurati made a face that said he was pleased, and bowing mockingly to King Nebuchadnezzar, left without further words.

Nebuchadnezzar watched as, from all around the city, down in the streets, hundreds of alien creatures emerged and walked to the furnace, disappearing into the portal in a single file until only Samfurati was left—and he too entered the flames.

The pulsing glow of the ensorcelled fire extinguished and the courtyard grew black and quiet. The sounds of weeping and the wails of his people filled Nebuchadnezzar's ears: the creatures were gone.

ZONE 3: TRAITORS TO GUESTS

"Ptolomaea," Azubah read aloud from the chiseled words on the stone sign. A slick layer of ice shimmered like diamonds. "Traitor to one's guests."

Obadiah's teeth chattered. He looked over the frozen lake but saw no one. "Where are they?"

Azubah studied the ice. "Underneath," he said, pointing down toward the immersed, frozen souls.

"How do we find a soul to interview if they're frozen out of our view?" Obadiah said between cold-induced bodily quakes.

"You're the angel with vast resources. I'm just your escort, remember?"

"Thanks."

"The ice looks darker in places. I speculate that beneath each dark patch is a frozen soul."

"Sounds logical." Obadiah was eyeing the giants. He waved his arms in order to gain their attention.

"Don't do that!" Azubah said. "One of them will come down here!"

"That's my intention."

"*What*?"

"I'm going to have a guardian loose a soul for us so we can complete this task. We certainly don't have time to dig a traitor out from the ice." Obadiah looked pleased when he saw one of the giants descending the stone steps. "Ah, here comes one."

Azubah sighed. "I'll go tell him our objective and escort the soul to you."

Obadiah found a block of lopsided ice to sit upon. "I'll be here," he said, and rubbed his hands to warm his frigid fingers.

SCOURGE OF THE FOREST

Four stone chimneys belched black smoke into the graying twilight. Drums beat like continuous heartbeats surrounding the great hall. *Boom.*

Boom. Boom. Boom. Women scurried like rats weaving between benches and the long tables, filling wood mugs of mead. Huge, fat pigs roasted on iron spits, turned by the hands of servants who, though tired from the preparations, were glad to be warm. The wind howled like a shrieking witch as the sun sank lower on the horizon, black barren trees etched against gold like exquisite lace. Across the walled courtyard the horses neighed from hitching posts and dogs barked at the sound of harps and pipes. From all over the countryside warriors came awandering to the busy hall to celebrate their victory against Rolf the Red with feasting and cavorting with beautiful women captured in their raids and battles.

This was the hall of their fearless leader, The Scourge of the Forest, Lord Nathaniel of the Black Wood. His name drove fear into the hearts of their enemies, and pride into the spirits of his warriors. Tonight, finally, after many years of battle and bloodshed, they would celebrate triumph over Rolf the Red and plan for a new future of peace and prosperity.

Snorri coughed into the bitter cold as he made his way toward the hall. A stable boy escorted his horse to a long pole where other horses whinnied to one another and munched on fresh hay.

"Will you dance with me tonight you hulk of a man?" a woman's voice, followed with a giggle, reached his frost-nipped ears. It was Celeste, daughter of Sigord, who'd been killed by a lance through the heart in the Battle at Two Rivers. She was the very definition of woman. Ample breasts spilled over her girdle. Long hair the color of the blackest night swung in a solitary braid to the back of her skirt-swallowed knees.

Snorri wasn't a man of many smiles, but Celeste was a woman a man couldn't help but smile for. "Hello there, goddess among women!" He popped her on the ass, bent her backward, and kissed her on the mouth. Her eyes sparkled at him with mischief and a hint of what might come after the feast. She laughed light-heartedly, for everyone was merry tonight. Snorri threw an arm around her shoulders and led the way into the hall, which bustled with activity. Music mixed with uproarious conversation amidst a flurry of dancing and loud boasting from drunken soldiers dreaming of farming, safety and fat children. The din echoed from the stone walls, reverberating with metallic clangs of swords, shields and cooking kettles.

Celeste twirled in voluminous skirts of red, purple and nut brown—around and around—her thick braid flying on the air like a silk rope. Snorri held her small pink hands in his big calloused ones, and only saw the joy fixed on her perfect face. He laughed from the bottom of his soul, happiness bubbling like a fresh mountain spring. The battles were fought. The battles were won.

"Three cheers for Nathaniel of the Black Wood!" someone shouted.

"Hip Hip Huzzah!" the crowd roared. Cups thumped on tables by hands connected to enthusiastic warriors. "Three cheers for the Scourge of the Forest, victor over Rolf the Red!"

"Hip Hip Huzzah!" the chorus rang loud. Even the dogs that ran between legs and under tables seemed to howl their approval. More cups slammed tables, and now the sound of swords banging shields filled the night air with an insistent battering. "Na—than—iel! Na— han—iel!" the men chanted for their leader, their general, their lord.

A thick tapestry at the center of the wall parted and an old woman, the seer, the crone of fortune, emerged. She'd ridden with them into every battle and they showed their reverence for her by banging swords to shields even louder. A smile cracked her wrinkled face, revealing a black-toothed mouth. And, then, still dressed in the bloody clothes of battle, stepped forth the very man the throngs of warriors demanded: Lord Nathaniel of the Black Wood, conqueror of Rolf the Red, the Scourge of the Forest.

Lord Nathaniel smiled, his pale flesh nearly translucent in the amber glow of the firelight. He held hands in the air to quell the fevered masses. Servants ran between the sweaty men, clumsily filling empty mead horns.

The crone handed the lord a cup of wine. He gripped the worn wood and held it high over the heads of the quieting crowd. "The battle is over, my friends! The victory is ours! Together as a band of brothers we've slain the red beast that has plagued our lands, burned our crops, and raped our women! Together we've driven the vermin from our boundaries, vanquished the disease that preyed like a rash that couldn't be healed. Rolf the Red is dead! Behold!"

From behind the tapestry came the chained widow of the enemy leader, gagged with rope, and around her neck swung a heavy pendant: the head of her dead husband, a gold chain threaded through empty eye sockets. A look of terror marred her beauty; the abuse heaped upon her in the days since her defeat was evident.

Lord Nathaniel sidled beside the woman, raking a thin hand through her unkept locks. Delicately he ran a finger over the rope tied around her dirt-streaked cheeks that cut into the soft flesh around her mouth. Tears rolled over her face and her whole body racked with fearful sobs.

Nathaniel licked her face and neck as the widow whimpered, instinctively recoiling at his touch. He laughed.

The crowd laughed with him.

With a graceful swoop, he seized her throat and squeezed her larynx in iron-hard fingers. Flesh split and blood sprayed, pumping in bursts over her body, over the swinging head of her dead husband, and over the torso and face of Nathaniel. The room grew quiet. The Scourge of the Forest bent the widow's head back at an awkward angle, as she sunk to her knees, collapsing in his waiting arms. He buried his open mouth in the spurting fountain of her blood. He drank deeply and then tossed her spent corpse onto the straw-strewn floor. Dogs ran to the broken body, tugging and yelping, growling and snapping at each other, fighting for their prize.

Lord Nathaniel's men stood in silent bewilderment. The servants and women froze where they stood. Only the chewing of the dogs and the howling of the wind was heard. Nathaniel moved from his place to the old crone and wiped the blood from his face onto a piece of cloth offered by her hand. He smiled again—thin-lipped—a twinkle in his features, and realized the room was stunned. "Well, go on then! This is a feast! A celebration! Shouldn't we revel in the blood of our defeated foes?" He laughed loudly, and turned to the musicians. "Music! Dance! Dance!"

The musicians hurriedly and confusedly let fly with an unorganized melody that betrayed their state of mind. Only the old crone was unmoved by the death of the widow. Whispering was followed by conversation, followed by laughter, followed by dancing and before long the crowd was celebrating as before and Lord Nathaniel sat in his chair observing his warriors and the whirling women in their arms.

The night grew later and the servants were dismissed. As the warriors guzzled copious amounts of mead, the women, too, began to slip from the hall and into the cover of darkness. Until, all that remained were the drunken soldiers, the silent crone, and Lord Nathaniel on his throne-like chair watching the men boast of battle and rutting.

The crone stood slowly and leaned close to her master. "I bid you goodnight, my lord. Drink deeply."

Lord Nathaniel smiled, patting her veiny hand. "I will. It's good knowing that I need them not now that our enemy has been trampled under foot."

"Spare none," the black-toothed hag said.

Nathaniel kissed her hand. "When have I?' His smile curled his blue-hued lips. The crone shuffled through the tapestry divider and into the shadows.

The Lord of the Black Wood stuck out an arm, clutching the shoulders of the nearest man. With a yank that rent the man's arm from the socket, he pulled the warrior into an embrace. A crunch of bone and the man's neck folded like leather. Nathaniel's teeth plunged into his vein. He drained him dry without even a glance from the other warriors.

Another, Krogdon of the Stone, a fearless soldier, had his back to him when Nathaniel slipped behind with the agility of a cat, and grasping Krogdon's head between each hand, he twisted: snapping his neck. He plunged a taloned hand into the man's chest, up under the sternum, and ripped forth his pumping heart. Greedily, he sucked the hot blood from the organ, squeezing it like fruit to glean every last, salty drop.

Two bodies in the straw. Three, with the widow. The drums and pipes continued.

Nathaniel preyed upon the men asleep beneath the tables, drunk and in a stupor, lying in the piss of the men and the shit of the dogs. He quenched his thirst until the men remaining grew less and less.

Six looked about them at the carnage peppering the floor. Ribcages splayed open like the Blood Eagle of the bastard Norse. Entrails strung like purple ribbons over limbs and ground. A horror worse than any battlefield because this mayhem occurred right under their noses within the confines of their feasting hall while they were unaware.

The drums continued. *Boom. Boom.* The walls quivered like thumping hearts.

Two men stood, wobbling, and ran as best they could to the double doors.

"It's bolted!" Hugar shouted. "It's bolted from the *outside!*"

Lord Nathaniel sauntered between the bodies of the massacred, stripped to his leather breeches, his pearl-white flesh streaked with scarlet and caked with gore of unimaginable revulsion. The warriors dug wildly in the straw looking for fallen weapons that servants had stealthily removed for their own safety. Nathaniel grew nearer.

"My lord! The door's bolted and something evil moves amongst us!" a warrior, more boy than man, shouted.

"What do you think this evil is?" Nathaniel said, pausing for an answer.

"I don't know. A monster? A spirit? *A demon!*"

Lord Nathaniel tossed back his long hair and laughed, his laugh resounding through the great hall. The men clutched their ears. One, more persistent than the others, pushed against the big doors with all his strength, slamming his brute shoulder against the wood as if a battering ram of flesh. Nathaniel pushed another aside and grabbed hold of the battering warrior, raising him by the throat, from the ground. He held him here, feet swinging as if upon the gallows, the man's eyes bulging. "The door is bolted, my friend. There's much celebration to be had!" Nathaniel gave the warrior a shake and broke the thick neck with a loud crack. The man didn't die, but fell, motionless in a heap, face in the bloody straw. The Scourge of the Forest dropped to one knee, lifting the man by his sweaty hair. "If you truly want out of my hall, I'll grant your wish." He picked up the warrior and with the force of a demon from hell, rammed the man through the wood door, leaving only his lower legs visible from the inside.

• • •

When the sun rose over the frozen countryside, the old crone commanded the hordes of servants to clean the great hall. The feasting had been glorious, the celebration triumphant. She brushed back the ebony tresses of her sleeping lord, satiated and full from his night of revelry. She smiled upon her master, her son, the Scourge of the Forest, Lord Nathaniel of the Black Wood.

ZONE 4: TRAITORS TO LORDS & BENEFACTORS

Hail blasted the angel and demon, stinging their flesh as they entered the final realm of Hell.

"We're almost finished," Azubah said. "Judecca: zone four. Home to traitors to their lords and benefactors."

Obadiah made a mental note of the sign—frozen over by dangerous icicles—hanging from an iron gate. The gate creaked loudly, rusted and un-oiled. The sound emitted forced Obadiah, nerves on edge, to jump. "I'm glad. This has been a laborious task, but I do thank you for your help."

Azubah shrugged. "I have to admit I wasn't pleased with being assigned to you, but the deed did get me out of my monotonous routine and let me see parts of Hell I've never experienced."

"And what do you think of the greater areas of your domain?"

"I'll be happy to return to my circle," Azubah said, stopping to shake snow from his hooves.

Obadiah looked around at the desolate area of the lake. A narrow ravine separated two glaciers, sloping downward in a treacherous path. "It's down there, isn't it?"

The demon saw nowhere else the sinners could be, but he was hesitant to commit to Obadiah's hunch. "I don't know."

The angel trusted his own intuition and shuddered at the thought of what awaited them in the very center of Hell. For the first time since beginning this journey, it was he, not the demon, who assumed the lead. "You don't have to come if you'd rather not."

"You'd go on *alone*?"

"I have nothing to fear. I cannot be touched by evil. I'm consecrated to God. You can't be slain, friend," Obadiah said. "But you can be tortured by one of the many hideous punishments we've witnessed on our trek together."

The demon sighed. "You speak truthfully, but I'll continue with you. I've come this far. I'd be a coward to turn back now."

Obadiah smiled. "When I reach the end, there may not be time for farewells. Suriel may recall me to Heaven immediately."

"I understand."

"You may be left to handle whatever situation unfolds—alone."

Azubah's face grew sorrowful, but determined. "To the end."

"To the end, then," Obadiah said, and clasped hands with his unlikely companion.

The path was too narrow to allow them to enter side-by-side, so Obadiah pressed onward in the lead. The path was steep and icy. Both angel and demon clung to the jagged ice to steady their footing. Azubah's rigid hooves slipped so much that the demon slid more than he walked. The path of ice leveled, stopping in front of another section of the frozen lake. Obadiah gasped. Azubah stared transfixed: the last time he beheld his general, Lucifer had been a gloriously beautiful being. Azubah's black-lipped mouth gaped. Eyes traveled upward—up, up, up the massive beast frozen into the lake. Three faces stared with questioning eyes that constantly wept. Lips snarled over bared gums and six black wings beat ferociously, whipping the winds about them, further hardening the ice. The condemned souls of the traitors to their lords and benefactors lay around the monster: chewed, severed, chopped, gnawed and torn limb from limb. And yet, they would never, could never die. Azubah, all too aware of the penetrating stare of the Prince of Darkness, seized the closest soul and yanked the legless man to one side, propping him against a chunk of ice.

ACELDAMA: FIELD OF BLOOD

"But, I don't understand why you'd deny me this request, uncle. Have I not always done your bidding? Have I not served you well? Your coffers have tripled under my careful management. Do you not trust me with the protection of your daughter? I love her more than life itself." Simon was on both knees, hands wringing his velvet cap.

His uncle, Lord Hampstead, sat behind an enormous table piled high with scales, coins and measures of weights. Ledgers and ink bottles cluttered the remaining portion. Hampstead's red face, swollen and purple-veined, looked uncomfortable over the lace of his collar. "I've said no and that's the end of the matter. Why would I turn my daughter over to a pauper such as yourself? Everything you have I gave you! Your miserable parents died without leaving you a single penny. All that you are you owe me and you have the gall to ask to wed my daughter too!"

Simon choked back sobs threatening to burst from his throat. He knew bawling like a child wouldn't help his plight. His uncle was a mean, hardened old man who tolerated no weakness in anyone. "Perhaps you'll reconsider after some time, my lord? Katerina and I are in love. She wishes–"

"*Love*? Marriage has a lot to do with many things, my boy, but *love* is *not* one of them! If men left important decisions like marriage and property rights to women, we'd all be in trouble. *Love* is for girls and pre-pubescent boys. *Marriage* is about alliances, power and wealth. It's high time you figured out the difference and become a man. I'll find you a wife suitable to your station as my ward. You aren't entirely penniless thanks to my generosity. You won't be burdened with some shrew. I'll make sure of that!"

Simon stood defeated. There was nothing more to say. Lord Hampstead waved him away. "Go on about your tasks now, nephew. There are books to be kept." The conversation was over.

Simon placed his hat upon his head and left the chamber, heart heavy and head throbbing. He didn't go to the mill, however. Instead he wandered to the edge of the forest and sat beside a brook to collect his wits. He skipped a few rocks across the rippling waters. His glance continued to linger over the shadowed trail leading into the darkness of the woods. The forest was said to be home to the Witch of Aram. An ancient crone who was once young and beautiful and wed to a crusader returned home from the Holy Land. She was rumored to be powerful and many women sought her counsel on all manner of subjects. Being a man, and a Christian, Simon had no dealings with witchcraft and knew not whether the witch was a witch or just an old woman living the rest of her days out in a secluded hovel.

Perhaps the witch can help, he thought. The wind blew through the trees, whistling and chattering. Birds called to each other in the heavy boughs, and the babbling stream seemed to sing a song of hope. *Wouldn't hurt just to speak with her*. Simon stood, brushing the dry grass from his hose, and slinging his cape over one shoulder mustered the courage to enter the dark wood.

The trail continued for some time.

He came to a dilapidated cottage in sore need of re-thatching and repair. A tidy herb garden bathed in a scattered spattering of sunlight through the trees backed against one side of the hovel. Climbing roses and ivy crawled over the collapsing fence and up cracked mortar. Smoke curled in tendrils from the chimney, and Simon knew someone was home.

Before his hand could rap against the warped wood door, it swung open, loose on its hinges, and a hoarse voice asked: "Who is it that has disturbed my meditations?"

Simon began to speak, but only a stammer came forth. "I—I—I-"

"I—what? Have you a tongue, man?" The voice belonged to a hag who hobbled into view as she questioned him from inside.

"My name's Simon, nephew to Lord Hampstead."

"Pompous windbag, that one. What do you want?" Her tone was clipped and impatient.

"I came seeking your help."

"My help?" The crone laughed. "How can I, an aged and impoverished woman, help you, nephew to a lord?"

Simon shook his head. "I'm not a wealthy man. I've been my uncle's ward since I was a child."

The old woman looked Simon over, clucking and clicking her tongue against her teeth. The wind lifted the thin wisps of gray hair from her balding head and she reached to her shoulders and pulled a black shawl over her crown. "Come inside. There's a chill in the air," she said, and hobbled inside, leaving Simon to close the door.

She sat before the fire on a wood stool and gestured to another across from her. Simon sat. "Now, tell me why you think I can help you."

Simon watched the fire pop, eating the wood within its orange belly. "I heard that you're known as the Witch of Aram."

She cackled. "And from *whom* did you hear such tales?"

"Servant girls, mostly. Some older women in the village. They say you help with birthing and illnesses."

The old woman pushed a black kettle on a hook over the fire. "Supplying healing salves and ointments for stretched skin are hardly the products of a witch, young man."

Simon felt foolish. "I'm sorry. I didn't know." He stood.

"Where are you going?"

"I don't want to trouble you. I'm sorry I came." He inched closer to the door.

"Sit! I'm not finished yet."

Simon sat immediately. The old woman's voice commanded obedience. If she wasn't a witch, perhaps she'd been a queen.

"Now, it's true, I'm sometimes called the Witch of Aram. Although that title was used many, many years ago. I'm more curious as to *how* you found me."

"I just followed the trail through the woods."

The crone laughed. "There's no trail through these woods, man. The only ones who find me are the ones who've been here before. Trail, indeed! I should just put the noose around my own neck if I should have a trail leading right to my doorstep."

Simon frowned, puzzled. "But there is a trail. See–" He stood and pulled open the door to point the way, only when he did so, there was no trail in sight. Only a drift of dried leaves and broken branches. "Well, it *was* there!"

"Close the door. You're letting in the cold." The crone plunked two wood mugs onto the hearth. "Tea?"

Simon grew afraid.

"Oh, don't look so terrified. It's only tea!" she said and poured water over fresh leaves that smelled vaguely of mint.

She passed Simon a mug and clutched her own to her chest, letting the steam warm her face. "The trail is of no matter."

Simon breathed a sigh of relief.

"Tell me why you braved a haunted forest to seek my aid."

Simon told the whole pathetic tale of love and loss and denial.

"Lord Hampstead always was a cold and hard man," the crone said. "Taxes his people beyond shame. I once watched him step over a dying child without even a glimmer of care."

Simon nodded. "That's my uncle."

The old crone tapped the side of her head with a single finger. "He'll not let you wed his girl while he has breath."

"I know."

"So, we must find a way to cheat him of the rest of his life."

Simon felt his eyes widen. "I can't *kill* him!"

"Not you, dear boy, but you'll have to lead him to his doom."

He pondered this for a moment. "Won't it look like I killed him?"

"You haven't even heard me out yet," the witch said. She took a drink of her tea, and cleared her phlegmy throat. "There's a field, a field of blood, called Aceldama, where grows a bewitched tree possessed of all the spirits that have died by the hangman's noose, the demons of the insane, the criminal, and the pure evil. If you lead Lord Hampstead to this tree, the tree will murder him most certain."

"*A tree?*"

"I know it sounds like the ranting of a lunatic, but I assure you this tree exists. You'll have to visit the tree beforehand, for it will demand payment for the deed and this payment must be pre-arranged."

Simon drained his mug and sat it on the hearth. "Like what?"

"That's between you and the tree. The tree never asks what cannot be given."

"What do you ask in exchange for the location of this foul tree?" Simon clinked the few silver coins he had in his purse. He didn't have much.

"I don't want your silver, if that's what you fear. When you are wed to Lord Hampstead's daughter and became a lord yourself, I'd ask that you pay a tribute of food and wine to me according to the seasons."

Simon thought that sounded reasonable. The crone only asked for what she needed. "I promise this will be done.

She smiled a gap-toothed grin and pulled a small, rolled parchment from behind a loose stone, putting it into Simon's hand. "Here's the map. Guard it well, and when you know the way, bring the map back to me."

He unfurled the scrap and studied it. Conveniently, the field of blood wasn't too far out of the length of a normal ride. He could take the lord hunting as a plausible excuse for their excursion. Simon stood, anxious to locate the tree on the morrow, and to get home before nightfall.

"Thank you," he said.

"We shall see."

• • •

The tree. At first glance it looked like any other ancient tree with low-slung boughs of knotty wood, hollowed holes where forest animals might nest, and branches that looked strangely arm-like against the backdrop of a rising moon. Upon closer inspection, it was anything but ordinary.

Simon, staying a cautious distance, studied the gnarled tree. If a tree was really what it was. The whole thing looked—*alive*—to him. Not alive like any other vegetation, but alive as in sentient, knowing as if human, or something once human. He shuddered.

Thick sap bubbled over bark in a goopy, red mixture. Red. Like coagulating blood. And, now that he really looked at the tree, those hollowed holes for nesting animals looked more like gashes in flesh—open, jagged and raw.

Simon stood still. A pulsing throb penetrated his boots. The ground quaked with tremors like a heartbeat.

"Hello?" he asked, feeling quite foolish. He looked over his shoulders to make sure no one was around to see him talking to a tree. The wind blew through the tree's branches, scattering a few leaves. "What else did I expect?" he said to himself, aloud, disgust at his own desperation, ringing in his voice.

"Indeed. What *did* you expect?"

Simon looked around. "Who's there?"

"Don't you know? You came here seeking—seek and you shall find," the voice replied. Low. Slow and deliberate. Primal, almost a growl.

Simon stared at the trunk. One of the gashes, horizontal in cut, twitched as if lips on a mouth. "Tree?"

"That's what you seek, is it not?"

"Aye, it is. I just didn't expect you to–"

"Speak?" the tree said. "How else were you to make a pact with me? I can't very well write without fingers."

Simon shrugged. *True enough.* "Do you know why I'm here?"

The tree laughed a booming sort of echo. "Let's begin with *how* did *you* get *here*?"

"The Witch of Aram lent me a map."

"The Witch of Aram? Is she still alive?"

ANGELINE HAWKES

Simon nodded enthusiastically, hoping this was what the tree wanted to hear. "And well."

"Oh, she was a sight to behold, a beauty! True beauty. Came to England on a black steed with her crusading knight. Hair as black as the horse, eyes the color of emeralds."

Simon allowed the tree to reminisce.

"Not many witches left with her powers," the tree said.

"Not many witches left at all. The church has burnt them."

With the mention of the word "church", the tree's trunk twisted and turned. Somehow the bark looked blacker, darker, more sinister. "The church–" The tree's voice was venomous.

"I didn't come to talk of this, however," Simon said quickly, not wanting to incite an ensorcelled tree into a demonstration of rage.

The tree huffed for a moment before uncurling its branches and relaxing. "If the Witch of Aram has sent you to me, then you have a pact to make in exchange for a life to take."

"Aye, how did you know?"

More laughter. "This is what I *do*, man. There's no other reason to speak to me."

"I want my uncle dead so I can marry my cousin, Katerina. He refuses to allow it."

The tree chuckled, as if it expected such a blurting request. "An uncle is it?"

"Aye, Lord Hampstead."

"An uncle and a lord?" the tree said. "My, my. Very ambitious, indeed."

"Will you do it? Will you kill him?"

"Bring him to me."

Simon felt a sense of elation, relief. "That's it? That's all I do?"

The tree laughed longer than before. "Of course not, you idiot! Do you think I quench the force of life so lightly? Do you think I grant the requests of sniveling mortals such as yourself out of the goodness of my heart?"

"No, no, I–" Simon began. "What do you want?"

"What do you *have*?"

Simon thought of how little he possessed. The words of the crone rang in his mind: *The tree never asks what cannot be given.* "I'm not sure."

"If I kill this uncle, you'll wed his daughter, correct?"

"Aye, aye."

"And you'll have children, correct?" the tree asked.

171

"Most likely, aye."

"You'll give me your first born child, dead or alive, I care not, but you'll bring the babe to me."

Simon glared, horrified, at the tree. "Our *child*?"

"There will be others. What's one to you when you can have so many?"

"But, what will you do with it? How can you care for a child?" Simon said.

"Silence!" the tree bellowed. "These are the terms of our pact."

Simon sat on the ground, and buried his face in his hand. The steady booming beat reverberated beneath his backside, under the surface, beneath the soil. *What choice did he have?*

He had nothing else to offer and the tree seemed to already know what it wanted. But, their *child*! What would the tree do with a baby? Simon shook his head, hands grasping hair like a madman. He didn't want to venture a thought on *what* the beastly tree, the murdering fiend of a tree, planned to *do* with a baby. His baby. His and Katerina's baby.

"Alright. Aye, my first born," Simon said, exhaling loudly.

The tree laughed mockingly. Its voice changed to one of taunting, evil. "Poor Simon the peasant boy kills a man, to own his toy."

"Stop it. That's not true. I'm not a peasant. Just unlanded."

"Simple Simon met a pieman going to the faire. Said Simple Simon to the pieman: pies of blood are rare!"

"Stop it!"

Laughter. "Simple Simon killed the pieman, slit his scrawny throat. Ate the pies, took his coins, and even stole his coat!"

Simon stood. "What's wrong with you all of a sudden?"

"Nothing with us is *all of a sudden*. This tree is home to all the souls who've swung on its gallows beneath its branches, or on wood cut from our boughs. We are many. We are legion. Imprisoned here by wickedness. Ensnared here by our seething desire for vengeance, for our greedy quest for pain."

Simon backed away from the tree.

"Bring us this uncle, this lord. Bring him to us." The tree's voice changed again.

Simon shouted: "On the morrow, I shall bring him. Do your part and I'll do mine."

The tree laughed, its branches shaking, leaves cascading to the ground in a flurry. "Oh, you will. *You will.*"

Simon set off for home, wishing he could banish the perverse laughter of the possessed tree from his mind.

• • •

It wasn't hard to persuade Lord Hampstead to go pheasant hunting. Simon lied a lovely tale of how he stumbled upon a new hunting spot. He packed a meal for two and his uncle brought a bottle of wine.

They hunted until noontime when Simon led the lord to the tree. "I've a good spot for our meal," he said. He handed the bundle of food to his uncle. "See that tree over there, set us up beneath it. I've a need I must attend to in the bushes."

His uncle laughed and took the lunch and the horses to the tree. He untied the bundle and uncorked the wine while Simon peered between a thicket of branches watching the scene unfold.

Lord Hampstead sat upon a large root growing above the earth and ate a leg of roasted fowl. "What's taking you so long, boy?"

"Be there shortly!" Simon called.

The tree inched an arm-like bough toward the dining man. Near Lord Hampstead's foot a thin root, long and rope-like, lifted itself from the clinging soil and snaked around the man—not touching, just about an arm's span away.

Simon inhaled sharply. Two other branches, twisted and black, crept ever closer to his uncle, sneaking behind him—waiting to make the kill.

A sound like that of a whipping lash—and the branches and root moved simultaneously, entwining around his uncle's body like a suffocating viper—tighter, tighter they squeezed.

Lord Hampstead couldn't even shout for a branch had wrapped around his neck like a woody noose and squeezed until the man's face grew purple, his lips tinged blue and his eyeballs threatened to explode from his skull.

Simon exhaled as his uncle's body went limp. The tree pulled him into the leafy boughs, shedding his fine clothes, dropping the fabric to the ground. A horrible, sickening crunching sound like the popping and cracking of breaking bones and dislocated joints sounded and Simon recoiled from the noise. Blood coursed in streams over the black bark, running in rivulets to the roots lapping at the soil. The entire tree sucked and inhaled, branches shuddering and shaking as if in ecstasy, until at last it grew silent and all was finished.

"We'll see you in due time, Simon," the tree said, its voice an awful lot like Lord Hampstead's. "In due time."

Simon leapt upon his horse and rode away, the mocking laughter chasing behind.

• • •

After the necessary mourning period, Simon and Katerina were wed without much celebration. The joy of the union had melted away that fateful day with the tree just as Lord Hampstead's life had oozed from him. The tale Simon told was that of a jovial hunting day, then his uncle just went missing. A search party was organized in an area far from the actual location, no body was located, and he was presumed killed and robbed by thieves after villagers found the lord's fine clothing—planted by Simon near a grove of intensely overgrown trees.

Within a year, Katerina was with child and bigger than the midwives thought was healthy. As her time neared, Simon grew anxious. She didn't look well. Her skin was an ashy pallor. Her appetite waned, but the babe inside of her grew even larger. So large, it looked as if her belly might rent itself in two.

Under the cacophony of thunder and cracking lightning, Katerina birthed a monstrous child: deformed in face and limb. Her blood gushed in great puddles beneath her, and there was nothing the midwives could do to quench the flow.

"Simon!" she gasped, fear, black within her eyes. A haunted, frenzied expression marring her beauty. "Simon!"

"I'm here, my love. I've got you!" He clutched her to his chest as if holding her so tightly would chase off the Reaper. Her clawing fingers eased to limpness as her life flooded from her womb: what gave life, took life, a cycle of doom. The babe whimpered in the cradle like a mewing kitten.

"You can't allow it to live, my lord," the midwife hissed. "'Tis a monster! A demon!"

"Murdering beast!" the other woman whispered.

"Give it to me," Simon commanded, moving as if in a nightmare, his life dead along with his Katerina.

The midwife bundled the babe in blankets and thrust the deformed creature into Simon's arms. "The Good Lord preserve us from such a monstrous evil," she murmured, crossing herself.

Simon mounted his horse and rode through the pounding rain, through the night, and into the forest to the tree. Its yawning maw opened wide to drink in the waters of the Heavens as it caught sight of Simon on horseback with a bundle in his arms.

"Here!" he shouted above the din of the storm. "I've brought you my firstborn as promised. Take it! This beast killed my Katerina. It was for her that I entered into this devilish pact! Now, she's gone."

The tree laughed. "Amusing how things turn out." It stretched out two branches to accept the wailing babe. A thin branch, so hand-like, pulled back the swaddling to reveal the deformed monstrosity: a lump of grotesque flesh with hair where hair should not be and limbs where bones should not grow. "What's this?"

Simon pulled back on the reins to calm his bolting horse. "The babe, as promised. Take the murdering monster. It belongs with the likes of you, foul creature, hellish tree!"

"This is not a baby. This is a monster! This is of no use to us!"

"Aye, as you are a monster! Rot in Hell together!" Simon shouted and turned his horse to depart.

Branches shot from the demon tree, gathering Simon in its clutches, pulling him toward the trunk. "You have reneged on the bargain! And so, we claim *you* as our payment."

Simon screamed as branches yanked him upward, into its boughs of death.

• • •

The sun rose on a wet landscape, raindrops sparkling like a million faceted diamonds on grass and flowers and ground. Nestled in a cluster of roots, woven like a rocking cradle, was a monstrous babe cooing as the tree extended a finger-like branch into tiny clenching fists.

The tree sang a lullaby, dead now to the ages, in an ancient tongue and tune, as the souls of those who met their grisly deaths poured into the child, ready to live again. The tree smoothed the twisted flesh and reformed bent limbs, remolding the beast into the form of a baby so that they could live again, kill again.

The baby cried; its cries carried on the wind to the ears of a passing peddler woman out to sell her wares. "What's this? An orphaned babe?" she said, and gathered the child into her arms.

"Come home to us," the wind whispered.

The old woman glanced around. "Who said that?" But she was alone with naught but the babe. "My ears! I've gone deaf or daft! So old I am!" she said, and laughed, jostling the baby comfortingly. "Let's go find you a mother to lend a breast and love."

The tree watched the babe going off to the world. The others watched in envy. There was no more room in the child. They must wait for another.

Satan and Those who have Committed the Ultimate Sin Occupy the Center of Hell: Treachery Against God

OBADIAH CLOSED HIS BOOK, content that his job was finished.

"Do you see *him*?" Azubah asked, shuddering.

"Who?"

"Judas Iscariot, the most wretched and reviled man, even in Hell." Azubah didn't dare point and draw attention; instead he slightly nodded in Judas's direction.

Obadiah gazed upon a most horrific scene. Clasped in the mouth of Satan, Judas wailed and thrashed as he was perpetually gnawed. The perverted trinity was complete with Lucifer raking taloned claws over the crimson-ribboned flesh of the most hated of all traitors.

"Thirty pieces of silver," Obadiah muttered.

"What a price to pay–" Azubah said.

A deep growl reverberated through the air encircling angel and demon with its booming intensity. The two immortals looked nervously at each other. The growl grew thunderous and then transformed into a voice: "You! Angel! Doesn't Suriel want to hear *my* story?"

Obadiah stared goggle-eyed into the hideous visage of Lucifer, once the most glorious of all angels. Obadiah looked away from him, not being able to hide his revulsion.

"You look upon all the evilness that Hell's walls contain, yet you turn away from me—whom you once called *friend*?"

Obadiah swallowed hard. Azubah's eyes darted from the fallen prince to the angel.

"If it weren't for you, these souls wouldn't have found eternity a place of horror and misery. They languish here for your vanity!"

"You were friends?" Azubah hissed. Obadiah waved him silent.

Lucifer laughed. "Vanity. Isn't there an old adage: *Vanity, thy name is woman*? Memory is foggy. Vanity, thy name is Lucifer lacks the same ring to it, don't you think?"

Obadiah fiddled with his pen, wishing Suriel would choose this moment to recall him, but that didn't seem to be happening. "The quote is *frailty, thy name is woman*." His voice betrayed his annoyance. "I'm on a schedule here, Lucifer. Why don't you tell me your story? I'm sure Azubah would be entertained by whatever distorted tale of filth you create."

"Don't say my name!" Azubah hissed sharply, spittle flying from his ebon lips.

Obadiah gave him an apologetic glance.

Lucifer paused, seemingly searching his ancient memories, choosing the slice of life he cared to repeat for the angel. "You might remember this, *friend*."

MORNING STAR DESCENDING

Carnage. Blood running like swollen streams over the muddy battle-field. Carved carcasses with broken, mangled wings littered the grassy mounds in heaps. Golden spears and pearl-handled swords lie among the clutter and debris of the dead and dying.

What could not be: was. What could not happen: did. All because of one angel's vanity and inflated self-worth and a particular talent for spectacular oration. He managed to flatter and persuade thousands with his silver tongue, convince them that a new order was upon them: where all would be as god, and no longer beneath or subservient to a higher power.

The army of Heaven clashed with the army of the archangel, Lucifer.

• • •

"Lucifer, why? Why this plan? I beg you to reconsider what you're about to do!" Obadiah said.

"What's done is done."

"Nothing is done yet. There's time to call it off. Bring back your troops."

"And what?" Lucifer hissed with a sneer. "Fling myself onto the mercy of God, beg forgiveness at his feet?"

"Yes!"

Lucifer laughed. "Are you that naïve? Do you think Yahweh will just let me say *I'm sorry* and everything will resume as before?"

Obadiah didn't answer.

The archangel—and Obadiah's best friend—pointed a finger at him. "Ha! You know the answer to that question yet you don't speak! You shouldn't have come here."

"I thought I could change your mind while there's still time, the sun is not yet up–"

"Join me! Join my side of darkness and we will bring a veil down over Heaven the likes of which has never been seen before! We'll scatter angels as far as the world is wide and no being will ever have to grovel at the feet of Yahweh again!"

Obadiah was filled with sorrow. "I do not grovel at the feet of my god, Lucifer. I show him respect and great admiration."

"For what? Because he has set himself up on a higher throne than ours? Who is he to call himself a god?"

Obadiah shook his head. "I'm afraid you've gone farther into your own madness than I thought possible. My heart is sick with your betrayal."

"My betrayal? You have betrayed me!" Lucifer shouted. "Did you betray my location too? Will you turn on me, betray me and our friendship for *your* god?"

"He's your god too."

"I am the only god I wish to worship!"

Obadiah bowed his head in defeat. His efforts had failed. "Very well. Then it is as you've said: *What's done is done.*" He stood and moved to the mouth of the cave that served as Lucifer's hideout and headquarters. "I'll not betray your location, but I cannot fight with you. My loyalty lies with Yahweh."

"You'll betray me, friend. Before the battle is over, you'll betray me to your god."

Obadiah walked into the twilight of the dawn and quickly to his camp. The horns would sound at daybreak. The battle would begin for the independence of the rebels rallied under Lucifer's banner. Heaven had never seen a civil war and for this time only Yahweh bestowed a free will upon every last being in the heavenly realms with the dictate: *choose!*

Also for the duration of the battle, Yahweh suspended their immortal lives. All angels could and some would die. Just a reminder that all life sprang from the Father and all life returns to him at his will.

Obadiah crept into his tent and readied his armor. He slung his belt around his hips, securing his scabbard. One third of Heaven waited on the other side of the mountain with friend and now enemy, Lucifer. *Misguided, misled fools.* How easy it is to fall to golden words and empty promises.

The trumpets blared and all fell into formation. The marching phalanx assumed attack positions as Heaven's archers let fly a million diamond-tipped arrows into the approaching army of Lucifer.

It began.

Blood spurted in unholy founts over warriors clad in white and red. Lucifer's troops donned crimson tunics, easily distinguishing them from Yahweh's forces. Their numbers suffered great losses. At one point several of Yahweh's soldiers intercepted and relieved a unit of Lucifer's troops of their red tunics. Disguised as warriors of Lucifer, Yahweh's angels rejoined the fray and wrecked much havoc and confusion by slaughtering their crimson-shirted comrades. Chaos ensued until Lucifer's angels cut them down.

The sun rose higher in the sky and the clang of steel still sang a gruesome dirge amidst the trampled, fallen angels. The air was alive with flying feathers, dirt and the salty smell of wasted blood.

Blood. It was everywhere. On everything. In his ears, nose, mouth. What once had never been seen, smelled or tasted, was now a rushing river at his ankles. Obadiah spat on the ground, not wanting to see if his spittle missed the many corpses there.

The battle progressed. If only Lucifer could be captured, his troops would break rank and run. There were no leaders among them save the morning star himself. He had gathered to him every weak-willed termite in Heaven and now, the battle waned, the number of dying increased, and all that held the loose knit, raggedy bunch of rebels together was their ill-placed belief in the success of Lucifer and his insane dreams.

The call rang out. God wanted this nightmare over, and he wanted Lucifer in chains. It was only a matter of time. What Yahweh intended to do with Lucifer once he finally had him was a topic of interest. Obadiah shuddered. Lucifer would be better off dead than face the punishment he deserved.

Afternoon faded into the silver-lavender of evening. The sun grew heavier, a golden fireball on the darkening horizon.

Obadiah swung his sword, hamstringing his foe, twirling, thrusting, running the unfortunate cherub through the gut with his blade. Swinging swiftly overhead and back, he blocked an oncoming assault from behind. Twisting and taking the gold-curled skull from the shoulders of the angel, Obadiah let loose an animal-like shout. Blood spattered his white robe, flecks of gore and shards of bone clung to the fabric.

A red-tunicked warrior darted in front of him. Obadiah sprang over the bodies of two entwined angels, and, with his outstretched sword, tripped the enemy. The angel tumbled into a pile of filth and death, flailed defensively, trying to retrieve his fallen weapon. Obadiah was upon him. Sandaled feet pressed into the angel's neck as Obadiah rolled the struggling being over onto his back. It was Lucifer.

Obadiah leaned on his sword just enough that a trickle of blood pooled in the well around the silver point of his sword. Lucifer snarled, growling with fierceness so primal Obadiah questioned the angel's true origins.

"Do it! Kill me!" Lucifer demanded.

Obadiah frowned, but didn't move.

"Coward! What are you waiting for? Kill me now!"

Obadiah considered the option. Scowling, he shouted over his shoulder: "Father! I have him! I have the Prince of the darkness that has befallen Heaven!"

Trumpets blared. A rush of angels with beating wings blasted Obadiah from all directions. Lucifer remained on his back. He clutched Obadiah's sword, sharp blade slicing the flesh of his hands. "Kill me! Don't let me suffer whatever fate Yahweh will shackle me with!"

General Michael arrived and his troops, bound Lucifer in chains, and loaded him, shrieking curses upon all involved, into a cart. As the cart rumbled toward the golden streets of Heaven, Obadiah stood, blood dripping from his sword onto the dead beneath his feet.

• • •

Obadiah glared grimly at Lucifer as he finished his tale. "Are you satisfied now? I have your story. You've been heard."

"It's not *my* story as much as it's *yours*," Lucifer said. His wings whipped a gale force wind around Obadiah with frigid icy blasts. The Prince of Darkness waved a taloned hand. "*This*, all of this, is *my* story."

"One that need not have been written had you listened to me on that fateful morning," Obadiah said.

Lucifer laughed, his tone mocking and spiteful.

A tinkling bell sounded somewhere in the Heavens and Obadiah sighed, relieved that Suriel was recalling him at last. He glanced at Azubah. "Get those blankets back to Astrial soon," he said, and smiled. Azubah smiled in return.

Lucifer mimicked Obadiah's voice with mockery. "Do you look upon your friend, this demon, the way you looked upon me before you allowed me to be chained and led away broken before all of Heaven?" Lucifer hissed. "Will you betray *his* friendship too?"

Obadiah shook his head. "The only one here who has betrayed Azubah is you, Lucifer. Him and thousands like him. *You damned him.* You *betrayed* him as you did Almighty God."

Obadiah began ascending, sailing over the pits, ditches, and ravines of Hell, back to Suriel and his order, and back to the Realm of God.

• • •

"What's to become of Azubah?" Obadiah asked, after all of the documents were validated and filed.

Suriel looked up from his stack of papers. "The demon?"

"Yes. He served Heaven well on my journey through that most foul place. I would never have completed my assignment without his assistance."

"I took this into consideration when his file came up for review," Suriel said.

"Review?"

"Millennial Performance Review."

"Oh."

Suriel closed a book and rearranged the stacks of papers on his desk. "You'll be happy to know he was promoted to Purgatory."

"What of his form?" Obadiah asked.

"He was returned to his former being, but his wings have been clipped to always denote his status as a rebel against Yahweh."

Obadiah smiled. "Thank you."

Suriel shrugged, pointing toward the golden throne room of Yahweh. "I just carry out orders. I don't make them."

Obadiah nodded knowingly and left the chamber. He paused, looked toward the throne room of God and whispered again, "Thank you."

ABOUT THE AUTHOR

A 2006 Bram Stoker Award finalist, ANGELINE HAWKES has seen the publication of novels, novellas, collections, fiction in 40+ anthologies, and over 100 short fiction publications. Angeline often writes collaboratively with her husband, Christopher Fulbright.